Death Brings Victory

T. M. Hunter

ISBN: 978-0-61564-115-7

This book is a work of fiction. The names, characters, places and incidents are products of the writer's imagination and are not to be construed as real. Any resemblance to persons, living or dead, actual events, locale or organizations is entirely coincidental.

Other Titles from T. M. Hunter

From the Aston West Universe:

Heroes Die Young

Friends in Deed

All Good Things

Before the Dawn

Seeker

Fallen

Stormrunner

The Cure

Dead or Alive: An Aston West Collection

Dirty Dozen: An Aston West Collection

Crossfire & Other Stories (a Kasey Reynolds collection)

The Max McCannor Series (w/ Lyndon Perry):

Escape

Runaway

Eureka

The Demonkiller Series:

Chosen

Tempted (coming soon)

Prologue

"Hold your fire."

Rione Sc'lari ran to the command room's center, background klaxons giving her a splitting headache. The black-haired Lazarian female stood out, not for her jet black jumpsuit, but being the only bronze-skinned beauty in a room full of pale Torians. Men and women in olive green uniforms sat at terminals around the perimeter walls, keeping close watch. She focused on the holographic imager displaying the station and its surroundings.

A small bull-nosed craft drew closer to the station. She moved in, her nose almost touching the projected image. The ship would have been considered derelict had its main engines not switched to full power as soon as it dropped below the hyperspace threshold. Being at war, station defenses went on full alert as soon as its trajectory had been determined; it was headed straight for them.

The weapons officer called out across the room. "Target remains acquired." His curt tone said everything. He was on edge, as they all were.

All of the station's new laser cannons were trained on the mystery vessel. Rione couldn't shake a feeling of familiarity. "Is it transmitting an ID code?"

The station's communications officer looked up from her station nearby. "Sierra-tango-four-two-four."

Princess Lucian Wren, in a flowing white Torian dress, stepped up behind Rione. “Isn’t that code...?”

The Lazarian jerked her head around, ridges protruding just forward of her ear turning pale white. “Aston’s ship?”

The communications officer interrupted, “Still no response.”

Rione’s forehead creased as she mumbled to her friend, “Lucian, something’s wrong.”

The Princess gave the next command. “Have it proceed to landing bay two.”

The officer turned her attention back to the sensor screen and her communication gear. There was no verbal response, but the ship’s thrusters fired, altering course.

“I’ll meet him.” Rione rushed for the exit, hoping the silence was merely an issue with outgoing communications.

She was already out the door when Princess Wren called, “Report back when you find out more.”

The ship’s response to their instructions was a good sign, but Rione had already made a paranoid leap. Pushing on her jumpsuit’s collar, she responded through its embedded transmitter. “Will do.”

Far below the circular walkway, Rione passed an unsuspecting commons area. The station had once bustled with life, before Toris had plunged itself into civil war. Now the entire facility seemed like a ghost vessel, the emptiness below broken up by an occasional trio or quartet of dark green Rulusian troops.

The landing bay entry doors split open along the outer wall and Rione raced inside, only to stop short. Aston’s ship sat at the room’s center, its lights dormant. The hull was scarred and burned, residual ice melting off in waves of cloudy smoke. The station’s two AFI-5 fighter-interceptors rested against the far wall. Her skin crawled as she forced herself closer. She wanted to find out why Aston hadn't already exited his ship, but feared what she might find.

The entry hatch on the ship's right side popped loose, causing her to jump. Motors ground out their rhythm as the door lowered toward the hangar floor. Relief finally flooded over her, until she heard Jeanie, the ship's computer, calling from inside. "Come quick!"

Rione scrambled up the stairs, intense fear burning through her heart. She jumped inside the ship, then caught a gasp in her throat.

Aston lay haphazard atop the near wall cot, unmoving. Strips of fabric were wrapped around his left shoulder, torn from sheets piled on the floor. Everything under him and below the cot was coated dark red.

"Aston!" she called, but received no response. Her rapid breath formed misty clouds as she rushed to his side. Shoving him did not wake him, either. Her entire body shook violently, not only from the cold, but from building fear.

His breath wasn't visible as hers was, so she reached up to his throat. Expecting the worst, she felt for signs of life. At first, she found nothing, then pushing a little deeper, a flicker of hope rose as she finally found faint beats, shallow and slow.

Rione's hands shook as she pressed her transmitter. Her voice chattered. "Emergency medical team to landing bay two. Now!"

Jeanie spoke, almost sorrowful. "He told me to bring him here. He knew you would be able to help, Rione."

The Lazarian female spoke into the emptiness. "What happened to him?"

"Aston instructed me not to explain the circumstances behind his injuries. I must comply."

Rione crossed her arms, holding herself tight. "Why is it so cold in here?"

"I reduced the temperature to prolong his life."

Rione backed away as the bay doors opened outside the ship and personnel stormed toward them. She whispered, "What happened to you, Aston West?"

Chapter One

"There it is," I muttered. An orbiting superstructure rotated on the viewscreen before me, silhouetted by the bluish-white planet. This monstrosity was far smaller than its sibling, the Torian orbital station, but still far larger than the Rulusian vessel we rode in.

I studied the hulking mass of dark gray metal which symbolized so much pain and suffering. A long boom, half the length of the satellite, jutted toward the planet. At the very tip, a sensor sphere conducted scans of the planet. Beams penetrated deep under the planet's surfaces and bounced back to large cupped blades surrounding the satellite's cylindrical body. The strength of these beams tracked the planet's citizens, rooting out large gatherings of anti-government forces. Violent executions had run rampant, and had to be stopped.

That's why I was here.

A Rulusian Captain sat stoic at my right, his black dress uniform fitting tight. Three golden rings on each shoulder pad caught the light, nearly blinding me. He lifted his bald green head and tilted it to either side, neck bones cracking. Sweat formed and rolled down my skin, from the extra-humid conditions Rulusians preferred. He smirked. "Well, Aston, shall we get their attention?"

"Sounds like a plan," I told him.

Thousands of blue organic crystals comprised the sensor sphere and supplied the transmitter's tremendous power. The pit of my stomach tightened into a knot, just below the Mark II blaster holstered outside my black jumpsuit. I'd unknowingly delivered those very crystals into the hands of the Torian king during my last visit to this system. In essence, I'd assisted his plan of genocide.

Sweet satisfaction would come with the satellite's destruction, and appeasing my guilt an added bonus.

He turned his attention to one of the stations along the round bridge's right wall. "Helm, set a course just this side of the border."

"Aye, Captain." The planet shifted left off the screen as our massive aft engines kicked in for the maneuver.

"We greatly appreciate your help, Captain." His actions placed him at great risk, even with his home world.

"Glad to do it. Hopefully you remember we're not officially helping you."

I let out a brief chuckle. "Well, you're doing a fine job of not officially helping us."

The ship's first officer, whose name I couldn't remember, spoke up from the opposite side of the bridge, her feminine voice steady. "Captain, a Torian heavy cruiser is on an intercept course."

Behind us on the left, the communications officer announced, "They're hailing us."

"As expected." The Captain stood and pulled his uniform taut. "Put it through, Lieutenant, audio only."

"Connection's live."

"This is Captain Dillager of the Rulusian freighter Green Four." He clasped his hands behind his back.

A rough, low voice broke the silence, each syllable heavily emphasized. “Captain, I demand you vacate this vicinity immediately!”

The Captain’s attitude ratcheted up a notch. “With whom am I speaking?”

“Commander Roth Sevil, Torian Planetary Defenses.”

“Commander, double-check your sensors. We are within the borders of interstellar space, and will continue as we see fit.”

“Unacceptable! What is your destination?”

“My crew and I are simply doing a little sightseeing.”

I barely kept from laughing. The cruiser’s Commander didn’t take the rebuke so well. “I demand you leave immediately! Do not force us to open fire.”

Dillager narrowed his eyes at the cruiser drawing closer on the viewscreen. “Commander, two Rulusian destroyers are currently protecting the Toris orbital station. They would be happy to settle any dispute you have with our flight path.”

A few moments of silence passed. “Ensure your flight path does not stray. We will open fire!”

The communications officer alerted us to the obvious. “Connection’s terminated.”

The male Rulusian keeping an eye on the scanner system piped up. “Two light cruisers now on an intercept course from the satellite.”

The Captain unclasped his hands and folded his arms across his chest. “Any other ships around the satellite?”

“No, sir.”

Dillager turned to me. “It seems you have your distraction.”

“Thanks again, Captain. We’ll catch you at the rendezvous point.” I started toward the back of the bridge.

"Happy hunting."

A doorway slid open and I walked through. The grill plates under my feet echoed with each step I took through the dimly lit corridor. Rione Sc'lari, my good friend, rested on one knee along the corridor, tightening one of her bootstraps. She wore a dark body suit similar to my own; mine made me feel naked. Judging from the sight of hers, I worried it wasn't just paranoid feelings. At least she had better curves.

She looked up when I told her, "Looks like they're taking the bait."

"Everything should be ready."

She lifted a disintegrator cannon sitting beside her feet. My heart skipped a beat seeing the long-barreled weapon; the first time we'd met, what seemed so long ago, Rione had tried to kill me with one.

I placed my hand on a small display screen nestled in the wall. After a quick scan, it beeped its approval and a series of clicks followed as the bay's hatch hissed open.

"So, how's the shoulder holding up?"

I lied, even as the joint in question objected. "Couldn't be better."

"Glad to hear it."

She walked inside, immediately calling out to the rest of our strike team. "Suit up!"

I looked to the far end of the bay, where a tiny ship rested. Three pale-skinned Torians in similar body suits rushed over to the inboard wall, their feet squishing against the landing bay floor. They opened up a set of hard plastic lockers, pulling out bright white pressure suits. Rione and I strolled over.

"Sure you don't want to take along something more?" She nodded toward my Mark II blaster and its holster.

"It'll be fine." Like an old, comfortable piece of furniture, I knew every nuance of the weapon. It fit me and never let me down. The thought of swapping it for something new never entered my mind.

"You'll be sorry."

Ordinarily, a Rulusian freighter's cargo bay would only be wide enough for an ordinary transport container. This particular ship had been extensively modified, turning three bays into a single hangar. I watched Rione slip inside her white suit before opening up my own locker. The stench of stale air invaded my nostrils.

This freighter had been modified specifically for covert missions such as this. So had its predecessor, a freighter designated Green Three which Rione had operated as Captain.

She walked in front of me, green eyes penetrating. "You have the tool?"

I searched the suit in front of me, and pulled a slender metal rectangle from its left breast pocket. "Right here."

"Distracted?"

The Torians headed off for the miniature ship. Rione had already closed up her suit, save for the helmet stuck in the crook of her arm.

"Sorry, just thinking."

"Hopefully you'll get all of that out of your system." She stepped away to join our Torian counterparts.

"I will." I pulled my holster off, then slipped into the pressure suit and returned my weapon where it belonged.

Grabbing the helmet, I rushed to catch up with Rione. Just like the freighter, this Rescue Operation Craft had been modified to fit this specific mission. The short, squat craft was meant for medical transport and evacuation. The modifications had been minor, but would be a huge part of our mission. I was just disappointed they hadn't installed some weaponry on the ship itself, maybe a heavy torpedo or a plasma cannon. That would have made our task far simpler than it was bound to be.

Rione spoke to the nearest Torian. "Is everything ready?"

"Pre-flight checks are complete."

"Good," I said.

"Glad to see you made it, Jake." Rione's lips curled in a smug expression.

His cheeks beamed. "You think I'd miss this chance?"

I shifted my helmet to the other hand. "I didn't think space ops were your thing, Falcon."

"Cripes! A guy gets sick off a bad batch of Borolo one time and he's labeled for life."

Rione smiled. "Take the gurney seat."

"I swear I won't puke on anyone."

She caught a laugh in her throat. It was time to get down to business. "Grab your weapons."

The Torians stepped over to an open weapons locker and pulled out three automatic burst rifles, along with belts full of energy clips. Jake grabbed another, this one filled with explosive charges, handing it to Rione.

"I think these are yours."

She wrapped the belt around her waist, and it dropped slightly to her hips.

The pale-faced Torian turned to me. "You want a different weapon?"

"This will be fine."

He raised an eyebrow. "You have extra energy clips?"

The one thing I hadn't thought of. I decided against cursing my luck and shook my head.

Rione was insistent. "Aston, take another weapon."

I looked over at the weapons locker and found a stubby-barreled weapon. To appease everyone, I pulled the thing from its mounting rack by a pair of handles, one on the side and one on top.

One of the other Torians piped up. "Firedart launcher. Nice choice."

"Sounds dangerous," the third one noted.

Jake nodded. "It is."

I nodded. "You definitely don't want to be on the receiving end of one." I examined the launch tube. Empty. "Hope you loaded some ammo."

Jake snagged a belt of energy clips out of the locker and pulled out a black bag before handing both over to me. I snapped the bag onto the belt before checking on the dozen red, elliptical shells inside, then wrapped it around my waist. I opted to wait until we were on the station to load the chamber. There was no sense accidentally setting one off and making this a suicide mission.

"Then, let's move."

I scrambled over and climbed the ladder first, taking the co-pilot's chair. Jake slid down through an access hole between the two rear seats. He eased into the gurney area, a small pressurized enclosure meant for transporting critical victims. He closed a hatch behind him.

The other two Torians took their spots before Rione eased into the pilot's position. We stowed our weapons where we could. She hit a button on the center panel, causing slow grinds to bellow in the makeshift hangar. The boarding ladder spun aft and retracted into the side of the craft while our spherical canopy lowered.

Rione reached for the middle display in the forward panel and tuned the screen to a secure channel. An image of Dillager appeared, sitting in his chair.

She started, "We're ready, Captain."

"Remember, turn on the noise generator before you get too far from us."

"Will do."

"Stand by." The Captain motioned off-screen and a modified bay door rose along tracks above our heads. Loud ratcheting echoed through the canopy.

Rione flipped a few more switches below the middle display and grabbed the yoke as thrusters came on-line. She eased it back and stomped the left-hand pedal at her feet. The ship was responsive, rising and turning toward the empty starfield. We jetted forward into the darkness.

Rione focused on the display. "We're clear, Captain."

He nodded off-screen and the transmission ended; the screen switched to a short-range sensor scan. I touched the screen where red triangular symbols marked the two light cruisers closing in on the Rulusian freighter's full green circle. The heavy cruiser was still electronically masked from our sensors by the dingy white whale beside us, which also blocked our visuals out the translucent canopy. "Looks like they're still taking the bait."

Everything was going according to plan. Rione put her finger on a scabbed-on switch to the right of the yoke. Four massive, bell-shaped nozzles cast a bright blue glow over the canopy. We eased past the freighter's aft end and she flipped it up. A deep hum started in the back.

"Ready or not..." She banked toward the satellite.

I kept my eyes on the sensor screen. "Light cruisers are still heading for the freighter." I took a moment and watched them through the canopy, dagger-like silhouettes piercing across the bluish-white backdrop.

One of the Torians piped up from the back seat, his voice tense. "They can't see us?"

I fielded the question. "If they had windows on their bridge, they could. Our noise generator should cancel out our radiation pattern, make us invisible to scanners."

"Let's hope so."

"Almost there." Rione corrected course slightly as we ventured unimpeded toward the satellite's crown, a convex metal housing which held the primary control center.

Rione shut off the noise generator as we got close enough to be enveloped by the mammoth structure's sensor signature. She eased the ROC down on the wide rim surrounding the crown. The landing skids barely even thumped against the hard metal. Embedded in the hull plate in front of our ship was an access hatch. One of the two Torians in the back pulled open the center hatch, and we all stared at Jake, whose pale face was tinted green from the trip.

"Enjoying yourself?" Rione smirked.

He swallowed. "Immensely."

She shut down the engines and we all donned our helmets. Dim blue light tinted the inside lower half of my visor. Rione gripped her disintegrator cannon before opening the canopy and her voice sounded off just beside my ears. "Let's destroy a satellite."

Moving across toward the access hatch, I reached into my pocket, pulling out the tiny pad. I eyed the four edges, even if there didn't seem any visible method of removal.

Rione peered over my shoulder. "Sure this will work?" I smashed the pad against the access hatch. A red light in the tip flashed, barely visible through my visor.

I held my hands against the right side of the hatch. "If not, this will be a pretty short mission."

Jake moved closer. "A lot of folks lost their lives for detailed station specs. Don't worry, it'll work."

We watched for any sign of operation, but the pad did nothing but flash incessantly. The folks who'd supplied it to us insisted that it would override the security system and unlock any external hatch without alerting the crew of the station.

Moments passed, before Rione spoke through the speakers. "How long should this take?"

"Not much longer." My words were prophetic as the hatch finally popped loose. I held the panel tight, easing up just enough for the panel to rotate out on a pair of hinges. Vapors escaped the airlock chamber we exposed.

I turned to Rione, motioning toward the opening. "After you."

We scrambled inside as quick as our pressure suits would allow, and I tugged the hatch shut. The entire team knelt under the compartment's low ceiling. Rione stared at me through her blue-tinted visor. "So, where to?"

I'd studied the blueprints of the satellite until I saw them in my sleep. Three doorways led away from here; we wanted the one directly across from the outer hatch. I crawled toward it, grabbing hold of the large metal wheel.

Cranking the wheel with all of my might, the seal popped and revealed a rectangular maintenance duct beyond. Miniature yellowish-orange wall-mounted lights presented the path along the floor, while wiring flowed overhead in mesh conduits. I led the way on my hands and knees.

Moments later, I came upon a ventilation grate in the floor. Ducking my head down, I peeked through the mesh.

"See anything?" Rione whispered.

Dingy gray walls adorned the empty hall. A lone guard stepped toward the external hull. He turned on his heels and marched back the other direction, passing below us. His dark blue uniform seemed more like something I'd expect out of a palace guard than on a military base. He wasn't even wearing any sort of body armor. Bad for him, good for us.

I waited for him to move out of sight, then whispered to the others, "One guard." I gingerly pulled the grate up, then pulled my Mark II from its holster.

Just as he walked back into view, he looked up at the gaping hole. I fired off a three-shot burst into his chest and he dropped like a pile of rocks.

Thankful there weren't any automatic blast sensors to trigger an alarm, I jumped down and peered along the short corridor while the rest of the team joined me. Another hallway along the interior wall crossed ahead of sliding doors; the control center. That hall ran a complete loop around the station. We'd take a different path.

"Take your positions," I instructed.

Everyone ducked behind exposed frames on the corridor's sides. I sprinted to the right wall, where Jake and Rione waited.

He smiled. "This will be easier than we thought."

I frowned. "It's never easy. Trust me." Halfway along this outer corridor was the other maintenance hatch we needed. I turned to face Jake. "Rione and I will head down to the reactor and meet you back here."

She interrupted, "Once the charges are in place, we'll set the evacuation alarm. The timers will be set for fifteen wertals."

Jake's eyebrows scrunched together. "Isn't that plenty of time to disarm the charges?"

I exhaled a deep breath. "The charges will blow ahead of schedule if they try to."

"Let's hope they don't, then."

Rione slapped his shoulder. "Everything will be fine."

Holstering my weapon, I trotted across the hall with Rione on my heels. She stood guard, her disintegrator cannon propped on her thigh. Thankfully the internal hatches were all quick-release types, with a thumb latch in each corner. Making quick work of those, the panel fell out of place and struck the floor with a muffled clang.

"Stop right there!"

I turned as three more guards appeared at the corner, their dress uniforms identical to their fallen comrade.

"Attack!" Rione bellowed. With one quick pull of her trigger, the disintegrator cannon blasted the lead guard square in the chest. The other two jumped away, watching wide-eyed as his body decomposed. Blood-curdling screams filled the hallway and my skin crawled.

They scrambled back around the corner as Rione fired another shot. A bright orange mark glowed on the wall, marking the point of impact.

Rione shouldered her weapon. "Let's go."

A flurry of crossfire echoed in my ears. I climbed through the opening and grabbed the rungs in front of me. Rione rushed after and we scrambled down the shaft. I pushed a button on my helmet's side, lighting up a bright white lamp which penetrated the dark abyss as I glanced down.

"There should be a vent duct around here." A small grate similar to the first lay in the wall behind us, a few rungs down. "Found it."

Once directly across from it, I reached back, barely touching the small metal bars with the tips of my gloves. I clutched the rungs and collected myself, then stuck one foot against the far wall to balance myself, shoving my fingers into the holes. A sharp tug proved this one to be a lot more secure than the last.

Rione's impatience grew. "Can you pull any harder?"

I swung back and gripped the ladder. "Not like this."

She stepped down a few rungs and without warning, kicked backwards at the grate. The echo of distorted metal rang out.

"Try now."

I positioned myself once more, grabbing hold of the grate. This time, it pulled out easy. I dropped it down the shaft, listening as it clanked off the walls.

"Showoff," I muttered.

"Let's move. We're on a time crunch."

This next duct was like the one we'd entered the station by, except smaller and lacking such benefits as lights. A klaxon echoed through the ductwork, while a red light reflected throughout the shaft we just left. Odd shadows shot past us with each flash.

"Looks like news travels fast," I remarked.

"Hopefully, it isn't too far," Rione mumbled.

"It isn't." I crawled along, before a thought popped in my head. "Hopefully the cruisers won't be diverted, as we planned."

"Trust me, they won't bother. Not until the crew starts evacuating."

I grimaced. "That's reassuring."

I reached another intersection and headed to the right. My helmet's beam reflected off the walls and nearly blinded me. Rione bumped into me from behind.

"I didn't think it was this far from the specs."

I squinted. "Trust me. This left is the last one."

"I hope so."

We turned the corner and reached another panel identical to the other ventilation grates we'd come across. I kicked out the cover and dropped to the floor. Automatic lights flickered to life as I landed and scurried over. Rione fell beside me.

Pipes coated with condensation stood along one wall. Small shelves rested in the corners, stocked with cleaning and maintenance supplies. A lone doorway stood before us. I once more pulled my Mark II from its holster.

Rione motioned toward the doorway, lifting her weapon as a precaution. "Lead the way."

I pressed an oversized silver button along the frame, and the hatch slid open. I peeked out into the empty hallway. As hoped, the station's crew had been summoned to the main deck to counter the invasion squad.

The two of us jogged along until the inside of the corridor became a half-wall, exposing the satellite's guts. A huge gaping expanse filled the area, broken only by a cylindrical metal pod at the very center.

The reactor core.

Above the pod, interlaced trusses ran in six different directions, doubling as supports for the vessel's antenna blades outside. A metal footbridge led down a level from where we stood to the core and its circumferential walkway.

"Two, maybe three inside?" I asked as we ran down the nearest bridge

"If the reports we received were correct."

"Shouldn't be a problem, then."

"Just don't launch off a firedart in there. I'd rather not become a martyr if I can help it."

I didn't bother bringing up the fact I still hadn't loaded the weapon bouncing off my hip with each step. I just wished the core room wasn't heavily shielded from the outside, so I could use it from here. No, the only way to take out the reactor was from the inside. "You're the one who wanted me to bring a weapon along."

"I didn't figure you'd pick that thing."

"Surprise."

We scurried down the footbridge, reaching the core's narrow walkway. I was immediately leery of its edge protected only by a slender pipe railing and widely spaced vertical posts. We reached the single hatch and its security keypad.

Rione mumbled under her breath. "Let's hope the code's still good."

"Everything's been as they told us so far," I offered.

She punched in a series of numbers and a green light flashed on the keypad. The hatch slid open and we rushed in, catching two pale Torians in white lab coats off-guard. Rione fired off a shot as one of them grabbed for a laser pistol resting on the counter.

His body decomposed amidst gut-wrenching screams, and her cannon whined through its recharge cycle. The other technician tried to take advantage of the respite and grabbed for the same pistol.

I fired my blaster, striking his arm with far less dramatic effect. He grabbed the injured limb, cursing.

"Step away from the console," I demanded. "You get shot in the chest next time." He glared at me, but complied once Rione's weapon reached full power and fell silent.

The air inside the core room was bitter and cold. Two consoles being used by these technicians sat along one wall while three enclosed cabinets stood opposite them.

I stared our captive down, speaking to Rione. "Make it quick."

At the very center of the room was a clear cylindrical chamber filled with a luminescent green fluid. Rione slapped each charge against the reactor's thick glass wall as she rushed around it, then strung wires between each charge. The green uroplasm rotated slowly, while palm-sized white spheres floated within, releasing fractum into the mixture. The reaction between these two chemicals ensured enough power generation to run the station.

I glanced past our prisoner at display screens. Most showed data collected inside and outside the reactor, but two provided visuals of the transmitter hanging off the station's boom. Fine details of the blue organic crystals were magnified for inspection purposes. Seeing them only boosted my resolve.

I spoke to Rione. "Are you ready yet?"

"Got it." She slapped the last charge in place, mounting the timer box next to it and synchronizing to her sleeve's timepiece. Then, the countdown started.

She turned to the technician. "I suggest you find an escape pod."

At first, confusion reigned in his face. Then, Rione turned to a nearby console and slammed a large, red button. Klaxons outside changed to deep, long rhythmic tones accompanied by a booming female voice. "Core failure imminent! Proceed with station evacuation!"

His eyes grew wide. "What are you doing?"

"Saving as many people as I can. Evacuate!"

"Stop this madness!" He jumped toward the timer box, but she fired another round. He joined his comrade, their ash piles intermixing.

"Some people just don't listen," Rione said with a grunt. "Let's go."

She rushed out the hatch and weapons fire stuck the core's outer shell. The shots caught her off-guard and she dropped the disintegrator cannon while tumbling past the railing. Her screams echoed throughout the chamber.

Chapter Two

I clutched the back of Rione's suit just below her helmet. Pain radiated through my damaged shoulder, and I yelled inside my helmet. It hadn't been smart to come on this mission without being fully healed, but I wasn't about to let Rione run off on this mission alone.

Another volley of shots struck the platform near us. Rione yanked on my arm with both hands, trying to get a grip. Her actions only ratcheted up my agony, as if my entire arm would rip off. I gritted my teeth, forcing the screams down while focusing on our attacker as he trained his blast rifle on us from behind the half-wall. I lifted my Mark II and flipped the selector switch to automatic.

"Aston, give me your other hand!"

My shoulder was still on fire in her grip. I fired the entire clip, but the guard dropped behind the wall before they reached him. I tossed the weapon aside and grabbed Rione with my other hand.

I looked in both directions, nodding to my left. "Go for the post."

Shots flew over us as she finally clamped onto the metal railing. I released my grip, my left arm now useless as I tucked it against my gut. Rione pulled herself to the platform. "We need to get out of here!"

I pulled the firedart launcher up, fighting hard to load an elliptical shell one-handed. Evading another volley of shots, I rested the barrel on the pipe railing and centered the electronic sight crosshairs on him.

Two more guards joined the first. Bad timing on their parts, as a solid yellow light filled the sight's upper left corner. I pulled the trigger and watched the shell launch toward the three victims. A trail of gaseous fumes trailed behind, which ignited at the launcher only a few moments later. Flames raced along, catching up to the explosive compound shell when they reached the target. A chorus of screams echoed throughout the cavernous chamber as a fireball erupted, enveloping all three victims.

Rione grabbed her disintegrator cannon and scrambled up the footbridge. "Go! Go! Go!"

I grabbed my blaster from the deck and let the empty launcher return to bouncing against my hip, racing up behind her. Flames still licked the walls when we reached the corridor. I was glad my helmet was airtight, because the stench from the three charred corpses spread across the floor would have been unbearable.

Rione's labored breaths rang out over my helmet's speakers as we scrambled down the corridor. "Glad we have a faster way out."

"There's the service lift." It was too bad we couldn't have used this lift for a faster trip down here, but meeting up with troops trying to kill us would have put a few kinks in our plan. "Hopefully the station crew's evacuated."

"If not?"

I raced past her and led the way. "Then, we'll have to fight our way through."

Someone had propped the lift doors open with a metal rod jammed into the frame. My guess was the now-dead guards intended to make a quick exit after checking the alarm.

I pulled the rod out with a grimace, my arm still in excruciating pain. "At least we won't have to wait."

"Good for us."

We climbed on board and the door slammed shut. The lift pod rose effortlessly.

She turned to me. "How's the shoulder?"

"Terrible."

"You should have told me you weren't fully healed."

I ignored her. As we came to a stop, the doors spread before us. An eerie calm hung over a wispy cover of gray smoke.

I spoke into the helmet transmitter, hoping we were in range of our team. "Hold your fire! We're back!"

"All clear!" Jake responded.

We eased out into the corridor, a dozen corpses lining the floor. Our three Torian teammates waited at the tee intersection we'd left behind what seemed forever ago.

"Glad you made it back."

Rione mumbled her response. "Almost didn't."

"That sounds like a story I should hear." His eyebrow rose, and then saw my arm tucked. "Looks like you two got the worst part of this mission."

I piped up, eager to leave. "We need to get out of here. Clock's ticking." Rione had already escaped death once and I'd done the same more times than I could count. I didn't want fate having another chance at either of us. We jogged back toward the duct we'd used for entry.

Rione turned to Jake. "So, have any trouble?"

"Nothing we couldn't handle."

"I expected to see at least a few holdouts."

“As soon as that evacuation order came, it was a mass exodus. Rather boring wait until you got back.”

One of our other teammates helped us into the duct. Jake stepped over, then looked back to Rione. “Ladies first.”

She smirked. “Then what are you waiting for?”

He laughed despite it all, shaking his head before climbing up. Rione turned to me. “Your turn.”

I wasn’t about to argue. Jake pulled me up into the duct. I grimaced with each jarring blow, crawling toward the outer chamber. When I got back to the freighter, I’d need to get my shoulder fixed up again.

Back in the airlock chamber, I finally had time to ponder what had happened, and shuddered in response. Rione had nearly died. I couldn’t let her, not after the last friend I’d lost.

Rione slammed the inner hatch closed, grabbing my attention. “Go!”

I twisted the release latch and the panel burst out with a shot. As we climbed out, I looked up and watched the heavy cruiser approach, flanked by the other two ships.

“Load up!” Rione checked her personal timer. “Four wertals left!”

Everyone scrambled into the ROC, taking their same spots as before. Rione was frantic as she pushed buttons and flipped switches. The three cruisers made wide sweeping turns as the canopy dropped.

One of the two crewmen grabbed my headrest. “They’ve seen us!”

“No! They’re searching blind!” Rione whipped her head around and I saw her emotion ridges through her visor. The small branches of raised skin along the left side of her face had turned white, making me believe she was putting on a good show for the team.

We lifted off from the pad and Rione guided us back toward the interstellar border. The engines accelerated to top speed, as she shifted her hand to the noise generator switch. She kept a close eye on the satellite's distance on the center display before switching it on.

I looked out the canopy as the cruisers continued their random search of the area. I breathed a sigh of relief before remembering the larger issue.

"How much time left on the charges?"

She swung her hand up and panic filled her face. "Brace yourself!"

I looked back out through the canopy as the satellite's center section bulged and buckled as violent blasts ripped through the core. A moment later, chain reactions ripped through the outer hull, the inferno racing through conduits of uroplasm spanning the entire structure. It reached the primary storage tanks just below the main deck and ripped the satellite to shreds in an explosion just short of a supernova.

Sonic shock waves raced away from the cataclysmic epicenter. Our original plan had been to leave soon enough that we'd have plenty of distance between us and the satellite. Any effects of the explosion would have been negligible. Unfortunately, our delays caused us to be right in the blast's wake. The ROC buckled and shook, and by the time Rione finally brought the craft back under control, the noise generator's gentle hum was gone.

We were completely exposed.

Rione cursed, attempting to restart the device with repeated flips of the control switch. All three cruisers broke off their original flight path and raced toward our defenseless ship. We weren't capable of hyperspeed, and our engines weren't enough to get us back to the station before those cruisers caught up to us. All in all, there were a million other places I'd have rather been at that moment.

A voice dropped inside our helmets through the cockpit audio link. It was the same one I'd heard on the Rulusian freighter's bridge, Commander Sevil from the Torian warship. "You're under arrest, terrorist scum!"

I looked over at Rione. "Maybe we can ignore them?"

The voice returned. "Come to a full stop and power down, or prepare to face the consequences!"

Rione pointed at the display screen. "They're still out of weapons range."

I glanced down. Tapping on the lead ship's red triangle, I watched the distance-to-target figure drop faster than my heart did to my stomach. "It won't take long with that closure rate."

Rione was deadpan. "Ready to be a martyr?"

"Not today." I pressed my lips tight.

Commander Sevil became more irate. "Power down, now!"

I looked down at the screen again. All three cruisers reached weapons range, locking on to us in unison. Red warning lights flashed around the lower canopy sill, and dual concentric red rings flashed around the symbol representing our ship. High-pitched, rapid beeps blasted our eardrums through the helmet speakers.

We were about to become space dust.

Another voice interrupted. "Unidentified vessel, do you require assistance?" It took a moment to place it.

Captain Dillager.

I jumped into the conversation. "Yes. We seem to be experiencing a mechanical malfunction."

"We extend our assistance to your vessel in distress as specified in the Code of Interstellar Wayfaring, section two-point-five-dash-one."

Commander Sevil interrupted our happy reunion. "You are meddling in an affair of Torian sovereignty. We consider this an act of war!"

Dillager kept his cool, which I'm sure did nothing but infuriate the Commander more. "I really think you should get your sensors checked. If you look closely, you'll see the vessel in distress is clearly outside of Torian territorial boundaries. By attacking them, you would be in violation of the Code and several interstellar treaties."

"We will destroy you both!"

"We thought you might not see it our way. Our destroyers are en-route to help settle this dispute."

At that very moment, the destroyers joined the mishmash of contacts on the display, two more full green circles. The cruisers came to a full stop.

"This is not over." Sevil hissed. His transmission terminated with three quick beeps in the headset. The klaxons returned in full force.

All three cruisers kept their targeting computers locked on the ROC. I wasn't sure if it for posturing, or if they truly were ready to start an interplanetary war.

The constant ear-busting alarms gave me a splitting headache. "Is there a way to turn this noise off?"

"Afraid not." Rione adjusted course for the freighter.

"That's what I was afraid of."

"Think they'll do it?" Rione peered at the three dark cruisers behind us.

"Let's hope not."

Off the port side, the Rulusian cruiser approached, with a destroyer on each side.

I suddenly had a thought. "Problem."

Rione turned. "What?"

"How are we going to dock with Dillager's ship? This thing doesn't have an airlock." Rione cursed, knowing I was right. The Torians would keep a close eye on us, and returning to the freighter's docking bay in their line of sight would be admitting the freighter was modified for our use. The Rulusians had gone to a lot of trouble to make sure no one knew they were involved in this planetary skirmish. If Commander Sevil discovered they'd been backing the rebels, it would provide all the justification he'd need to engage the Rulusians.

Looking down at the data displayed, we also didn't have enough fuel to get back to the station. There hadn't been enough capacity to do so in the first place, thus our original plan for a rendezvous. Our team would have to board the hard way.

I turned to face Rione. "Take us to a spot just over the airlocks."

"You want me to land on the ship? Are you crazy?" Her eyes went wide and forehead scrunched.

"Just temporarily."

She shook her head, but adjusted course all the same.

I contacted Dillager. "Captain, if you don't mind opening the outer starboard airlock..."

"Acknowledged."

"We'll be in momentarily."

"Acknowledged."

A couple kilpars in length, the smooth lines of the freighter tapered from its nose to a constant rectangular cross-section around the first quarter. Rione gently brought us down and settled the ROC atop the main hull. The canopy lifted and the ladder extended. Our Torian team members exited the craft, including Jake Falcon out of the gurney bay, then we made a slow crawl along the hull.

"I'm setting the engines for a full burn. We'll pick it up later," Rione told me.

She climbed out and I followed. Once we reached the airlock, the ROC's engines fired off and it bolted off toward the Torian orbital station, a dark shadow in the distant starfield.

I maneuvered over the airlock lip, before a flash of light caught my attention. My skin crawled as the ROC exploded. The fire extinguished, while the debris field scattered.

Rione exclaimed. "What was that?"

I turned and looked at the gathering of Torian warships, having no doubt what had just happened. "I have a pretty good idea." Grimacing, my skin crawled at what might have happened if they'd decided to fire on us earlier.

We climbed into the cramped airlock, and the pressurization sequence finished quickly. We raced down the corridor and through another open hatch.

Dillager held up his hand to keep us silent as we scrambled onto the bridge. He was already in the middle of an audio-only conversation.

"Commander, we demand to know why you intentionally fired on an unarmed vessel in interstellar territory."

"I would think a Captain who spouts off sections of the Code of Interstellar Wayfaring would know that any derelict craft posing a travel hazard must be disposed of."

"The Code intended for derelict craft to be retrieved."

Sevil spat his words. "The Code is vague on that point."

"The intent was obvious."

"You take care of derelict ships your way. We'll take care of them in our own."

An odd irony, since derelict craft were usually my first choice when searching for, and then taking valuable cargo.

Unfortunately, that wasn't actually allowable under the Code, either.

Dillager turned to his communication officer. "Terminate this conversation." He received a nod in return.

His first officer stood looking over her scanner screen. She glanced over at Dillager. "Captain, all of the Torian cruisers are holding position, just the other side of the border."

I finally remembered her name. Jaclyn.

The Captain let out a deep breath. "Shame about the ROC. That noise generator modification wasn't cheap."

I knew he was right, having done the same to my own ship long ago. "At least he didn't retrieve it, I suppose."

Rione pulled off her helmet, sweat pouring off her face and hair. She chuckled. "Ever the optimist."

One thing I'd never been accused of.

With all of the defying death going on, I'd forgotten about my shoulder. The pain screamed back with a vengeance as I reached for my helmet.

"Need some help?" Rione asked.

I bore down on the pain, pulling it off my head. "I'm good, thanks." Sweat flowed off my head as well, but even with the tropical temperatures on-board this freighter, I still felt the blessed touch of semi-fresh air.

"Serves you right for going on a mission with a bum shoulder," she told me.

Jake caught our attention from behind, his helmet tucked into the crook of his arm. "If you don't mind, we're going to get out of these suits." The trio trudged around the circular bridge, exiting aft into the cargo hold.

Jaclyn nodded toward me. "You injure your shoulder over there?"

Rione answered for me. "Re-injured it, more like."

The Rulusian female walked down from her spot. "Let's go get you fixed up."

Dillager plopped himself in his chair. "Jaclyn doubles as our ship's medic."

I turned to Rione. "I'll catch up with you later."

The Lazarian frowned in response, which I thought odd, before she followed the team out. Jaclyn motioned in the direction we'd come, and the two of us started back toward the crew quarters.

• • •

We stepped inside, where about half of the stacked bunks were empty. She helped me unzip the white pressure suit, and I stepped out of it before plopping my butt down on an unused cot. Facing Jaclyn, I watched while she stepped over to the corner, rummaging through a wall-mounted medical supply cabinet. I stared at her thin, green figure in its black dress uniform.

She grabbed supplies while she talked. "It looked like they were going to blow your ship to bits out there."

I hadn't been so scared of death in quite a while, but played it cool. "I've been through worse."

"I'm sure."

She shut the small metal cabinet door, walked over and sat beside me. A small medication dispenser was in her right hand and a flexible pad in the other.

"Strip," Jaclyn commanded.

I chuckled. "We barely know each other."

She rolled her eyes. "You want me to fix up your shoulder or not?"

I reached for my right side, but pain roared through my left shoulder as I did. Clenching my teeth, I changed hands and awkwardly grabbed for the zipper at my neckline.

“Let me help.” Jaclyn placed her gear down, then reached across my chest. Her face drew near mine, with her silky smooth skin close enough to touch. A floral scent invaded my nostrils. She gave a little smile and winked before pulling the zipper down to my waist. The slick, black body suit slid off my chest, the material falling in a pile around my waist. Beads of sweat formed all over the exposed skin, and rolled down toward the bedding. She moved away slightly and stared at the various scars on my chest, the largest in particular running a quarter of the width across my torso.

“This must have a story behind it.” She raised an eyebrow, running a finger just below my ribs along the old wound. It took every bit of willpower I had not to jump at her touch.

I pursed my lips. “Bar fight.”

“The other guy must have been pretty upset at you.”

I didn’t even remember what we’d been fighting about. Strange, since I’d almost died.

“I imagine so.”

She pulled her finger away from the scarred tissue. “Looks like you’re lucky to be alive.”

“Guess so.” The other guy wasn’t so lucky. I omitted that tidbit of information.

She noticed the scarring in my shoulder. “Another fight?”

I grimaced, not willing to talk about that one. “You could say that.”

She lifted an eyebrow, but sensed my reluctance. Others tended to push for more, but Jaclyn simply pointed past me. “Turn.”

I followed her instructions, then felt the medication dispenser prick my shoulder. A numbing fog spread throughout the area and brought instant relief.

“Thanks.”

"Don't thank me just yet."

I heard the rumpling of plastic and looked back as she scrunched the pad back and forth in her hands. It wasn't something I'd seen before. I scrunched my eyebrows. "What exactly is that?"

Her light green eyes sparkled. "You'll find out soon enough. Don't worry."

For emphasis, she leaned over and planted a kiss on the back of my damp shoulder. It would have served a little more use if she hadn't used the numbing agent first.

Finished with her work on the pad, she laid it onto my shoulder and I nearly screamed as the fire-hot surface bypassed the numbing medication completely. I swore it burned the first three or four skin layers off.

"Aren't medics supposed to do no harm?" I complained.

She chuckled. "You forget this isn't my main job. Now, stop being a baby. It'll be over soon enough."

And as Jaclyn suggested, the heat passed into my shoulder and the pad normalized at a lower temperature just before she ripped it off. It felt better, but I wasn't sure the excruciating pain had been worth it.

"Thanks." I started to stand.

She pulled at my suit, sitting me back down. "Still not done."

Then, she massaged my shoulder with her soft, green hands. The numbing agent was wearing off and it was almost as if my shoulder was good as new. I decided the pad had indeed been worth it, if only for Jaclyn's touch.

I smirked, still facing the other direction. "So, you often take a hands-on technique in doctoring your crew?"

"No." She planted another kiss. This time, the sensations raced full steam ahead.

I stumbled over my words. "Well, then..." She gripped my shoulder and massaged a bit deeper. I stopped talking.

Then, another voice interrupted. "What is this?"

Rione stood in the doorway when I turned to look. Her pressure suit was off, but she still wore the black body suit, while her long black hair was matted from the heat and humidity. Her emotion ridges were deep red in anger.

Jaclyn kept her focus on me. "Fixing Aston's shoulder."

It didn't faze Rione. "Captain Dillager wants us to join him in his quarters. All of us." She stormed out.

"What's her problem?" Jaclyn pulled her hands away.

I shrugged, before easing my body suit back on. She helped me with the zipper, her face right next to my own when she finished. "We'll continue this later."

Chapter Three

Dillager's quarters were just off one quadrant of the round bridge. They weren't much in appearance, but still reigned as the only individual quarters on a Rulusian freighter. The Captain and Rione sat at a circular glass table with silver and black chairs. He motioned Jaclyn and me to the open chairs, uncorking a dark green bottle more than a little familiar to me.

I sat on the table's far side, Rione and Jaclyn on either side of me. My friend's emotion ridges were still visible, never straying from dark red. Her eyes remained on our host, avoiding me and Jaclyn. The episode in the crew quarters burned in my mind. Why had she reacted that way?

Dillager nodded, pouring the green liquid into four waiting glasses. "Glad you all made it back in one piece."

Rione was despondent, moist hair sticking to her face. "Wish it could have gone a little smoother."

Jaclyn interrupted. "We have an old saying back on Rulusia. 'When it comes to survival, the goal concerns itself not with the efforts.'"

Rione didn't bother looking at her, while Dillager chuckled. "I prefer another saying, 'Victory always calls for heavy drinking.'" He handed out the glasses.

Someone who spoke my language, even if this particular dialect was one I didn't care for.

"Mind telling me what this is before I drink it?" Rione frowned at him.

I answered instead. "Jungle Juice."

The Captain set the bottle aside and smiled, his jagged teeth resembling a monster's far more than they should have. "Nectar of the gods."

"Just make sure not to drink too much." I smiled. "It packs a punch."

Jaclyn chuckled. "Only for amateurs."

I turned to her and snorted. "Unless you're Rulusian, everyone's an amateur."

Rione brought us back to business, her hand on the filled glass. "Captain, what's the status of our situation with the Torian cruisers?"

"No situation," he waved. "The Commander knows better than to provoke Rulusia into an all-out war."

His first officer interrupted, solemn. "I imagine that to be inevitable."

"Perhaps. But a mere Commander doesn't want the infamous distinction of being listed in the history books as starting it."

Jaclyn shook her head, her lips tight. "Hopefully, you're right."

He leaned back and clasped his hands behind his head. "I am. He knows, as we all do, this entire situation is all a matter of perceptions."

I leaned forward. "Whose?"

"Everyone. The Rulusian public sees this exercise as a humanitarian mission, as do most surrounding systems."

"And if shots are fired?"

He flashed those brown, jagged teeth again. "Just so it doesn't look like we started it."

I grunted. "A Rulusian freighter draws off Torian cruisers shortly before their satellite is blown apart, then offers assistance to the fleeing vessel. You're not worried anyone will connect the dots?"

"Not particularly, no." Dillager grabbed his glass and bellowed. "To victory."

"To victory," everyone repeated.

We raised our glasses. The two Rulusians downed theirs in the blink of an eye. I knew what Jungle Juice did to me and merely sipped my own.

Rione took a drink far larger than she should have, and her face soured while returning the glass to the table.

"Potent?" I smiled.

"A little." At least she spoke to me.

Dillager topped off everyone's glass. "So, now that the satellite has been destroyed, what's next?"

Rione ran a finger across the rim of her glass. "Rebel forces should be able to gather in larger numbers now, since the king won't spot them so easily."

I lifted my glass. "Which means they'll have to devote forces to find them manually."

Rione nodded. "And fewer guarding potential targets."

Dillager smiled and repeated the toast, "To victory!"

The two Rulusians again gulped down their drinks. I tipped my glass until the fluid reached my lips and pretended to drink. Bad things happened when I drank too much Jungle Juice, and I had no intention of passing out before I wanted to.

Rione, however, finished the whole glass off.

"Careful," I warned.

She laughed under her breath. "This is supposed to be a celebration, isn't it?"

"That's the spirit!" Dillager poured another round.

Jaclyn looked over at me. "So, how'd you ever get involved in this skirmish, Aston?"

I chuckled under my breath. "Fate, I suppose."

Rione laughed. "Aston has a unique ability of being in the wrong place at the right time."

There was no disputing that. Had I not stumbled upon her derelict freighter destined for destruction, she'd be dead. It had almost been a case of fate ensuring my arrival in a nick of time, if you believed in that sort of thing.

Jaclyn chuckled. "I can imagine."

Rione pointed a finger at me, her hand still around her glass. "That reminds me, I owe you again." I knew things were headed toward an unhappy ending when she tossed another glass down her throat.

"Don't worry about it."

Both Dillager and Jaclyn seemed confused, but the feeling faded as Rione swayed in her seat. I grabbed her shoulder to steady her. True to form, her eyes rolled up and her head slumped forward. I eased her down until she rested on the tabletop.

Dillager smiled. "Guess she reached her limit." He slammed back his own glass.

Jaclyn smiled. "Amateurs."

A speaker recessed into the wall behind Dillager squawked, "Captain, we've reached the station. Two transport shuttles have been dispatched to dock with us."

He leaned back on two chair legs, shoving a thumb into the transmit button. "Acknowledged."

Jaclyn glanced across the table. "Some timing."

Rione's head was flat against the table, her hair out of place and emotion ridges visible. They'd turned pink, a shade I never remembered seeing against her golden-bronze skin before. I'd need to help Rione back to her quarters in her current state. This wasn't something the Rulusian crew, or our Torian teammates, needed to witness.

"Captain, you mind asking for a third shuttle?"

• • •

Fortunately, the station spared us an extra transport with no questions asked. I buckled Rione into one of a dozen forward-facing seats forming four columns in the empty aft compartment. Then, I left her to sleep it off while walking up the center aisle. Our docking clamps clunked loudly as we disengaged from the freighter.

Jaclyn turned to face me from the pilot's seat as I entered the cockpit. "Will she be okay?"

"Her head will feel like it was at the center of that satellite explosion, but other than that, she should be."

I sat in the right hand seat while she guided us toward the grim station.

Jaclyn held her lips tight. "I noticed you weren't following her lead."

I gave a nervous laugh. "I've been through bouts with Jungle Juice before, and try not to repeat my mistakes."

"Don't tell me you're an amateur, too."

That elicited a smile. "Not at all. I'm more a Vladirian liquor kind of guy."

"I'll keep that in mind."

"You asked for a docking port close to her quarters?" The last thing I wanted was to foul up her dignity even more than had already been done.

"It should be just down the corridor."

As if they heard us, a set of flashing lights winked at us next to one of the docking ports on the inner ring. The compartment fell into silence as we continued in and docked. The clamps engaged once more, while Jaclyn powered the ship down. The interior lights dimmed.

"So, any plans once you drop off Rione?"

"Head back to the landing bay, and get some sleep."

She nodded in understanding, then thumbed toward the back. "Going to need any help with her?"

"I could use an extra hand getting her through the airlock tube, but after that, I can handle it myself."

She motioned me back. "Well, pressurization should be equalized now, if you'd like to lead the way."

I started to the aft compartment, where Rione was still passed out in her seat. Jungle Juice was dangerous in the wrong hands, and as much as she'd ingested, it wouldn't surprise me if she didn't wake up for a few rotations.

I unfastened Rione's restraints and hoisted her up, then started for the airlock hatch which Jaclyn opened. A short, dark tube led toward a gray corridor beyond.

I nodded toward the tube. "If you don't mind holding her a moment, I'll pull her through from the other side."

"No problem."

Jaclyn placed herself under Rione's other arm and shouldered the burden while I climbed in feet-first. Then, I grabbed Rione by the underarms and pulled her through the tube. This really wasn't the place to be boarding a station unconscious, but bringing Rione in through one of the normal landing bays would have created far more problems.

Jaclyn followed behind. "How's the shoulder?"

"Great. I need to get with you later and find out what you gave me. Maybe you can leave some with me."

She smiled. "I'll see what I can do."

Shortly, I stood up in the drab station corridor, hoisting Rione up. "Thanks for the help," I told Jaclyn.

"Sure you don't need help getting to her quarters?"

"I'll be fine."

"Catch you later." She waved and started off in the opposite direction.

I lugged Rione's limp body through the hall. She was a lot heavier than she looked; either that, or she'd found a way to somehow soak up the alcohol like a sponge. Not wanting to chance the shoulder treatment wearing off, I'd draped her across my right shoulder. All the while, I kept thinking I should have taken Jaclyn up on her assistance.

"Remind me not to let anyone give you Jungle Juice again," I mumbled with silence her only response. I smirked and chuckled. "Glad we could come to an understanding."

We finally arrived at her personal quarters, and I was fortunate not to have stumbled across anyone else along the way. I definitely would have gotten attention, dragging an unconscious woman down the corridor.

I leaned Rione up against the wall and moved her hand against a recessed pad beside the door. It glowed fluorescent green and performed a quick scan before releasing the lock with a clunk. The hatch slid aside and I pulled her through. As soon as we made it inside, the door closed and everything went pitch black.

"Lights."

Nothing happened. I tried other variations without success.

I sighed. "Perfect." We stood there until my sight grew accustomed to the darkness, at least where I could make out a nearby chair to put Rione in.

Once she was down, I started back for the doorway. As I approached, the sensors picked up my presence and the hatch opened once more. With a vast swath of light, I did a quick scan of the room since it was my first time inside her quarters.

It was larger than most I'd seen on space stations, but still cramped, made even more prominent by having no windows. Along the far left wall, an open doorway led to a second room. Another closed hatch lay just beyond the divider, which by the power of deduction, I figured led to a lavatory.

Directly across from the door was a couch similar in color and style to the chair Rione was using. In the far right corner, a bed rested, aligned with the wall. It hardly looked used, compared to the cot on my ship, which was always in disarray. At the foot of the bed was a storage trunk with a cushion-top lid. A dresser was nestled between the bed and couch. On the opposite side of the couch, against the lavatory wall, a small table with a dark gray metallic lamp.

Bingo.

I scanned the cleared path between me and the lamp, then started a very slow and careful walk toward it. The door closed and bathed us in darkness again, but at least this time I knew where I was going.

I gingerly felt for the lamp when I thought I was nearby. Touching the base was enough to cast an eerie glow around the room.

I looked over at Rione, who hadn't budged at all through this entire ordeal. I debated how to get her into bed, and finally settled on cradling her. I picked her up and gently carried her over, placing her limp body on top of the royal blue covers.

I stood and stepped back, smacking my elbow against the dresser. I cursed up a storm under my breath. A quick glance at Rione confirmed she was still out, but there was a slight smile on her face. I couldn't remember whether it had been there before or not.

I turned and saw a picture frame which had landed on the floor. Careful not to injure myself further, I reached down and grabbed it. The electronic image brightened in response, while I placed it back atop the dresser.

I studied the image. Rione stood on the right, in a loving embrace with a pale-skinned Torian. I'd only met Malone once before, during my last visit to the station. He was one of the rebel forces' top leaders down on the planet, and seemed like a top-notch guy from our one meeting. Based on how they were intertwined, and the skimpy clothes both wore, the photo was not one of comrades in arms, but lovers.

Both had huge smiles on their faces, standing on a sandy beach. I wondered where the picture had been taken. Toris was an icy wasteland incapable of sustaining life, leaving no alternative but underground caverns for the population to live.

Feeling a bit snoopy, since I'd never really gotten to know my friend all that well, I looked at the other two objects beside the frame. A necklace lay at the center, composed of two joined strands. Each of the wires was strung with shells and stones of various shapes and sizes. It was quite possible they'd all come from that same beach Rione and Malone stood on.

My eyes strayed to the only other object in sight, another picture. I let my hand touch the frame and the image brightened just as the first. This photo was of Rione and another man, this one with skin as bronze as her own. I'd never met him. The two of them were crouched on a sandy beach, but a young child knelt in front of them.

I'd never known Rione had a child.

Something bothered me about this second picture, but I couldn't quite figure out why. I drew in closer with an intent stare, then did a double-take while looking back at the first picture. Trading glances between the two, it finally came into focus; the rock outcropping along the horizon on the far left side of the shot. It was the same location in both pictures.

Then my eyes drew upon the little girl in the second picture. A necklace hung around her neck. I debated whether to touch the necklace on the dresser, since I'd intruded enough already. Curiosity got the better of me, and I reached for it. My heart jumped out of my chest as Rione mumbled something incoherent. I watched a moment to make sure she was still out, then continued my exploits.

I picked it up and turned the piece around. On the largest stone, stuck at the bottom of the outer wire, was crude lettering marked with what appeared to be a laser etcher. It read, 'To our beautiful daughter, Rione. Love, Mom and Dad.'

I looked back at the photo again. That wasn't Rione, but her mother? They were identical in appearance, which wasn't odd, but still struck me as spooky. She'd returned to the same site with Malone. Her parents had died long ago, as had my own. Returning to this particular spot had been some sort of remembrance.

I suddenly felt dirty and attempted to return the necklace to its same spot. I touched the lamp again, sending the room back into darkness before walking toward the door. It was time to return to my ship and sleep, as the adrenaline rush from the mission was crashing down.

Moments later, I climbed the steps to a second level, making my way to the landing bay where my ship was parked. To my surprise, Jaclyn stood just outside the doors, her dress uniform unbuttoned down to her chest. She had a bottle of Vladirian liquor and a smile on her lips.

"Figured you might like to celebrate with something besides Jungle Juice."

Chapter Four

Jaclyn and I sat in my living quarters, the outer hatch closing us off from the rest of the station, nursing the Vladirian liquor she'd brought. Had I known someone would stop by, I might have cleaned up the place before the mission. Cleanliness wasn't one of my finer points, but the ship had become far more of a sty than normal.

Jaclyn didn't seem to mind. "So, you just live here on your ship? No quarters on the station?"

"No sense in taking space someone else could use."

"You don't have to sell me." She took another look around. "I think it would be exciting, travelling around the galaxy whenever and wherever you want."

"Other than finding your next job, so you can pay for food and fuel," I mused while drinking my glass dry.

Jaclyn was still off in her own little world. "I thought my time in the military would be exciting."

"Recruiters like to make you think so."

"That they do." She drank down a glass, then lifted an eyebrow. "You were in the military?"

"Gryphon Defense Force, flew space fighters." Joining them as a young man had been my only chance at survival. The fellow who'd signed me up had still gone to extremes.

"I could see you doing that."

A sigh passed over my lips. "A long time ago."

I refilled our glasses with the sweet yellow liquid. Silence surrounded us. Jaclyn took a longer drink, truly a woman after my own heart. As she placed the empty glass on the table, she wiped the outside of her mouth with a long, thin green finger. "I suppose it's good I'm getting out of the service soon."

I held my own drink just off my lips. "Getting out how, exactly?"

"I'm about ready to retire. Should be done by the time we head back to Rulusia."

My forehead scrunched. "What'd they do, enlist you right out of the womb? You're too young to retire."

A laugh escaped her lips. "That's nice of you to say, but I'm far older than I look."

I gazed upon her smooth face and blonde hair, and couldn't believe it. I wanted to ask how old she really was, but intelligence collected a rare win.

"Oh, before I forget..." She turned and reached into her uniform's pocket, pulling out a small pouch which she handed over. I pulled open the clasp and peeked inside at the medical dispenser, several pads, and a small foil pack filled with vials. She continued, "I stopped by the station infirmary and picked up some medicine for your shoulder."

I reached up and gently touched my wound. "It certainly feels better."

She raised her glass. "Rulusian medicine is the best in the galaxy."

"Won't get any argument here."

The side of her mouth curled a bit as she set her empty glass down. "Almost as good as our massage therapy."

I chuckled and put mine next to hers.

“Shall we continue where we left off?” Her hand reached for my leg, and excitement wove through my body.

Dumbfounded, I didn’t bother responding. She grabbed my hand and led me to my cot. Sitting next to me, Jaclyn leaned across my chest to pull my body suit’s zipper down to my waist. Her smile was wicked, and my heart thumped with the anticipation of things to come. The suit slid down to my hips and she pointed toward the cockpit.

“Turn.”

The tips of her fingers probed while her palms kneaded my shoulder. Pain lingered below the surface, but was just barely able to maintain my composure. “You have an excellent touch.”

“Thanks.”

I felt her warm breath only a moment before moist lips touched the back of my neck. Tiny shivers raced across my skin. Her head moved toward my injured shoulder, then pulled away. The scent of lust lingered.

“It’s been a while, hasn’t it?”

I gave a nervous laugh. “That obvious?”

“You’re really tense. How do you normally relax?”

“Drink heavily.”

Her hands pulled away. It wouldn’t have been the first time I’d screwed up, and likely not the last. But then, her uniform flew past and landed on the floor.

“Let’s find some different ways to help you relax.” Jaclyn pressed against my bare back, kissing along my shoulder blades. Her arms reached around me, stroking my chest. Primal urges rose within me.

It had been so long since I’d felt the touch and caress of a female body, I’d almost forgotten what it was like. I didn’t know what I was feeling most out of the jumble. Scared, maybe. Excited, yes. Confused, definitely.

"Just relax and let it happen," she insisted, as if reading my mind.

Her hands moved down my chest, caressing and exploring every spot they could. Then, one reached my waistband, where the body suit still rested. My mind and body were debating what I should do, and in the confusion, Jaclyn slipped past undetected. A moan escaped my lips, and suddenly my mind had no say in the matter. She moved her face closer to my own.

I turned to look her in the eyes and my mind gave one last valiant attempt at stopping this. But before I could say a word, she silenced me with a long, passionate kiss and my body readied itself for what was to come. We broke apart from one another and she pulled her hand free.

She rolled onto her back and a smile filled her face. I moved my hands up her body, skin soft and silky against my rough fingers. I called out to Jeanie, "Dim the lights."

• • •

I stared at the ceiling, arms tucked behind my neck. Jaclyn lay beside me, her head resting on my chest. She drummed her fingers against my skin, keeping time with my heart speeding right along.

She let out an exasperated sigh. "Even better than I imagined."

"Yes, it was." It was something I hadn't had in a very long time. Thankfully, I hadn't forgotten how the dance steps were supposed to go.

She looked up with a gentle smile, then ran a hand through my hair. We kissed one more time, before she reached for her clothes on the floor. "Well, I need to take care of a few things before heading back to the ship. I'd like to see you again before we leave, if you'll be around."

The thought of continuing where we'd left off made my heart jump a few beats. "I don't plan on going anywhere."

I followed Jaclyn's lead as far as dressing myself, then escorted her toward the outer hatch. She leaned in for another deep kiss as we reached the exit. Taking the unspoken cue, Jeanie opened it for us. "Thanks for a wonderful time."

"See you soon," I told her, grabbing the door frame and watching her walk off toward the landing bay doors.

Then she was gone.

"Close us up, Jeanie."

I walked back over to the table and grabbed the Vladirian liquor. Not bothering with a glass, I tipped the bottle back and finished it off.

"I never had the chance to welcome you home, Aston," Jeanie stated.

"Thanks."

"I trust your mission was successful?"

I hadn't told her the specifics of what we'd planned doing. As odd as it sounded for a machine, I figured she'd worry. "Yes, it was."

"Then, you were celebrating with your new friend?"

I stared at the empty bottle, unsure of what to say. Of course, I knew Jeanie saw every spot aboard the ship. It just hadn't occurred to me she would bring it up, let alone take an interest in why it was happening. At least she hadn't asked while Jaclyn and I had been in the heat of the moment. "I guess you could say that."

"So what do you plan to do now?" She asked me.

My lips pressed tight, while I tossed the bottle to the floor. It clunked in a pile of dirty laundry. "Probably stick around here a little while longer, until I come up with a plan."

"Do you believe Elijah will discover your location if you stay here too long?"

Just the mention of his name sent my blood boiling and my head throbbing. Even my shoulder started to ache. "Even that sadistic freak knows better than to enter a war zone."

At least that was my theory. It allowed me to sleep, even if I wasn't sure I fully believed it. Elijah Cassus was insane enough to do it, despite the risk. I'd killed his brother and revenge was a deep and hearty motivation. Heck, my need for retribution was just as strong, and when the two of us met again, we'd see whose drive was stronger.

"Then it would be better to stay here permanently?"

"Perhaps."

Even normally, I wasn't one who stayed in one place too long. This was anything but normal. Elijah wanted me dead, but I wanted the same of him for ordering his brother to kill a friend I'd wanted to save. I knew it wouldn't be easy to get to him, not with him commanding an entire organization of mercenaries and pirates. That's why I needed to come up with a plan first.

I looked over at my shoulder. The medics on-board the station had done a fine job of repairing it, but there'd be no getting around the scarring, not with the damage I'd gone through. It probably wouldn't look so bad, if not for all the bruising intermingled with pale raised flesh. All of my other scars had taken on a more dormant appearance, and this one would too. Eventually.

Gently, I reached up and brushed my fingers along the wound's remnants. It hadn't been the wisest move to go on a mission without being completely healed. Unfortunately, my sense of obligation had gotten the best of me. That tended to be a recurring theme in my life.

Jeanie's voice called out. "Are you okay?"

"Yes." I closed my eyes and took a deep breath. "Just a little worn out, that's all."

"Perhaps you should rest?"

"You read my mind." I flopped down on my cot. Staring at the ceiling again, I couldn't get past what had just happened. Certainly, it had been enjoyable, every moment. But there was something still nagging at the center of my being.

Tossing and turning for what seemed forever, I finally gave up the fight. I couldn't sleep with the scent of sweaty lust still in the air. Instead, I walked over to my closet. Reaching inside, I pulled out a clean set of pants and a fresh shirt. The light blue fabric was soft and cool against my chest as I buttoned it up. Rione had purchased it for me as a get-well present during my recuperation.

I stared at a small mirror inside the closet door. At least I was minimally presentable.

I spoke to Jeanie. "I'm going for a walk around the station, clear my head."

She didn't bother responding, but opened the hatch for me. I left the landing bay and took in my surroundings. The lights above were dimmed, to mimic a nighttime feel. Not a soul was visible in the commons area below, which suited me fine. I needed the silence and solitude. I ventured around the circular walkway, then down a set of stairs into the station's hub.

I already knew how this would end. I couldn't clear my head by just walking around. The only tried and true way was to drink myself to oblivion. It was a method I'd developed over a lifetime. Vladirian liquor, as much as I loved it, wouldn't do the trick. There was only one drink which knocked me out quick, and that was Jungle Juice.

An old familiar sign hung over an entrance doorway, spelling out 'Stardust' in bright yellow tubes. I made a direct line across the commons area. The regular sounds of joyous laughter and pleasant conversation were absent. Most shopkeepers and residents took advantage of this time for slumber, but the emptiness also had a lot to do with the escalating Torian civil war. Many businesses had lost so much foot traffic that they'd closed permanently. The Stardust, on the other hand, still enjoyed a lively crowd from time to time.

Thankfully for me.

A bartender looked up as I walked inside. Our regular barkeep was nowhere to be found, and the pale Torian currently tending couldn't have been much more than a teenager. He gave me an odd look with his deep blue eyes.

He smiled, uncomfortable as I took a seat on the stool in front of him. "How are you tonight?"

"Terrible," I muttered.

He nodded knowingly. "What can I get you?"

"Jungle Juice."

"Certainly, sir."

I cringed. "Don't call me sir."

"Okay, s..." He stopped himself, then smiled. "No problem."

"I'll take the whole bottle if you don't mind."

He nodded, then reached under the counter and pulled out a familiar green bottle. "Certainly a lot of interest in this stuff."

"You must be new, kid."

"This is my third night. Bottle will be ten credits."

I flipped a golden twenty-credit coin onto the counter. "Keep the change."

He stared at the green rim, eyes wide. His smile spread rapidly. "Thanks!"

"It's because you have two Rulusian warships parked out there keeping watch over the station." One of the reasons this place had even survived was ongoing visits from Rulusian troops on the abbreviated equivalent of shore leave. They certainly loved their Jungle Juice, even more than I did Vladirian liquor.

"Oh."

"Anyone else, and they likely couldn't get through a glass or two without losing consciousness."

His forehead scrunched. "You just bought a bottle."

I grabbed my purchase and stood. "Yes, I did."

"Want to talk about it?"

"Not tonight, kid, not tonight." I gave a slight wave and headed out the door.

It didn't take long to return to my ship. Jeanie spoke as soon as my feet touched the floorboards inside. "Were you able to clear your head?"

It was almost like being married, or at least what I'd always heard about it anyway. "For the most part."

I walked over to my cot and sat down. I placed the bottle at my feet, removed my shirt and pants, then stared at the bottle. My drinking really needed to stop. It wasn't serving to eliminate my problems, only a temporary fix.

But I had yet to find a permanent one.

"Dim the lights."

Jeanie did so.

What was my mind so hung up on? I'd had a great time with Jaclyn, but there was something nagging me. And then, in a moment of clarity, I finally admitted it to myself. This had just been a fling, something that I had done off and on again throughout my life. But my feelings, my heart, it yearned for another, and I couldn't have her.

I uncorked the top and lifted it high. The fruity green liquid flowed faster than I could swallow, and dribbled out the sides of my mouth. I lowered the bottle to the floor beside me. I felt myself under its effects almost a heartbeat later, as my vision swayed, so laid down and closed my eyes to help the process along.

Chapter Five

"Aston..."

I blinked my eyes open, hearing Jeanie's voice. Pulsing slammed around inside my skull, making it seem like a landing pad for starship pilots' training. "What is it?"

"Rione has entered the landing bay."

Jeanie had impeccable timing, as rapping echoed against my hull. I grabbed my head, stumbled to my feet and weaved over to my closet. Tossing on a white shirt and black pants, I mumbled to Jeanie, "Open it up."

Even through my jaw, I felt the gears grinding while the hatch lowered. Rione stood there with no sign of the hangover she should have had from her own battle with the green demon known as Jungle Juice. She smiled when I stepped out. "Looks like you had a rough night."

I put my hand up to shield the light. "I'd think after all you drank, you'd have worse."

She sighed. "Other than not remembering how I got back into my quarters, it wasn't all that bad."

"Lucky."

Her face flushed. "I assume you took me home. Thanks."

"No problem. I didn't figure you wanted to stick around on the freighter."

"Lucian wants to see us." She rushed toward the exit. I followed, hoping my headache would disappear before talking with the Princess. We exited out onto the familiar second-story circular platform looking down upon the commons area.

More stores were open since I'd made my nocturnal visit, but the crowd was still thin. Rulusian troops mulled about, and a handful of civilians. We continued around the elevated platform toward the Princess' office.

I had a question that really needed to be asked, but I wasn't sure if Rione would answer. Even so, discretion needed to be tossed aside. "Why'd you go on a drinking binge back on the freighter?"

Not receiving an answer for some time, I figured I'd overstepped our friendship's boundaries. Then, she surprised me. "It's not often you almost die."

I was caught off-guard, mostly because defying death happened to me all the time. "Understandable," I mumbled.

She changed the subject. "Care to grab a bite to eat after we're done here?"

I decided not to push any farther. "Sounds good."

Rione pushed a button beside Lucian's office entrance. The hatch slid open a moment later. The room was small and cramped, more so than you'd expect for someone in line for the throne. Princess Wren faced away, standing and gazing out through small circular windows embedded in the hull, while long blonde locks formed a waterfall down her back.

I saw the Rulusian freighter we'd used for our mission off in the distance. Thoughts of Jaclyn, who'd be heading back to her ship before long, came to me. I was still conflicted between our actions and my feelings for another.

The doors behind us slid shut and the Princess turned on her heels, motioning at two chairs. "Thanks for coming." She sat behind her carved wooden desk, while we took our seats. Her weathered pale skin and dim blue eyes told me more than words could; Waging war against her own father had taken its toll.

I got down to business. "You wanted to see us?"

Lucian smiled. "We wanted to hear about the mission."

Malone's voice carried over small speakers in the corners. "I'm here."

I watched Rione, figuring she'd be pleased to hear from him. Her lips formed a thin line.

We sat in uncomfortable silence until Lucian began. "The rest of the team indicated you ran into trouble."

Rione forced out her words before I had a chance to explain. "No trouble at all."

Malone's voice went cold. "You told Jake the two of you, and I quote, almost didn't make it back."

Suddenly, a huge knot welled up in my gut. We hadn't done anything wrong, but there was a definite air of being called into the principal's office here.

"We ran into a little more resistance than we'd expected after setting the charges. That's all." Rione folded her arms across her chest. Her emotion ridges grew deep red and the room fell into more awkward silence.

Rione spat her words, deciding not to wait on anyone else to make the first move. "But we made it out. That's the important part."

I grew antsy and wanted to defuse the situation. "So, with the satellite destroyed, what's next?"

Malone continued in an emotionless monotone. "Without the satellite to hinder our efforts, we expect to build our forces for a high-profile attack."

"If the target is high profile, it should prove to be a boost for the rebellion." Princess Wren smoothed out her silky white robe.

"We have a plan in the works," Malone informed us.

Rione smirked. "Count me in."

Malone was adamant. "Too risky."

She fumed, and was about to lose it. I continued, "It can't be any more dangerous than what we just did."

"I couldn't live with myself if something happened to her," Malone told us.

"Nothing will happen to me," Rione complained.

"Exactly right, because you're not coming along."

Rione fidgeted in her chair. It was good Malone wasn't here in person, or she'd have choked and beaten him to death where he stood.

"But you *would* be safer down here," he conceded. "The station isn't the safest spot in the universe."

She turned to Lucian. "Are we done here?" The princess was caught off-guard and didn't respond. Rione bolted for the door. "I'm staying here, end of story."

Wren turned to get answers from me, but I simply shrugged my shoulders and rushed after Rione.

• • •

She slammed the tray of food onto the table and sat. "I can't believe what an arrogant bastard he is."

My forehead scrunched as I took the seat across from her. "Malone's only concerned about your safety."

"He doesn't have to worry about me. I can take care of myself."

"I have no doubt about that. I'm sure Malone believes it too. But you're not invincible."

Rione fell silent and picked at her food. Finally, she responded with a depressed tone. "Never said I was."

The Stardust bar had once been a vibrant, thriving business, but like the rest of the station, it was barely surviving. One of the changes they'd had to make to stay in business had been the addition of Rulusian food items to the menu. I sliced into a tender Borolo steak and savored the tasty morsel.

She looked up from her plate, her expression sour. "Speaking of being invincible..."

I chewed slowly, having a fairly good idea where she was heading. I had no intention of sharing. There were some things which transcended even close friendships, and my recent past was one of those.

She asked anyway. "What happened to you? When you came back, that is."

I feigned ignorance after swallowing the piece of steak. "What do you mean?"

It was hard to believe her mood could have become any worse, but it did. "Cut the crap, Aston! You know exactly what I'm talking about."

I looked around at the empty tables. A pair of Rulusian males sat at the bar, talking with the same young barkeep I'd met up with earlier that morning.

"I'm just not sure what to tell you."

"You almost died. Why don't you start with how?"

My temples throbbed. Memories of Leah's death all returned with a painful vengeance. "It's complicated."

"Then start with something simple. How'd you get stabbed in the shoulder?"

"A knife."

She rolled her eyes and sighed. "Because?"

"Someone didn't like me much."

She pushed her plate away. "Why are you being so difficult?"

"It's not something I want to talk about."

Again, we fell into an uncomfortable silence. I'd lost my appetite as well, so pushed my plate away. The barkeep came out to retrieve our dishes.

He glanced down at the remaining food. "Everything taste okay, folks?"

"Fine," I muttered. "Weren't as hungry as we thought."

It seemed acceptable to him, as he walked off through a pair of swinging doors. I looked over at Rione, who watched the main entrance with eyes glazed over.

"I can see where Malone's coming from." I should have known better than to set Rione off, but there wasn't any point in delaying the inevitable.

She turned back to me, her stare burning red hot.

"It's just I can sympathize. I want you safe, too."

Rione turned away again. "He treats me like a child."

"I've dealt with you enough to know that's not possible."

Even from my vantage point, I saw her smile.

I was glad her mood softened. "So, what are you planning to do?"

"Find a way to get down to the planet."

I chuckled under my breath. "Isn't that what Malone wanted you to do anyway?"

She scowled. "I plan on joining his attack."

I shook my head. "So you're deliberately trying to upset Malone?"

"Don't worry, I can be very convincing."

That much, I already knew. A smile crossed my face.

• • •

I climbed back up to the second level, and around to the landing bay doors. As I entered, an evil foreboding flooded every part of my being. It was almost as if I was being watched, a target.

I shook my head to clear my thoughts and kept walking. I lifted my hand just a moment before remembering I didn't have my jacket, which I hadn't worn since escaping Elijah.

I looked into the dark shadows, and my skin crawled even more. Lars was dead, and Elijah was nowhere near this place, but my paranoia knew no logic. I jumped up the entry stairs two at a time.

"Close us up."

My heart raced while I glanced around the room, the hatch gears grinding in the background. Everything was just as it was when I left. Why would it be any different?

"Did your meeting with Rione go well?"

"Rione?" I took a moment, finally grasping the question. "Yes."

"Is everything okay, Aston?"

This sudden fear drove a stake through my heart, coming out of nowhere. "I think so."

I stepped over toward my cot and plopped down, my mind clouded and confused on an emotional roller coaster. My foot bumped against the bottle of Jungle Juice which had put me down before. I blinked and looked at it intently.

It used to be I'd only drink to pass the time between stops. Now I kept using it to mask the pain, to keep from remembering the death and destruction I'd witnessed.

Tears rolled down my cheeks as the memories flooded back, and I moved my hands up to wipe them away. Lars and Elijah had killed Leah, and I'd been unable to stop them. I'd barely saved Rione from death on our recent mission. Now, she wanted to put herself in harm's way yet again. I had a nagging suspicion I'd fall short again, that Rione would die because I couldn't keep her safe. My feelings for her went too deep to let anything happen to her.

I pulled my hands away, and jumped at the sight of blood. I attempted to smear it off on my pants, but it wouldn't come off.

"Jeanie, what's going on?"

"I do not understand."

My breaths were rapid as I rubbed my hands even harder on my pants, the sheets, anything I could find. "This blood on my hands!"

"Aston, you do not have blood on your hands."

I closed my eyes tight, opened them once more and looked at my hands, red from rubbing but otherwise clean.

"Should I contact the infirmary?"

"No," I muttered, my pulse returning to normal. This hadn't been the first time with hallucinations, and I feared things would only get worse.

I looked down at my bottle of Jungle Juice. One more time, I promised myself. I pulled the bottle up, uncorked the top and eased the pain the only way I knew how.

• • •

Rione had a wide smirk on her face as I stepped out onto the landing bay floor. My head begged for mercy from the vise grip Jungle Juice held it in. A bit ironic, having to put myself through so much physical pain in order to avoid the emotional kind.

She pushed stray hairs from the front of her face. "You look terrible."

I massaged my forehead. "I feel worse."

"Jungle Juice?"

I nodded.

Her forehead crinkled. "That's twice in as many rotations. What are you trying to do?"

"Develop immunity," I mocked.

While shaking her head, Rione's eyes told me she wanted to ask me more. Thankfully for me, she held back. "Maybe something to eat will help."

She turned and walked back toward the bay doors. It wouldn't, but that didn't stop me from following her.

I glanced around the area, which took on a decidedly more pleasant look than before my latest mental breakdown. Lights above were brighter and any shadows had retreated into the corners. My paranoia had subsided, drowned along with my sorrows and consciousness.

She turned her head as we passed into the corridor. "Unless you'd rather postpone."

"I'll be fine."

"Your choice."

I continued walking with Rione to the commons area, all the while squinting at the heavy illumination. I wanted to ask more about her plan to put herself into harm's way, despite everyone's insistence otherwise.

But I knew where the discussion would take us. An argument with Rione was something I didn't even want when I was coming off a stone dead sober sleep. I didn't even want to consider how things would go in my present condition.

We made it to the Stardust and headed off toward the corner, where our regular table was tucked away. The crowd was a bit larger than expected, but only due to the Rulusian troops taking advantage of their final break before the return home.

The same young bartender walked out to us. "Hi, folks. Same as always?" We both nodded. "I'll get it right out."

I was half-surprised they didn't just prepare it ahead of time, with the schedule we kept. As he left, I glanced over at Rione, who stared out at the Rulusians standing around the bar.

An uncomfortable silence fell once more. My mind had started to clear, at least I thought so. Nevertheless, I decided to risk setting off another war. "So, any more word on your plans to head down to Toris?"

"Not yet." Her mood immediately soured while she kept her eyes on the troops.

"You okay?"

"Fine."

Her tone said otherwise. "No, you're not." I leaned my chair back on two legs, supporting myself with the wall.

"I guess neither of us shares our problems. You don't want to tell me how you nearly died, and I don't want to explain my relationship problems."

I frowned, thoughts focused on my recent tryst. I wasn't exactly the fountain of knowledge when it came to relationship problems. But then, I realized I'd just learned more than she'd wanted me to. She looked down at the table, fiddling with her hands.

I tried to be considerate. "I doubt I'd be any help in the relationship department anyway."

"Here you go, folks."

We both turned as our server put two plates of food down in front of us, each having three Borolo slices and two Japali eggs. I forced out a smile. "Thanks."

He left us to our food, which we ate in awkward silence. I glanced up at Rione every so often, but she kept her eyes and attention fixed on her food.

She paused just before placing a morsel in her mouth. "Things just seem to be rocky..."

A familiar voice interrupted. “Hey, you two.”

We looked up as Jaclyn neared our table. I put on a polite smile and motioned to a seat beside me.

“Thanks.”

Conflict reigned heavy on my heart. Nothing could be more awkward than sitting here with one woman I cared about so deeply and another I’d just had a fling with.

Jaclyn sat down. “Looks like we’re pulling out of here sooner than I thought.”

Rione focused on her food, ignoring the two of us as I responded, “Oh?”

“The Rulusian President has ordered us to leave the area within the next rotation.”

I lifted an eyebrow. “Trouble?”

“I figure he’s worried about the fallout from our proximity to the satellite, since it was destroyed.”

“I think I suggested that very thing,” I reminded her while taking another bite of Borolo. She didn’t bother responding, which didn’t bother me. I knew I was right.

The same young man who’d helped us the first time stopped at our table again. “Can I get you anything, ma’am?”

Jaclyn waved him off. “Maybe later.”

The waiter walked off and Jaclyn turned to me. “I was hoping you might make your way to Rulusia sometime.” She reached out and rested her green hand on top of my own.

Rione bolted up, startling me. “I’m getting a drink.” Without another word, she stormed off.

Jaclyn watched Rione leave, eyes narrowing. “What’s her problem?”

I shrugged, though I was starting to figure it out.

Jaclyn turned, an evil smile crossing her face. She ran a slender finger down my arm. "I wanted to thank you again for your hospitality."

I smiled. "No problem. It was fun for me, too."

The corner of her mouth lifted wryly. "Hopefully it won't take you long to make your way to Rulusia."

I wanted out of this conversation, to hopefully smooth things over with Rione. "I'm sure I'll be there soon."

She wrote down her contact information on a napkin, placing it in my pants pocket. Her hand lingered a little too long. "Now, I do think I'll eat something. What you have looks good."

"It is." I popped the last Borolo slice into my mouth.

She stood from the table and walked back toward the bar, meeting an empty-handed Rione along the way. The Lazarian's scowl grew as they passed.

I raised an eyebrow as she made it back to the table and sat down. "Thought you were getting a drink."

"They didn't have anything I wanted."

I never ran into that problem.

Before I could say another word, she interrupted. "Let's go. I need to talk to Lucian about my plan."

I hadn't understood Rione's reaction at first, but it started making more sense. The drinking and her angry outburst, both took place in front of Jaclyn. For some reason, she was angry every time the Rulusian showed interest in me. It was absurd. She had Malone, and I had...

No one.

I pushed the thoughts from my mind and followed her toward the exit. I decided to face the situation upfront. "If there's something I've said or done to upset you, I'd appreciate you letting me know."

We stepped out through the large doorway into the central hub, heading for the opposite side of the room.

"It's nothing," she told me.

I heard an explosion before the shockwave knocked me to the ground. While confusion reigned, I looked back at the bar, engulfed in flames. They hadn't extinguished, so at least the outer hull hadn't been breached.

My thoughts were immediately on Rione. My vision grew narrow and darkened as I looked over at her limp body, unable to tell whether she was alive or dead. My instinct was to check her, but I couldn't move my limbs. Fear screamed through my body as darkness enveloped my mind.

Chapter Six

Random syncopated beeps filtered into my ears before I cracked my eyelids open. Female voices carried through the dark, blurry void. “Looks like he’s coming to.”

“I’ll let the Princess know.”

Footsteps clacked on the floor, moving away as my eyes adjusted and a sense of touch returned. A spongy mattress rested under me and the thin robe covering my body was unable to prevent chills from racing through my bones.

Above my head, a bright light drew closer as the first voice spoke again. “How are you feeling, Aston?”

“Terrible...and cold.” My throat was raw, and I suppressed a shiver.

A warm blanket was placed on me, helping a little. “Do you need something for the pain?” A pale Torian female wearing green scrubs came into focus over me.

I barely nodded, before she moved away. The physical pain was substantial, though nothing compared to the emotional suffering burning through me as memories flooded back. Then the sensations grew even more intense and fear rolled off my tongue. “Rione?”

She pressed a medication dispenser into my arm and injected me. Her mouth formed a thin line. “I’m surprised both of you aren’t more injured than you are.”

I frantically looked in both directions, seeing her body in the bed next to mine. The realization brought a momentary sense of relief, until I remembered Jaclyn had been inside the Stardust when it exploded.

A lump welled up in my throat. "Any other survivors?"

The nurse grimaced, shaking her head. I turned away, trying to find solace in watching Rione; it didn't help. Tears welled up in the corner of my eyes and streaked down my face. Certainly Jaclyn and I hadn't had a close relationship, two starships passing in the abyss, but I had the added emotional weight of knowing she'd been in the bar because of me.

The medic continued, breaking up my thoughts. "The blast knocked you both around pretty good, but neither of you sustained serious injury."

"I guess we're lucky." I looked up into the bright light, not feeling too blessed at the moment.

She turned to look at a data screen above my head, glassing over my emotional breakdown. "By all rights, you should both be dead."

"Story of my life," I muttered.

She looked back, her blue eyes warm and caring. "What's that?"

"Nothing."

"Well, I'll be back to check on you soon."

"Thanks."

I waited for the clopping of the medic's shoes to leave the area, then turned toward Rione again. Kicking my legs over the edge of the gurney, I started across the room. Fiery pain burned through every muscle in my body, most notably in my knee and shoulder. Injuries from my past had been revived.

Reaching back to close off my robe and keep some modesty, I stepped up to her bed. She was situated as I had been, a robe covering her still body and a sheet pulled over her legs. If not for the rise and fall of her chest, I may have thought her dead after all. I gently touched her arm. Her eyes flickered open.

"Welcome back."

Frantic, her eyes shot back and forth. She finally focused back on me. "What happened?"

"Bomb explosion."

Her forehead scrunched. "Survivors?"

I pressed my lips together. "Just the two of us."

"Jaclyn?"

I shook my head. Once more, a lump formed in my throat as I recalled the brief time Jaclyn and I had together; moments of passion and lust. Now I felt guilty for what we'd done, especially with her life snuffed out forever. I shook my head in solemn contemplation.

"Do they know how it happened?"

"No one has said, just that we're lucky to be alive."

She tried adjusting to a more comfortable position, but gave up. "I believe it. Feels like I was smashed between a pair of cargo containers."

"Need anything for the pain? I can get the medic, she's just outside."

"That sounds good, actually."

"Be right back."

I turned and started for the only doorway out of the room. She commented from behind me. "Nice view."

I looked back to see a weak smile on her face. My face flushed as I grabbed my robe flaps again. The medic walked into the room, blocking my path. "Oh, you're both awake?"

Rione's expression faded. "If I could have something for the pain..."

I shuffled over to my bed and sat down.

"Right away, Miss Sc'lari, but first, are you two up to visitors?" Neither of us indicated either way, so she turned toward the doorway. "Come in."

Princess Wren walked inside, Captain Dillager next to her. Deep, purple circles took refuge under her blue eyes. She spoke in a quiet tone, fiddling with her robe. "Glad to see you two made it."

The Captain mumbled while worry lines formed along his forehead. "Unfortunately, we can't say the same for eleven others, including seven members of my crew."

I felt the need to speak. "Condolences for your loss, Captain."

He waved me off. "It's part of the risk that comes with the job."

"There shouldn't be a risk in a public place where civilians gather."

"Perhaps," he told me.

The medic came back into the room, medical dispenser in hand. Conversation briefly stopped as she injected Rione. The medic started to do the same for me, but I waved her off, still good from the first dosage earlier.

Rione caught Lucian's attention. "Have they determined who's responsible?"

"Security is combing through videos taken before the blast."

The Captain tugged at his uniform. "I doubt it will be so easy."

Wren sighed. "Likely not. But short of motive, video evidence will be our only hope."

Rione interrupted. "Lucian, there's a war going on."

"My father knows better than to attack the station, even under the cloak of secrecy. It would give Rulusia the perfect reason to jump into the conflict."

Her words triggered a possibility I hadn't really fathomed up to this point, not seriously anyway. Maybe the explosion hadn't targeted the station itself, but was meant for me. The trouble with people making death threats was sometimes they carried through.

I'd doubted Elijah Cassus would enter a war zone to make an attempt on my life, but the complete disregard for collateral damage had his name written all over it.

Wren continued. "No one has been allowed to arrive or depart the station since the blast. If they're here, we'll find them."

Dillager clasped his hands behind his back. "Your highness, there is still the matter of my deceased crewmembers, as we discussed earlier."

"Yes, Captain. We'll wrap up the investigation as soon as possible."

"If we can be of any assistance, every single member of my crew would volunteer if it means we can get our comrades home for burial."

"My offer still stands. We can cremate their remains here on the station and launch them into our star, Torian custom since before we even built this station."

"Unfortunately, your highness, Rulusian burial customs are very specific. The body must be interred on Rulusia within three rotations."

I looked over at Rione. The Captain saw me and corrected himself. "When there's a body to be found." Which, in the case of her freighter, hadn't been possible.

"Very well," Wren noted. "I assume you have caskets ready on your transport."

The Captain nodded.

"As soon as we find out anything, you'll be the first to know."

"Thank you, Princess." He walked out of the room.

Once the coast was clear, Lucian stepped over to Rione, leaned down, and gave her an awkward hug. "I'm glad you're alive, my friend."

"Not as much as I am."

They separated, but held hands. "When I first heard about the blast, I remembered you and Aston spend a lot of time there. When I heard you'd both been taken to the infirmary, I feared the worst."

Rione grimaced. "After we walked out, I don't remember much until I woke up here."

"They tell me neither of you suffered serious injury?"

"Lucky us," Rione commented.

I interjected, wanting to find out if my latest theory was on target. "I'd like to check out those surveillance videos, if possible."

She let go of Rione's hand and turned. "That would be appreciated."

Shortly after, with both of us wearing fresh clothes brought in from another local store, Lucian led the way across the commons area. The whole area was a disaster zone, with guards stationed around the blast radius while others sifted through the debris. I suppressed a shudder at how close we'd been to death. It wasn't the first time, and likely wouldn't be the last, but it never made the experience easier to handle.

Wren took charge as the three of us stepped into the security office. She caught the guard's attention behind the counter. "We're here to check out surveillance videos."

Without a word, he walked the length of the curved room toward an open doorway in the corner. I remembered this room from my first visit to the station with a little less than fondness, considering my two separate incarcerations separated by an escape attempt. We exited into a booking area, and then moved into another side room. A second guard sat in the darkened chamber, scanning video footage at high speed on a flat panel display. Behind us to the right was a small window which looked into an interrogation room, which I had no memories of at all. They hadn't needed it at the time I'd been arrested.

Our escort stepped up to his comrade. "The Princess is here to see these."

He turned his chair to face us. "Great timing. I just finished my initial pass-through."

Rione jumped in. "Were you able to find anything?"

"I'll show you."

He turned and ran his fingers over a small keypad while he spoke. "One thing about the Stardust was the place was covered by cameras, except for a small dead zone in the back room."

It struck me as odd. "They didn't bother putting one there?"

"That section was added later. I guess the owners didn't see the need for another camera. They're not cheap."

Rione placed her hands on the back of his chair. "So, you found something?"

"We determined the blast originated from that dead zone. I've been analyzing other cameras in the vicinity to see who entered that area before the explosion."

Wren drew closer. "And you've found some suspects?"

He ran his fingers along a black control board in his lap. A still image appeared on the display.

"Only two. This is the first one."

Another few keystrokes and the screen split into six different viewing angles. The video started on each screen, and a pale, bald-headed Torian entered the establishment, a robe stretching down to his feet. He stepped to the bar and ordered a drink, then walked past a vast wasteland of empty tables before disappearing off camera.

It seemed odd for him to pass up the open seats, but not overly so.

The guard accelerated the video until he appeared back on camera, sans the glass, and out the door. The video cut off with a single move of the guard's hand.

"I'll spare you the painstaking details, but we have the full video montage all the way back to his ship."

Lucian remarked without emotion. "The station is still on lock-down, no ships arriving or leaving?"

"Yes, ma'am."

"Good, pick him up."

I caught everyone's attention. "There was a second suspect?"

"Yes." The guard pressed a few more keys and another sequence began. Like the first, a man entered and headed straight for the counter. This one wasn't Torian, though, judging from his long, black hair which covered his head.

After grabbing his drink, he turned and his hair swung out of place. He almost could have been a local, with his ghostly pale face. But a pair of beady black eyes gave him away. A chill ran up my spine.

"Uni," I whispered in panic, growing nauseous.

Rione grabbed my left shoulder. The medicine must have worn off, as pain roared through it. "Are you okay?"

"I know him."

Lucian spoke from my other side. "How?"

I looked at both of them, uncertain of how to proceed. Suddenly, the idea I'd considered didn't seem far-fetched. Elijah had sent one of his minions to do his dirty work, someone who already had an axe to grind.

"I'd rather not go into details."

The princess' blue eyes were more vibrant than they'd been recently. "Should we interview him?"

I couldn't speak, so just nodded.

She turned to the guard. "You have his location."

"Yes, ma'am."

"Bring him here."

Rione turned to me. "You sure about this?"

"He definitely has a score to settle," I muttered.

In other words, he wanted me dead.

• • •

It was odd seeing Uni again. I watched through the one-way glass as he sat stone-faced at the table. The room was lit by one main light hanging overhead, bathing both him and Rione in bright light. She'd taken it upon herself to conduct the interview personally, and I was glad to let her do so. If he'd indeed been sent to kill me, there was no reason for me to make an appearance and give him another opportunity. Certainly, he was shackled to his seat, but with his personal motivation, it might not have mattered.

Rione leaned forward. "So, Mister Zulch, we'd like to ask you a few questions."

Uni flipped his head, sending his black locks sideways across his forehead. His voice was still as high-pitched as I remembered, but with anger now laced into the words. "And if I refuse to answer?"

She frowned. "We have a holding cell in the next room if you'd prefer."

Uni's stare was cold. "Ask."

"What brings you to Toris?"

"Just passing through."

Rione lifted an eyebrow. "And where are you headed?"

"I guess I'll figure it out when I get there."

She paused, trying to read him. Then, she sprang the news. "You're a suspect in the recent station bombing."

Uni moved his shackled arms to the table and leaned forward, his features heavily illuminated. He laughed. "You've got the wrong man."

"Prove it. Let us search your ship."

"Search anything you want. I have nothing to hide."

Beside me, Lucian spoke to one of the two guards standing with us. "Notify the team to start their search."

They left the room and we were all alone. Maybe I'd been wrong about Uni after all. The guilty usually didn't volunteer for searches, and Uni wasn't the type to bluff.

Rione placed two elbows on the table and leaned forward. "How do you know Aston West?"

So much for maintaining anonymity.

My eyes grew wide. I no longer cared about Uni having another opportunity to kill me, but wanted my secrets to stay hidden. Bolting out into the corridor, I raced into the interview room. Uni looked up as I entered, and his mouth morphed into a menacing frown.

He spat his words through clenched teeth, slamming his arms on the table. "I want him dead."

At least I was right on one count.

Rione continued. "Enough to kill eleven people?"

"He's the only one I want. I'm telling you, I didn't plant any bombs on this station."

"Why do you want Aston dead?"

He raised an eyebrow, his stare firm on my face. "You didn't tell them?"

I knew where he was going and shook my head in a futile attempt to keep him silent.

Rione was insistent. "Tell us what?"

"Aston killed my baby sister."

Chapter Seven

I pointed a finger at Uni. "That's not true."

"You're the one who convinced her to escape." He pointed across the table. "You got her killed."

"She wanted to escape the twins. So did I."

His eyes went wide. "I told you to wait, to think through your escape!"

My chest tightened. He was right; I'd ignored him then, in a rush to get away from the twins. Leah had suffered the punishment for my mistake. "Lars murdered her. You should direct this hatred where it belongs."

"Except you killed him, too."

I clamped my mouth shut, but felt Rione's stare. Turning to her, bitterness flew off my tongue. "What?"

"I was waiting to hear that wasn't true, either."

"There are parts of my past I'm not proud of." Granted, I'd taken special joy in Lars' death, something I'd never felt before. Rione didn't need to hear that.

She almost choked on her words. "Killing people?"

"You've killed people in this civil war."

"That's different."

"I've never murdered an innocent person," I told her, focusing back on Uni. "Lars deserved to die. He murdered his sister, and then tried to kill me."

"You're still responsible for her death."

I pulled a chair out from under the table and sat down hard. We had an interrogation to complete, which wasn't going to happen if we kept hashing out the same argument, especially one I had no desire to continue.

I took a separate path. "I don't get you, Uni."

He scowled. "Why's that?"

"You're extremely intelligent, so how's Elijah duped you into doing his dirty work?"

"I'm not here for Elijah."

"He wants me dead. You're carrying out an execution."

"You put too much faith in Elijah and his power."

I snorted. "He has you under his thumb, along with the rest of the Brotherhood."

"Since Lars' death, Elijah hasn't been able to maintain control. Several others have made their escapes. I tried to convince you we could put a plan together. You didn't listen or even think through what you were doing." His shackles pulled tight as he lunged forward, straining against them. "You got Leah killed!"

"If I hadn't tried to help her escape, Lars wouldn't be dead." It was bitter irony; only through Leah's death did her dream of escape become reality for so many others. I looked down at my hands, and saw her blood coating my skin. I closed my eyes in an attempt to stop the horrifying vision. "She'd still be trapped by the twins, just like everyone else."

"Except she'd still be alive."

My eyes flashed open. I fought the tears off. "So, what now?"

"I still want you dead."

"Too bad your bloodlust is misdirected. Lars killed your sister, but Elijah was the one who ordered it done. Why don't you take him out instead?"

"Who says I won't? I can take it out on all of you."

The door behind us opened and Wren's voice called out. "Mister Zulch, our team has found nothing on-board your ship linking you to this crime."

"Since I had nothing to do with it, I expect not."

"You must stay on-board your ship until the investigation concludes. After that, you will be banished from the station, never to return."

Two guards walked in and stepped up behind Uni. He glared at me as they released the shackles.

"Don't worry. I'll find you again, when you least expect it. This isn't over, West!"

I added one more person to the list of those who wanted me dead.

"Take him away." Wren thumbed toward the door.

"Count on it!" He laughed maniacally.

Wren pushed the door closed, then turned to me. Rione cut her off. "Spill it, fly boy."

I stood and slid the chair back in its place. "Sorry, I don't feel like going into details."

Wren scowled. "Then give it to us in the broad-stroke version."

"You weren't paying attention?"

"Humor us."

"I tried to help Uni's sister Leah escape from a pair of brothers I considered friends. They killed her, tried to kill me, and I killed one of the brothers. The other one wants me dead, Uni wants me dead, everyone wants me dead!"

Their faces were both stoic, unsure what to make of my revelation. I frowned. "Is that a broad-enough stroke?"

They had no response for me. I folded my arms, frustration building. "Now isn't there a second suspect we should be interrogating?"

• • •

I stared through the glass at our last known suspect, Adair Black. At a glance, I knew we had the bomber, and not just because he was our only remaining suspect. The Torian's muscular build filled out the ragged clothes on his body and his leather pants. A scar ran down his pale right cheek, just below his bright blue eyes.

It was the callous attitude which clinched his guilt, as far as I was concerned. Adair leaned his chair back and picked at something on his pants. He then turned his attention to the glass and an evil smile filled his face. This wasn't his first time in the game.

Rione looked over at me. "Are we ready?"

I exhaled a deep breath. "Let's go."

Adair looked up and his expression soured as we finally entered the room.

Rione took the lead. "Mr. Black, we have a few questions to ask."

He shrugged and grunted.

"What brings you to the station?"

He set his chair down and leaned in close, with a low grumble from deep in his throat. "Sightseeing."

With a smile, he chuckled at his own wit.

"If that's the way you want to play, we'll cut to the chase. We know you planted a bomb on the station."

"Believe what you want." He went back to picking at his black leather pants.

"I'm having a hard time understanding how you can be so callous, Mr. Black. Innocent people were killed."

He stared at both of us in turn, his eyes cold. "Life is unpredictable."

"I'm sure you're aware terrorist activities are punishable by death under Torian law."

"So I've been told." He bared a set of rotten teeth and laughed. I smelled his putrid breath even from across the table.

Someone knocked at the door, so I checked on it. A guard slipped an envelope through as I opened it. I grabbed the package as he whispered. "Analysis of the suspect. His clothes are covered with the same chemical residue found in the wreckage. A team is searching his ship."

I smiled. We had him.

I walked back to the table and slapped the envelope down. "We have all the evidence we need."

He laughed. "You don't have anything."

Rione glanced through the packet and whistled. "You're going to pay big time for what you've done."

He was going to die for killing Jaclyn. Familiar stirrings flooded my heart.

He reached in his pocket and fished out a crumpled wad of paper. "This says I'm not." He tossed it on the table.

I smoothed out the page and read it over. I went back to the beginning and read aloud in the hopes my sight was deceiving me. "By order of the king, Adair Black is granted absolute immunity for any acts necessary in bringing Aston West and Rione Sc'lari to justice. Dead or alive."

"Impossible," Rione muttered. She pulled the sheet away, but couldn't read it any differently.

"Sounds like you made enemies out of the wrong people. Too bad you don't have one of these stay-out-of-jail passes." He laughed.

"And what are we being brought to justice for?"

"Terrorist activities. Ironic, huh?" He smirked. "You destroyed government property and murdered its employees."

My first thought was of the spy satellite, but it had just happened. There was no way anyone could already know about our involvement in the blast.

"What property?"

"A Torian heavy cruiser and its crew."

I blinked. "The one he sent to destroy this station?"

Rione and I had protected the station during my first visit to Toris and now we were in the crosshairs of the king. No good deed goes unpunished.

"I don't know the details, just how much I was paid for the job. And that I'm untouchable." Adair smiled.

The door flew open and Wren stormed in. She grabbed the scum's free pass. "This can't be an official document."

"Afraid you're wrong, Princess. That's your daddy's signature."

Rione and I both looked into Wren's face. We didn't like the despair we saw.

"So, if you don't mind placing these two under arrest, I'll transport them back to the planet for their trial and execution."

Lucian's face tinted red. "You are in no position to tell me what to do!"

I'd witnessed her temper before, and was glad to be on this side of it. Even the bomber seemed a bit taken aback.

"I plan on fully authenticating this document. Until I do, you'll remain in a cell."

She stormed off toward the door. "Aston and Rione, come with me."

"Don't go far, you two," the scum called out.

Guards swapped places with us as we followed the Princess out of the room. Back in the observation area, we watched them shackle Adair and lead him away.

Wren stared in disbelief at the paper in her hands. It shook slightly. "My father has gone mad. How could he do such a thing?"

I shook my head slowly. It didn't seem out of character in the least. "It's a war, Princess."

Her eyes were deep and sunken as she looked up at me. "Yes, I realize that."

Rione folded arms across her chest. "So, what are we going to do with Mr. Black?"

"I don't see many options. My father gave him immunity." She tossed the paper on the table I sat on.

I looked down at the document. "Isn't there anything we can arrest him on unrelated to the bombing?"

"Not unless we find something on his ship."

"Unlikely."

"I won't let him take either of you anywhere."

Rione moved her hands to her hips. "With immunity, what's to stop him from attacking the station again?"

"I can have him removed from the station."

I leaned against a table. "I don't see that as a deterrent."

There was a knock at the door. Captain Dillager's familiar green face peeked in. "Princess, the guards told me I'd find you here."

"Captain, glad to see you again."

"Doesn't sound like it." He looked us all over. "I'd think there'd be a more festive mood. I heard you caught the bomber."

Wren pushed Adair's pardon toward the Captain. "Unfortunately, we can't prosecute him for it."

Dillager's beefy green hands picked up the paper. His eyes grew wide while he scanned the document.

"So, he's going to get away with mass murder?"

I interjected. "It certainly appears so."

The Captain grew silent, moments before his face broke out into a jagged, evil smile. "Where can I find this piece of trash?"

Wren scowled. "We're holding him in a cell. He's under the impression we're authenticating this document."

"Take me to him."

We walked into the holding area a short while later and Adair stood from his cot. It was also good to be on this side of an energy field for a change.

The murderer focused on the Princess. "So, you found the paper is all in order. I'm ready to be released."

Her face tinted red once more. "Silence!"

Dillager stepped up to the field. "Young man, you are correct. This document from the Torian king is perfectly valid, and you will not face charges under Torian law."

Adair stood and started toward the front of the cell, anticipating his release.

"Unfortunately, it has no bearing under Rulusian law."

"What?" His entire face sank as he stumbled to a stop.

"Rulusia considers murder a very serious crime."

"But I have immunity."

The Captain drew a hair's width away from the energy field. "Not from me, you don't. You murdered seven members of my crew, and will be lucky if you make it back to Rulusia alive."

Our prisoner began blabbering. "But the king..."

"My father enlisted your services personally?"

He swapped glances between Wren and the Captain. "Yes."

Lucian clapped her hands twice and two guards entered the room. "Restrain this man and escort him to Captain Dillager's transport."

They lowered the field, placed electronic restraints on Adair's wrists and led him out of the room. He yelled his objections. "The king will hear about this!"

Adair fought against his captors until one of them called out, "Stop resisting!"

He wasn't at all interested in following the instructions, so one of them pulled out a small wand. A ball at the end rapidly changed from dormant to a bright white glowing globe, just before they released the captor and tagged him with it. Screams filled the room, just before the big man went down in a silent heap. I smiled at his misfortune.

The gentle face of the Captain returned once the criminal had been hauled out of the room. "Don't worry. He'll be punished to the fullest extent of the law."

Wren finally smiled. "Thank you, Captain. We owe you a debt of gratitude."

He nodded and walked out of the room.

Wren turned to us. "Now, we have a problem."

Rione sighed. "The king wants us dead."

Wren turned to us. "You need to find a hiding spot."

It sounded like a terrific plan to me. "The galaxy's a big place," I offered.

Rione, on the other hand, had different ideas. "You can run if you want to, but I intend to stay and fight." She turned to the Princess, exposing her deep red emotion ridges to me. "I don't take attempts on my life lightly."

Running would have been the smartest move. Everyone wanted us dead. But I knew Rione's temper wouldn't let her think clearly. I had to keep her safe, as I'd been totally unable to do with Leah.

All of that meant I was staying in a war zone, now with a bounty on my head.

Chapter Eight

"No, and that's final!"

"Malone, it's not open for debate."

I sat on the edge of Rione's bed watching her pack a duffel. We'd picked out another pair of black body suits similar to the ones we'd chosen for the satellite mission. Hers still drove inappropriate feelings through me, and I was just glad Malone was still down on the planet.

His voice spilled out of the ceiling speakers. "It's too dangerous for you to join us."

Given a choice, I would have ditched the discomfort of listening in on their private argument and taken refuge on my ship versus sitting here. Unfortunately, she planned to head for the planet as soon as she finished here, and I wasn't letting her out of my sight. There was a high likelihood she'd leave me behind otherwise.

She stopped what she was doing and stared off at the wall. "Aren't you the one who wanted me to come down to the planet in the first place?"

"Down to the planet, yes. Not joining our team."

"The king has a bounty out on us. Hiding won't help."

"Then maybe you need to leave Toris and lay low until everything settles."

As much as I agreed with Malone's sentiment, I already knew what Rione's reaction would be. Watching her emotion ridges redden, I tried defusing the situation. "Malone, that's not really an option."

He spat his words. "Aston, stay out of this."

I clamped my mouth shut and frowned. I didn't know him all that well, only having met him briefly during my first visit to Toris. We both wanted the same thing, to keep Rione safe. If he wanted to battle it out with her, then he could be my guest.

She stormed over to the small wall-mounted microphone box. "We're coming, whether you like it or not."

"Rione..."

She disconnected the transmission, before marching back to her dresser. Flinging clothes into her bag, she complained to me. "I can't believe how obstinate he is."

I sat there silent, knowing there was nothing I could say that would help at this point.

She picked up the electronic image of her parents I'd seen during my earlier visit, stared at them a few moments, then returned the picture to its place. She picked up the stone-and-shell necklace and ran it through her fingers, deep in thought.

Rione unhooked the clasp. "Help me with this?"

She drew closer to me, and I stood behind her as she handed over the accessory. I wrapped it around her neck while she held up her hair. I breathed in her skin's sweet flower fragrance until the clasps snapped in place.

"Thanks."

"No problem."

She turned to face me, her forehead scrunched. "You know, you don't have to stay with me."

"Yes, I do."

"This isn't your fight. Nothing's keeping you here."

I considered my answer a little longer than I should have. "Yes, there is."

Our stares met. She knew there was more to my answer, and I noticed her emotion ridges turning pink. She watched my lips, waiting for me to say something more, but I couldn't bring myself to. I turned and started for the door. "If you're ready, my ship's waiting."

• • •

"Sierra-tango-four-two-four, you're cleared for departure."

I responded from my captain's chair. "Acknowledged."

A klaxon belted out its warning beyond my hull as the massive bay doors above us opened outward. Rione sat next to me, staring at the forward viewscreen and the debris flying around the empty bay.

"Last chance to change your mind," I offered.

Rione stared forward. A nervous chuckle escaped my lips, as there hadn't been a chance. "Take us out, Jeanie."

The ship jolted and lifted off the bay floor. We ascended past the open doors out into the dark abyss. The bluish-white planet beckoned to us from afar. I couldn't make out the Torian and Rulusian warships from this distance, but knew they were out there.

"Jeanie, turn on the noise generator and take us in."

"Acknowledged."

Fortunately, my ship was better suited than the ROC we'd used for the strike mission. I had no idea when the noise generators kicked in, as they were far quieter than the scabbed-on units which had caused too much drama before. The engines kicked in full blast as we cleared the station traffic, and my seat enveloped me like a mother with her child. I needed all the comfort I could get.

Rione didn't seem interested in conversation, so I kept my mouth shut. We continued in awkward silence until the planet filled my viewscreen. Two Rulusian warships waited in the darkness, the same vessels which had come to our assistance after the strike mission's success.

Jeanie informed us, "Approaching the Torian border."

I looked toward the silhouettes standing out against the bright planetary backdrop. Our old nemesis, Commander Sevil, in addition to the two light cruisers loitered between us and the planet. Their dark gray hulls nearly made me shiver in the midst of a warm compartment.

Rione finally broke in. "So, this is your first trip to the planet?"

"Yes."

"Too bad it has to be on these terms."

I shrugged. Even during my first journey to the Toris system, the threat of civil war had hung over the inhabitants. Granted, I hadn't known it at the time, or I likely would have passed on the cargo run which brought me here. In a sense, stumbling into Rione and her derelict freighter destined for destruction had saved my life more than once. Granted, it jeopardized my life almost as much.

She continued. "Hopefully once the war is over, you'll be able to visit for pleasure."

"Hopefully," I muttered.

I watched debris, remains from the destroyed satellite, flickering in the planet's glow.

Rione noticed as well. "Glad that thing was destroyed."

I spoke without looking at her. "I hope it helps as much as everyone thought it would."

"Trust me. Rebel troops were getting massacred, since they could track us any time we congregated. Without the satellite, things will be far easier."

We drew closer to the Torian cruisers. One of them broke from the pack and headed in our direction.

"Jeanie, what's the status of our noise generator?"

"Everything appears operational."

"What's with that cruiser?"

"It is changing course."

I held back the curse on my tongue. "I can see that. Have they detected us?"

Rione interjected. "Are we in weapons range?"

I looked over, baffled. "This ship doesn't have the firepower to take on a light cruiser."

"Are we in *their* weapons range?"

The hairs on my neck rose. "Jeanie?"

"Yes."

Rione smiled, a bizarre move. "I'd say it's just random. If they spotted us, they'd be shooting already."

I looked to my left, where a sensor screen displayed all the contacts outside. "We're not across the border just yet."

She leaned back in her chair. "You forget you're a marked man now. They match this ship up with you and it won't matter where we are."

That didn't help me relax.

I watched the cruiser pass before us and continue on its way. "Jeanie, make sure to adjust course far enough behind them the noise generator isn't disrupted."

"Acknowledged." Positioning thrusters fired off.

Rione chuckled. "I wish I'd known about noise generators before. It's been easier sneaking weapons to the planet since we outfitted all of our transports with them."

"So, that's how you've been getting weapons down? But where are they coming from?"

"Rulusia has secretly been shipping them to the station."

"Sneaky," I muttered.

The hairs on the back of my neck rose as we passed behind the Torian vessel. I knew Jeanie had calculated an appropriate path for us to clear, but my fear couldn't help but imagine the worst. There was always the possibility we could be wiped out without warning.

I motioned toward the center console. "You're the only one who knows where we're going. Mind inputting the coordinates?" She reached over and tapped the display.

"Jeanie, take us in," I said once she finished.

"Acknowledged."

Our seats jolted as we adjusted course for re-entry and accelerated toward the insertion point.

• • •

We shot through the scattered clouds and I was forced to shield my eyes from the bright reflection off the planet's icy surface. I was glad Jeanie was navigating, as I couldn't see a thing, even once she dimmed the screen.

Rione interjected as we descended. "We'll need to get down low, and quick. Some of our ships have had trouble with rocket sites tracking them down with scanners."

Jeanie confirmed it. "I'm detecting scanners attempting to get a fix on us."

"You might want to buckle in," I instructed our guest as I did so myself. "Jeanie, you heard her. Get us to the surface as fast as you can."

"Acknowledged."

We fell like a lead weight out of the sky. My back sank into my cushion until the metal frame pressed against my spine. Blood rushed to my head and my hearing grew hollow. I only hoped Jeanie was monitoring our health.

Then, the engines powered back up and I sank toward the floor as we swooped down into a jagged canyon. The glare disappeared, drowned out by rock walls.

Jeanie spoke as my hearing returned. “I have calculated the fastest path using terrain mapping.”

“Without a doubt,” I commented.

We weaved back and forth through the frozen pathway, rocky crevices looming on either side. “Mind shutting that viewscreen off?” Rione’s voice mumbled from my side.

I forced my head to the side, glancing over. Her skin had a slight green tint. I idly wondered if her emotion ridges were too.

“Trust me, turning it off will just make it worse,” I told her. Of course, the wild and abandoned movements were nothing to me. It had been a long time since my times as a fighter pilot in my home planet’s Defense Force, but there were reasons I’d been selected. My tolerance for rapid maneuvering had been one of several.

The cabin shook and shuddered again as Jeanie jerked us around another stony crag. This wasn’t going to turn out well for Rione. She closed her eyes. “Please, shut it off.”

I sighed. “Jeanie...”

The screen went dark and a few moments passed before Rione opened her eyes again. Just then, the ship darted back and forth in such a fashion that even I felt nauseous. She covered her mouth and I knew the end was close. I thumbed toward the back. “Waste can, back there!”

She nodded and released her restraints. Unfortunately, she barely made it past the divider before I heard the unmistakable sound of vomit spewing onto my floor.

“You’re cleaning that up,” I called out.

"Sorry." She expelled some more, making me cringe as the smell wafted up in my direction.

"How much farther?" I asked Jeanie.

"Not long."

"I don't imagine Rione will be able to handle much more of this." To drive home my point, the ship rocked from one side to the other. I heard her vomit yet again, and only hoped she'd been able to find a receptacle.

Jeanie gathered my attention. "Would you like the viewscreen back on?"

I had a feeling that was causing my own issue. "Yes."

The screen flickered back to life, projecting the darkened icy wasteland we flew through.

"Our destination should be around the next turn."

"Glad to hear it," I muttered and prepared for the hard right, just a moment before the ship banked. I heard something tumble in the back, then Rione called out with a string of curses that even made me blush.

"You okay back there?"

"Fine," she bellowed. "Warn me before you do that."

Jeanie jumped in for my benefit. "We will arrive at our destination without additional turns."

I smiled, not bothering to respond. The ship accelerated toward a sheer face of ice. As my nerves jumped into gear, we descended toward a small dark opening. I let out a breath I'd been unknowingly holding.

Rione stepped through the entryway. "Good, we're here."

The nauseating stench grew even stronger. My eyes started watering. "I would have figured you'd have better control than that," I nodded toward the back.

"I was a freighter Captain. We didn't usually maneuver like that."

I grimaced. During my time in the Gryphon Defense Force, there wasn't a single flight, during peace or wartime, when we didn't have a sortie far worse.

I moved my conversation with Rione to our destination, as we continued through the cavern. "So, is this place safe that we're heading to?"

Jeanie switched on the external lights, which reflected off the orange-brown rock formed into a man-made tunnel.

"As safe as any other place on the planet."

That didn't make me feel any better. "You aren't worried the king will come looking?"

"We'd scoped it out as a potential camp site, but didn't plan to use it until the satellite was destroyed."

"Convenient."

She shrugged. "We had to keep some reserve locations."

The tight quarters just beyond my hull made me nervous. I hoped no one was flying the other direction.

Rione continued. "Malone knew to bring his squads here as soon as we completed the mission."

The walls drew even closer, offering very little room for Jeanie to maneuver.

"Couldn't have found anything a little easier to access from the surface?"

She gave out a curt laugh. "You're lucky there's even access to the surface at all. They had to excavate this tunnel as it was."

"They move fast," I marveled, taking another look at the rocky walls.

"They have a lot of practice."

I simply nodded. The walls completely disappeared as we passed into a massive chamber. In addition to hollowing out solid rock, these folks were fairly accomplished at moving equipment and personnel quickly. Makeshift fabric tents were propped up at the cavern's far side, near another dark tunnel.

A pair of transports faced each other on a flat landing pad. They were the only flying craft around.

"No fighters or interceptors?"

She shook her head. "Wouldn't do us any good, even if we could afford them."

"Really?"

"We don't have the ability to train pilots, and wouldn't have a chance against the government's warships."

"Set us down, Jeanie."

We descended toward the landing pad. I watched as personnel filed out of the tents and looked up at us. Malone stood there at the forefront with a handful of others, just as dust and dirt sprayed up from our thruster exhaust. His face was like stone, a frown chiseled into it.

I turned to Rione. "He doesn't look too happy to see us."

"He'll get over it."

The landing skids thumped down on the pad of stone and the engines shut down. The dust settled and Malone's face was still covered in anger and disdain. This definitely wasn't going to go well.

Chapter Nine

Malone started yelling as soon as the hatch opened. "What do you think you're doing?" A distinct odor of mold and mildew oozed inside my ship, making my eyes water.

Rione glared daggers in his direction until the stairs came to rest. "Joining your strike mission."

He pointed at her, making even me cringe. "It isn't safe for you here. Now, you're leading them right to us."

Rione brushed past him. "We dove below their scanner sweeps well before they locked onto us. I've done this a few times, you know."

Three pale Torians stood around Malone in black body suits identical to ours. Their faces were stiff, but their eyes and mouths were contorted awkwardly, just as mine were. Things got worse as Malone grabbed her hand and turned her around. Rione stood toe-to-toe with him, the silent angst building.

One of Malone's companions interrupted, a short female with ratty blonde hair over her shoulder. "We're ready to review the mission."

"Fine," Malone muttered and stormed toward the nearby tents. He had to know, just as I did, Rione would get her way.

Rione fell in line behind him. I followed, while the blonde Torian female eyed my holstered blaster. "You're Aston West, aren't you?" I nodded, and she continued. "You were part of the team that took out the spy satellite."

"So I was," I said. I didn't much care for extra attention, so hoped she would drop it.

"Well, don't expect special treatment around here."

I kept my eyes on Malone ahead of us. Despite the fact I hadn't wanted any attention in the first place, her attitude still caught me off-guard. "Wouldn't think of it."

"I'm Celine."

"Pleasure, I'm sure."

"Just don't get in our way. We like to run a cleaner operation than you pulled up there."

My face burned, but I didn't bother responding as we made our way to the middle of the compound and a small, private tent. We marched inside through an open flap.

A small metal table rested at the center. There were no chairs, so we all stood while Malone set out a small square device. A holographic image beamed just above the table, with accompanying Torian text. I hadn't bothered to learn the written language, so it was all gibberish to me.

Malone took control, placing both palms on the table and disrupting his edge of the map image. "With the spy satellite out of commission, we need to strike hard and fast. Keep momentum on our side."

He pointed to one end of the map. "This is our current location. There shouldn't be any major traffic on the transit lines and we should have a clear path." He moved his finger along a pair of thick red lines to the map's center. "Here."

Rione looked over at Malone's face bathed in the map's light. "A transportation hub? You think that's high-profile enough to get attention?"

A small smile broke out on Celine's face as she interrupted. "It's a primary terminal. Every transit line in this sector runs through that hub."

I was understandably confused. "Won't you risk civilian casualties?"

Celine crossed her arms. "The surrounding city has been abandoned a long time. We'll be arriving late at night, and most businesses inside the hub are closed for a planetary holiday. There shouldn't be anyone there at all."

Rione turned to me. "Anniversary of the collapse."

I grimaced. Toris had suffered a catastrophe of the worst caliber when their subterranean thermal generator plants had been destroyed in a cave collapse several revolutions ago.

Out of that tragedy, the Torian people had been led to rely on other races and societies. The entire episode had started them on a path into the civil war now being waged. I didn't imagine the timing was mere coincidence.

Malone pointed across at Celine. "Be sure to bring enough hardware to make it matter." She nodded.

He pointed to another Torian male to his left. "You and I will lead the strike squads. Break into packs of four and escort the demolition teams, just in case."

He turned the other direction, focusing on another male I didn't know. "You have the medical squad. Just hold at the exit point and keep the engines running."

He peered around the room. "We'll set the charges for remote detonation, and set them off once we're clear. Don't need to risk a timer going off before we do."

I could almost sense the heat coming off of Rione's face. It didn't seem like anyone else but Malone even noticed. He had his eyes directly on her.

She asked, "And what about Aston and I?"

Malone wanted to pass us by, but Rione's interruption made it necessary for a decision. "You're on my team. I'll be able to keep an eye on you both then."

She frowned in response, but maintained the silence. He looked around the room one last time. "This is going to be a crucial attack, everyone. It will get the public's attention and most importantly tell the government that we're not going to put up with their treatment anymore."

He crossed his arms. "So, everyone get some rest. We'll assemble the teams in approximately half a rotation." The rest of the room nodded their agreement. "Dismissed."

• • •

As we stepped out of the tent, Malone's three teammates took off in various directions. Once they were out of earshot, the two lovers started in arguing, right where they left off.

"I told you it wasn't safe for you to be down here," Malone's biting tone hissed past his teeth.

She snarled. "It wasn't any safer on the station!"

His lips finally curled into a smile, and a moment passed before Rione's did the same. They drew close and kissed, increasing my personal awkwardness. I looked back toward my ship and the sanctuary it would provide.

"I've missed you," he mumbled.

"I know," she responded.

Malone turned to me as I was on the verge of running off for solitude. "Aston, join us for some drinks."

I had a feeling he didn't have any Vladirian liquor laying around, but even if he had, I didn't really want to be around them, not together as the couple they were.

"I should probably rest before we head out."

"Join us, Aston," Rione pleaded. Her emotion ridges were light pink again, no doubt from being around Malone.

I shook my head. Malone moved over and clasped my shoulder; the good one, thankfully. "I still need to thank you properly for saving Rione's life."

"Really, I should head back to my ship."

He released his grip, finally getting the message. "Well, perhaps another time, then."

I gave a weak smile and nodded before the two strolled off toward a smaller tent. I finally made my escape.

Jeanie was quick to address me as I stepped inside my living quarters. "Was your gathering productive?"

I ignored her, walking to my cot. "Close us up."

The door gears drowned out my thoughts as I plopped down and rested my arm across my face. Jeanie took the hint and dimmed the lights. A moment later, the odor dissipated. I checked with Jeanie. "Any idea what that smell was?"

"The rock formations under the Torian surface are prone to decay, which produces a noticeable odor."

At least that gave me my answer, but didn't give me any idea how to combat it.

Jeanie continued, "It seemed your friends were interested in celebrating with you."

I adjusted my arm, trying to find a better spot. "How'd you hear us without me having my transmitter?"

"I interpreted their body language and yours."

I lowered my arm, staring at the ceiling. "Here I thought you'd picked up lip reading."

"I have not mastered that skill. It will take time."

I chuckled to myself, enjoying the golden silence. Jeanie interrupted again. "Do you mind if I ask what may be considered a personal question?"

It was the first time I remembered her ever asking such a thing. I hadn't figured she'd consider a question too personal. "Go ahead."

"Your actions and demeanor around Rione seem to have changed recently. Why is that?"

This was a question that would require heavy drinking, as I had no doubt Jeanie wouldn't let me slide on an easy answer. I rolled off the cot, starting for the cockpit where I still had one last bottle of Vladirian liquor stored away. "That's just how people get when they become friends. Over time, they become more accustomed to each other and act differently."

"I see." She fell silent.

I leaned over, opened up the small cooler behind the right-hand seat, and pulled out the brand new bottle. Unscrewing the cap, I smiled. That had been easier than I would have figured possible.

Then she fulfilled my original expectations. "I have not observed these same changes between you and your other friends, even though you have known them longer."

I lifted my bottle and sweet yellow liquid flowed down my throat. At least it bought me some time to consider my answer. "Everyone is different. Some friendships develop differently than others."

"So, your friendship with Rione is more developed than the one you have with Tabor Yurick, for example?"

I grimaced. Tabor was a distributor of fine goods, at least he made himself out to be. I knew better. He and I met shortly after I'd first gotten into the world of scavenging, when I needed to unload some cargo which wasn't exactly legal to sell.

I started back for my cot. "He and I have a different type of friendship. We do a lot of business together. Our personal lives are usually kept separate."

"So, you're personally attached to Rione?"

I sat down hard on my mattress and took another long drink. "More so than to Tabor."

"You seem to be pondering your answers carefully, as if you would rather not respond to my questions. Would you rather I stop?"

I really did, but Jeanie and I had progressed far beyond the master and slave relationship my home planet's citizens had insisted upon being installed in all computer systems. It wasn't my style to restrict her. "No, ask as many questions as you want."

"Is it common for your friendships with females to grow deeper than with males, and reach that stage quicker?"

My chest tightened. I should have taken her offer to stop the interrogation. "Why do you ask?"

"Your reactions to Rione seem very similar to those with the former first officer of the Rulusian spy ship."

"Oh." The mere mention of Jaclyn was enough to drive me into another long drink. At this rate, I'd need to break open another bottle.

The silence extended a little while longer, while I tried to anticipate all the questions Jeanie could ask.

She interrupted once more. "Do you expect to progress your relationship to the same point with Rione?"

I lifted an eyebrow and capped the bottle. I knew going down this path with Jeanie would be a disaster, but felt it necessary to explain myself, even as my chest tightened with sorrow at a lost life. "My friendship with Rione is deeper than it was with Jaclyn."

"Then you expect to engage in the same behaviors with Rione as you did with her?"

My face grew red hot, my tone tense. "I think we should end the questions now."

"Acknowledged." Forced to comply, silence fell again.

I knew Jeanie held no ulterior motive in her questions, but the specific answers she sought were sending me down paths I did not want to ponder aloud. I tossed my bottle onto the cot, and rose to my feet.

"Are you angry with my questions?"

I took a deep breath in, counted to ten, then exhaled slowly. "No, I just need to clear my head. I'll be back shortly. Keep the door open, I won't be long."

She opened the exit hatch without a response. I stomped down the steps and across the grainy rocks, holding my breath as long as possible to avoid the stench. With a glance around the reddish-brown cavern, I started toward the campsite.

The cavern was quiet and desolate as I stepped past the various tents. Everyone else was getting sleep, just as I needed to. My frustration built with each step, instead of abating as I'd expected. Rest was going to have to wait longer than I thought.

Near the far end of the compound, a larger tent stood with its flaps open. I peeked inside, seeing illegal munitions resting in giant piles. I wondered if any of them were part of the first shipment I'd caught Rione with on my initial trip to this planet. Another reminder of how fate had drawn me into this civil war. I just wished I knew why.

"Hands up!"

I jerked my arms into the air while my heart raced.

"Turn around, slowly."

As I turned, I came face to face with the female Torian team leader who'd been with Malone earlier, Celine. She held an automatic blast rifle in her hands, the barrel pointed directly at my chest.

Her scowl didn't help me relax. "What do you think you're doing?" She asked me.

I calmed myself. After all, we were all on the same team. "Just walking around before I settle down to rest."

She nodded toward the open tent. "And that was part of the tour?"

"Just curiosity on my part." Shivers ran through me as I realized she still hadn't put the weapon down.

"Curiosity isn't admirable, even in people I know."

I let her words slide away, then let out a deep sigh. "Mind if I drop my hands?"

One blonde eyebrow lifted. "Depends on whether I should trust you or not."

This reminded me of how I met Rione. I wasn't too sure how I felt about that. "I'm fairly certain you can trust me. I'm sure you've heard of me."

She tossed her head, her ratty hair flopping to one side. "Just because you help us destroy the king's toys doesn't mean you're trusted."

I frowned.

An evil smile passed over her face. "Put your arms down. You look like an idiot."

Maybe she and Rione were the best of friends. I lowered my hands to the side as she finally dropped her rifle's butt to the ground.

"Sorry, it's hard to know who to trust. We thought we could trust that slimy Rulusian politician Ba'lor Bilhari, and you know how that turned out."

I nodded. Ba'lor Bilhari had been deep inside the rebel cause, even setting up that first illegal weapons shipment from Rulusia. He'd ended up ratting out the rebel cause for his own political gain. Once I'd shown up and ruined the original plan, he'd taken matters into his own hands and ended up imprisoned. At least he had before I'd left the first time.

"Whatever happened to him?"

Celine let out a snort. "Executed."

"Couldn't have happened to a nicer guy," I mused. Considering the man had been involved in at least one direct attempt on my life, I didn't feel too much grief. He hadn't started off on the right foot by being a politician, and ending up a traitor had sealed the deal.

"Well, I'd better get back."

She nodded. "Everyone needs their strength for this mission, that's for sure."

I stepped past Celine and made my way back to the ship. Closer to the main compound, I looked back and she was already gone. It was definitely a bizarre exchange, but I put it out of my mind while I stepped between the tents of sleeping Torians.

When I stepped inside my darkened ship, Jeanie didn't respond as she had the last time.

"Close us up, Jeanie."

She obeyed the command without comment. I thought about asking about her silence, but knew she didn't have the ability for emotions. How silly would it be for a computer to be upset?

I sat back down on my cot, and grabbed the bottle of Vladirian liquor which rested beside me. It didn't take long for me to finish the bottle, and I tossed it onto one of the many stacks of filthy clothes lying around.

Feeling a bit more relaxed, I leaned back and placed my arm over my closed eyes. I gave one last set of instructions. "Let me know when you see Rione."

"Acknowledged."

I gave a weak smile. At least she had responded.

Chapter Ten

Jeanie's voice woke me. "Rione is approaching."

I had no way of knowing how much sleep I'd gotten, but from the sheer exhaustion crawling through my veins, it hadn't been enough. Blinking until the ceiling came into focus, I muttered my thanks, climbing to my feet. "I'll be back later."

The door gears squealed their objection as the entry hatch lowered. Rione stood at the bottom of the stairs as it struck the rock floor.

"Ready for this?" She smiled broader than I'd seen her in a long time.

My boots crunched in the gravel. "Looks like you had a good time."

The emotion ridges on the side of her face turned pink once more. She lifted one eyebrow. "You could say that."

"So, I take it you and Malone came to an agreement and he's letting you stay."

She let out a slight chuckle, but didn't answer me verbally. We started toward the center of the camp, where Torian rebels gathered into their teams.

Rione didn't bother turning to look in my direction, speaking as we trotted along at a brisk pace. "You, on the other hand, look terrible."

"Rough time sleeping," I explained.

"Worried about this mission?"

"Not that I know of." In actuality, I didn't want to get into the specifics. We all needed to keep our minds on the task at hand. This was neither the time nor the place for an in-depth discussion of my emotional issues.

Now was the time to get this mission started.

Malone congregated with his team leaders at the far end of the gathering. I stepped up beside Celine, who barely acknowledged my existence.

Malone tossed Rione a disintegrator cannon, and started to send an automatic blast rifle my way. I waved him off, pulling my Mark II out of its holster. He shook his head, before turning to each of his leaders. "Are your teams ready?"

Each responded, "Yes, sir!" The boisterous voices echoed off the cavern walls.

He started off toward the smaller opening in the far wall. "Let's go!"

I stepped up beside Rione and we rushed along with the small horde of Torians desperate for their freedom. Near to the cave mouth rested another big tent like the one I'd seen during my bout with insomnia.

"Mount up!"

Several soldiers stepped up and yanked on the flaps, pulling the covers off a dozen black, streamlined vehicles. Each had four knobby tires on a narrow wheelbase, accompanied by a set of smaller steel wheels currently raised off the ground. A driver's seat and an aft bench sat between the forward and aft wheels.

I watched as teams climbed onto the vehicles, two on the bench seats and one in the driver's seat. Another Torian took a gun turret position at the front. The throaty roar of combustion engines filled the cavern, before each wide unit rolled along the dusty ground.

"Aston," Rione called out. I turned and watched her riding a bench seat. I hopped up beside her as it rolled by.

We were third in the progression, giving us a clear view of the first two vehicles as they passed through the opening. Journeying through a small tunnel, we exited out into a much more refined passageway. Large amber lights hung from the tall ceiling, beaming down upon a set of parallel metal tracks.

The first vehicle reached the tracks and spun in place until it was in line with the rails. Slow grinding from below its undercarriage accompanied the lowering of its metal wheels which aligned the vehicle onto the tracks. It gunned its engines and sped off, followed shortly by the second in line, and then ours right behind.

Lights flashed past above our heads as we accelerated down the tunnel. The engines reverberated against the walls, and made any conversation impossible. I looked back and watched the remaining vehicles join our convoy.

The metal rails underneath us appeared older than most of the young people riding with us. Likely put in when the tunnel was first burrowed out, the metal guides had shifted and settled over time. I kept one hand on my blaster and the other on a support rail behind my back. My body was forced back and forth in rhythm with the tracks. I looked up at Rione's face, where the green tint of nausea had crept back, just as during our canyon trip.

Almost as if she heard my thoughts, she turned and glared at me. Orange lights changed to pale white as the surrounding cavern became lined with white tile. They rushed past in a blur as we exited the tunnel into another far greater chamber, housing an entire city. The vehicles decelerated as we rode through stone and clay buildings. I looked around, but didn't see a single citizen. Just as they'd told me, it still drove my paranoia wild.

As we continued to slow, storefronts and homes grew clearer. Those that weren't broken out behind black, iron bars were boarded up with thick planks. We drew closer to a large, blinding white clay building, and the first two transports disappeared inside another tunnel.

Darkness enveloped our own vehicle, until my eyes grew accustomed to the pale lights embedded in the walls. The tracks in this area were a bit more pleasant, without a noticeable jerking motion to accompany our travel.

"Feeling better?" I muttered to Rione.

She turned and faced me again, but breathed a sigh of relief before looking forward once more.

We entered another large room, filled with tracks switching off to each other, all of them separated by raised concrete platforms. A huge turntable rested at the very center of the room, with other lines venturing out of the room at different angles. We came to a careful stop next to a platform and climbed off the vehicles while the rest of the troops arrived.

I looked up at a black wrought iron lattice hanging from an overhead walkway connected by stairs to all four platforms situated at our entrance. The combined walkway then led to waiting areas on either side of the platforms. Each set of tracks had the same arrangement, completing the circle. Concession stands and businesses, all closed for the holiday, lined the outer walls in these larger areas, which also contained tables for commuters to wait on their particular transports.

"Massive," I noted.

Malone clapped my shoulder. "It should definitely get everyone's attention."

A deadly silence filled the air. My gut rolled. I couldn't shake the feeling still gnawing at my insides.

Malone called out to Celine and the demolition teams as they dismounted. "Set the charges. Make it quick."

She nodded, as they raced out of sight down the track.

Once the sound of their boots in the dusty rock could no longer be heard, I turned to Rione. "It's too quiet."

She snickered under her breath. "That's the point."

"Something doesn't seem right."

Her forehead scrunched, then she turned to Malone. "We might want to take a look around."

"There's nothing to worry about."

She thumbed toward me. "Aston has a knack for sniffing out these things."

He stared at me in disbelief, but finally made the right choice. He turned to other team leaders on both of the platforms we'd taken. "Spread out. Search for any sign of trouble."

Various personnel split up. Some of them climbed up onto the overhead walkway. Others jumped down onto the tracks and ventured off toward the huge turntable at the facility's center.

"Coming?" Rione caught my attention. I moved to catch up with her and Malone, then stomped up the stairs, the metal clanking and joining in chorus with the others.

While everyone dispersed throughout the facility, the three of us stood at the top center of a combined walkway. I leaned against the railing, blaster in hand while scoping out our surroundings.

Troops wove up and down the tracks and through the circular dining tables. Some knelt down and set their charges. I moved my gaze onto a maintenance yard at the far left end of the facility.

A glimpse of movement between parked tram cars under repair caught my attention, and I pointed. "There!"

"What?" Rione whipped her head around, but I'd lost sight of whatever it was I'd seen.

"Someone was moving over there. It wasn't one of us."

Malone pulled a small spherical transmitter off his belt. "Looks like we have some company. Team Alpha, check out the maintenance yard."

A jumbled response returned, and I watched the team of rebels converge on the target. They disappeared from view and a moment later, the retort of weapons fire echoed off the walls. A rainbow of colors reflected against shiny metal hulls of disabled transports, casting a virtual light show on the ceiling.

I turned to my friends, the hair standing on the back of my neck. "We need to run, now." Then, I bolted back to the stairs and raced down toward our waiting vehicles.

From the sound of their feet on the metal flooring above, they hadn't followed my lead. I looked back as they passed overhead and continued toward the platform's end. Cursing under my breath, I raced back up and followed them. I didn't plan on getting stuck alone in a firefight.

We raced down the end staircase, sprinting through the maze of tables in the closest commons areas. Screams bellowed out from the maintenance yard. Every part of my body begged me to make a break for it.

But I followed along as my two companions raced for the edge of the platform closest to the maintenance yard. Malone pulled his transmitter up. "Report!"

This time, the response was loud enough I could make it out. "Too many...getting massacred...need to..."

The communication cut off completely. I heard an accompanying scream echo in the distance along with more weapons fire.

Malone finally saw things my way, pointing back toward the overhead walkway. He screamed his orders into the transmitter. "Retreat! It's an ambush!"

I didn't need to be told twice, rushing for the metal staircase and jumping two, sometimes three steps at a time. When I reached the top, I looked back, seeing the other two right behind me. Another glance in the opposite direction and several pairs of rebel troops scurried around, along with government patrols with even deadlier weapons chasing behind. Their gray battle armor would need a little more power to penetrate. I flipped my Mark II blaster to its three-shot burst setting.

Though I'd been a fighter pilot in the Gryphon Defense Force long ago, they'd tried to recruit me into becoming a foot soldier. If there was something I could do fairly well, it was run and shoot at the same time.

I sprinted along the overhead walkway, firing off at the government troops. Some shots hit their mark, others didn't. Unfortunately for me, it drew their attention away from their immediate targets and they aimed their weapons in our direction.

A blast from Rione's disintegrator cannon struck one of those taking potshots at us. He screamed while his body decomposed from the inside out, the armor apparently organic as it succumbed to the same fate. Even more attention came our way, while I ducked and dodged incoming fire on my way down to our original platform.

Screeching metal filled the entire chamber as flatbed trams entered the hub from the other portholes. Dozens of troops stormed off onto empty platforms, all carrying heavy plasma cannons. They fired blasts into the running rebels.

I hit the platform and dove to my stomach, kissing the concrete as random shots flew over me. Rione's voice cried out behind me. "They're getting massacred!"

I looked up and watched as one after another, the crossfire struck targets, causing our comrades to ignite, rebels all screaming in agony until they finally fell as lifeless corpses.

I looked back as Rione and Malone jumped down to the platform in front of the first transport. He pulled up his transmitter. “Blow the charges! Blow them now!”

My eyes went wide. “You’ll kill us all!”

“Better to take them with us,” he stated coldly.

I had no intention of dying on this world, or any other. I jumped up and raced to the waiting transports.

He repeated his command. “Blow them!”

Yet there wasn’t an explosion, nor any response. Maybe they’d all died in the ambush. I’d ceased caring.

Then I remembered my internal promise about Rione and turned to watch her. Every part of my body lit aflame as I saw flashes of light near the two of them. Rione screamed, and my mind flashed through the possibilities. I raced for her as she and Malone both crumpled in slow motion to the ground. Her sobs hit my ears, which was a good sign.

At least she wasn’t dead. Not yet, anyway.

I raced around the first transport, where Rione cradled Malone’s body. Cold chills ran through me as I revisited Leah’s death from the outside looking in. Where blood had flowed freely from her, Malone’s lifeless chest was scorched from a blast of weapons fire. Rione looked up into my eyes, filled with sorrow and despair I knew well.

“Why?” She sobbed, something I’d never seen her do before. She turned her head as more rebels screamed in pain and suffering at the hands of the enemy. Her emotion ridges were deep blue.

A blast struck the staircase and exploded. I flinched, finally brought back to the reality of government troops moved in.

“We need to go!” I grabbed her jacket.

“I can’t leave him.”

I tugged even harder. “He’s gone, Rione. You can’t do anything more for him.”

She resisted my efforts, and more explosions went off around us. I drew deep down for even more strength, and raced toward the rear transport with her in tow.

As we reached it, I pulled Rione close and looked into her sorrowful eyes. “Can you drive this thing?”

She nodded, jumping into the driver’s seat. I climbed into the forward gunner position, grabbing hold of the triggers and firing green bursts of energy at the approaching tidal wave of government troops. The transmission clunked into reverse beneath us, and our tires squealed on the tracks as we accelerated away from the platform. I watched as the troops’ flatbed trams moved toward the turntable at the center of the hub. Unfortunately, we were moving far slower backwards than we had been forward. Action would pick up quickly.

“We’re not going to have much time,” Rione called out, confirming what I already knew. “They’ll catch up to us before we reach my ship.”

I turned, looking back at her. “Is there anything back there to help us?”

Keeping one hand on the throttle, she reached back with the other and rummaged out of site, before tossing a green duffel to me. In the depths of the fabric, I felt a small pouch sitting there all alone.

I pulled out the clay-like square. “We have another demolition charge.”

“But the detonator’s back with the rest of the transports.” She pointed toward the front, where a flatbed tram gained ground on us.

Enemy soldiers fired off rounds, exploding the rock around us as we passed by. Rione grabbed her weapon with a free hand, firing off rounds from her disintegrator cannon. One of the troops standing at the front of the tram was hit, his comrades jumping back from the strike. The victim's remains flew off the speeding tram as soon as they turned to ash, all the while his agonizing screams filling the corridor. Another potential victim jumped up into his place the moment he was gone. The tram grew closer.

I suddenly had an idea, reaching over the nose of our vehicle and dropping the charge on top of the tracks.

"What did you do that for?" She complained.

I ignored her and grabbed the handles of the mounted plasma cannon. The explosive device bounced and rolled along the tracks, the gap with oncoming troops closing. Focusing my attention on it, I belted out a sequence of shots, striking the device and sending a fireball roaring through the tunnel. Chunks of rock collapsed from the ceiling while the flatbed tram derailed itself in the explosion. Screams echoed against the rock as the dirt and dust bellowed out from the scene of the disaster.

"Nice shooting," she commented as we continued toward the secret chamber. "That should buy us some time, but the next group will just blast through the debris. We need to get back to the orbital station."

With the immediate danger behind us, I watched Rione as her tears flowed again. Not knowing how to assuage my own sorrow over Leah's murder, I didn't really have a clue how to help Rione.

• • •

We'd dumped the transport at the entrance, and raced into the chamber on foot, an eerie silence surrounding us as we scrambled for my ship.

"Jeanie," I bellowed as we drew closer. "Open up. Fire up the thrusters, now!"

The entry hatch lowered, debris pelting us as we raced for safety. An explosion rocked the chamber. I looked back, seeing a ball of flame erupt out of the access tunnel, which would have been our transport being eliminated by the government troops.

“They’re here!” I called.

Rione raced up the steps in front of me. I shouted out orders before my feet even touched my living quarters’ floor. “Jeanie, take us back to the orbital station!”

The thrusters blasted at full power, lifting us into the air while the door rose off the ground.

Rione grabbed my arm as I raced for the cockpit. “We can’t let them have any of this.”

“What?”

“If they get those weapons, they’ll use them against other rebels. We have to destroy everything.”

I knew she was right. Without looking away from Rione, I spoke out. “Jeanie, do you have our exit path planned?”

“Yes, Aston.”

“Target the munitions tent at the camp’s far end.”

She was hesitant, but I knew she’d comply. She had to. “An explosion in such tight quarters would be unwise.”

I stared into Rione’s eyes and knew it was a risk we’d have to take. “Do it.”

“Acknowledged.”

I broke free and continued up to the cockpit, plopping down in my seat as the viewscreen flickered to life. Jeanie maneuvered around until the munitions tent was into view. It was now or never.

“Fire!”

Green beams pulsed from either side of my viewscreen and lit the tent aflame. Troops scrambled into the chamber, moments before the munitions inside the tent went up.

Bodies flew in the air. Being inside our sealed hull, I could only imagine their screams echoing off the chamber walls as the fireball drowned them out forever.

Another explosion rocked the inside of the cavern. I called out to Jeanie as Rione took the second seat. “Get us out of here!”

Our ship turned and the aft engines fired off. We raced toward the escape tunnel, the same one we’d arrived through.

Jeanie announced facts I really didn’t want to hear. “The cavern is losing structural integrity.”

I’d been okay with the idea when face-to-face with Rione, but now the idea of my own mortality wasn’t all that appealing. “Jeanie, will we make it?”

“I recommend both of you strap in. I will need to begin evasive maneuvers.”

We slid into harnesses I never remembered using. “Are you going to need something to vomit into?” I asked Rione.

“I’ll make sure to aim it in your direction.”

If the situation was a little less dire, I would have continued needling her. Instead, I watched the tunnel entrance get closer in something far less than slow motion. Jeanie jerked us to the right to miss a large falling boulder, and the exit disappeared from the middle of the viewscreen. Another maneuver followed, then one more.

I kept one eye on Rione, just in case I needed to deflect bodily fluids. To her credit, though, she held her own as we dodged even more falling debris.

Jeanie finally skirted through the narrow opening, moments before I felt a shockwave hit us from behind.

She kept us informed. “The cavern has collapsed.”

I exhaled, finally realizing how fast my heart was pumping inside my chest. Attempts to calm myself only made matters worse, even while Jeanie steadied us through the tunnel's tightest spaces.

"Glad we made it," I muttered with my heart moving up to my throat.

Rione undid her restraints, tossing them aside. "We aren't out of this yet, flyboy. You can bet the government troops who survived back there are contacting their superiors."

I shivered on the inside.

She continued, "And rest assured, they'll have fighters and destroyers on us faster than you can drink a bottle of Vladirian liquor."

We burst out of the dark tunnel and immediately accelerated toward the upper atmosphere. The blue sky was a bright contrast to the darkness underground, until Jeanie dimmed the viewscreen.

To be honest, the sight was beautiful to behold.

And then, Jeanie ruined it with bad news. "AI-5s on an intercept course."

"Distance?"

"Fifteen kilpars outside of their weapons range."

Quite a distance, if we'd all been flying the same ships. Unfortunately, my small transport would barely make it to orbital altitude before they caught up to us. There'd still be plenty of distance to cover before we reached the Torian border, let alone the orbital station.

A shiver went up my spine as I remembered a crucial fact. There was still a trio of Torian warships out there.

All in all, it was a pretty dismal situation. I'd been through them many times before, and had always come out mostly unscathed.

So, in other words, I was due.

Chapter Eleven

"How will we make it?"

Considering Rione hadn't vomited during our escape so far, I'd actually forgotten she was sitting next to me.

"We will, don't worry." I spoke the words, but couldn't even convince myself.

"You don't have a plan, do you?"

I frowned. "Working on it."

Jeanie interrupted. "Interceptors closing at ten kilpars."

"Status of the cruisers in orbit?"

"Two will be in weapons range when we reach orbit."

The situation was going from bad to worse, and I had no clue how to get us out of it. I scoured my memory to find something which worked in the past. There was nothing.

"Interceptors at five kilpars. Their targeting arrays are coming online."

A thought flashed in my head, and I would have immediately dismissed it had our circumstances not been so dire. Instead, I chose this last resort.

"Jeanie, set up a hyperspeed jump. Hit it as soon as we enter the upper atmosphere."

"Destination?"

"Somewhere near the orbital station."

Rione flipped her head around, glaring at me. "Are you nuts? You can't do a hyperspeed jump in the same system!"

"Well, unless you've got a better idea..."

She mumbled to herself, "This had better work."

Jeanie inserted her opinion. "Such a move is unorthodox and not recommended by the drive manufacturer."

She was always right, with this time no exception. "Do we have any other options with a chance of success?"

She didn't bother answering, even though I already knew what her response would be. Instead, she gave us more pressing information. "The interceptors have reached weapons range. Two AIR-3s are inbound."

Adilphi Interceptor Rockets. I may have been able to evade them, but more would come, I was sure.

It was now or never. "Have we reached orbital altitude?"

"Yes, Aston. The two cruisers are in range, preparing to fire."

"Make the jump!"

"I highly recommend against..."

We didn't have time for a discussion. "Do it, now!"

"Cruisers are firing."

The static field generators began their normal operation and we accelerated into the field and jumped across the hyperspace threshold. The ship shook and shuddered, which I assumed was a result of the cruisers' heavy cannons unleashing a salvo on the spot we'd just vacated. Unlike every other jump we'd ever made, I watched an almost instantaneous field destabilization take place.

"What happened?"

"The blast from the cruisers struck just as we crossed the hyperspeed threshold. It damaged our atomic displacement coils and brought us out of hyperspeed."

"Are we across the border?"

"Yes, just barely past the Rulusian warships. We are out of weapons range for the Torian cruisers."

I exhaled a deep breath. "Continue course for the orbital station, full speed." As if there was any doubt how fast we needed to get there.

I calmed myself, even though I should have known better than to think we'd make it out of the danger zone. Jeanie announced, "Incoming messages."

"How'd they catch our frequency?" I glanced down at the communications panel.

"The message is being broadcast on all frequencies."

I lifted an eyebrow. "Put it through."

I recognized the voice immediately as that of our nemesis, Commander Roth Sevil. "Unidentified vessel, you and all occupants aboard are hereby placed under arrest for terrorist activities. Power down your propulsion system and prepare to be boarded." The message paused, then repeated.

"No chance of that," I mumbled.

At the next pause, a female voice interrupted the transmission. "This is Captain Porthia of the Rulusian battleship Red One. We extend our assistance to your vessel in distress as specified in the Code of Interstellar Wayfaring, section two-point-five-dash-one."

"Do not interfere with us, Captain! We have a valid warrant for the capture of any and all fugitives on-board that vessel, and we have every intention of serving it."

"Any Torian warship crossing the border will be considered a threat to the orbital station, and will be fired upon."

Commander Sevil returned venom for venom. "Any vessel that fires upon us will have declared war on Toris."

Everything went silent. I watched as the station grew larger in the viewscreen, albeit far too slowly. I went ahead and asked Jeanie, "What are they doing out there?"

"The two Torian warships I detected earlier are diverting toward the border. Another three warships, including a second heavy cruiser, are joining them from the surface."

I turned to Rione again. "This won't end well, is it?"

"I need to get a secure transmission to Lucian."

I motioned to the panel. With a few keystrokes, she established contact. Princess Wren's head and shoulders filled a smaller window along the side of the screen.

Her eyes went wide, the worry lines deep. "Rione!"

"Your highness, we need help out here."

"What happened? Why are you returning so soon?"

The mood sank inside the compartment. Rione choked down her tears, even as her voice cracked. "Lucian, we must contact Rulusia to bring more warships into the area."

"It will only provoke the current standoff situation into a full-blown war."

I interrupted. "I think we're too late to worry about that, Princess."

Jeanie confirmed it. "The Torian cruisers have crossed the border and have powered up their weapons systems."

"Show us."

The other half of the display zoomed in on a mob of warships. Wren had to be seeing the same thing in her office, her eyes shaking back and forth. I'd considered war a foregone conclusion to the act of placing warships in someone else's backyard. The only question in my mind had been when the breaking point would be reached.

That time was now.

"What are they waiting for?" I asked, with no evidence of the firefight having begun.

"The cruisers are at a full stop," Jeanie told us.

"On which side of the border?"

"They are in interstellar space."

Rione snorted through her nose. "They're taunting the Rulusians, daring them to shoot first."

I stared at the screen. "I'm surprised they haven't."

"So am I."

Princess Wren interjected. "Neither side wants to be the first into the conflict, not until they're given no other choice."

I shook my head. "Or have an airtight excuse."

"I'm sure both populations will demand it of their governments," Lucian responded. "The Rulusians are seen as a highly superior fighting force, and any appearance of bullying the Torians could have widespread consequences."

Rione and I both grimaced, as Wren continued. "So they won't initiate anything, not before reinforcements arrive, which will likely lead the Torians to start shooting."

A glimmer of hope permeated Rione's voice. "So, they're sending reinforcements?"

Wren finally offered a weak smile, and weight lifted off her shoulders. "The politicians were able to spin the altercation with their transport to persuade the public more peacekeepers were needed. A battalion is on its way."

"Hopefully in time," I muttered.

Lucian agreed. "Hopefully."

Rione focused on the ships filling my viewscreen. "This has gotten way out of hand."

"Wars do that," I said with a sigh.

"Along with killing the ones you love," Rione said.

The Princess focused her concern. "What's wrong?"

Rione's hard-hearted tone couldn't hold back the tears any longer. She choked up. "He's dead, Lucian."

Wren's forehead scrunched, eyes full of sorrow. "How?"

Her emotions overwhelmed her. "Ambushed. Government troops. Everywhere."

Princess Wren pondered everything she'd just heard, then looked up with furrowed pale eyebrows. "It sounds like we still have a leak somewhere."

I looked over at Rione, and knew she was in no condition to continue these discussions. It wasn't completely the same, but I'd been right where she was. Trying to figure out where she'd gone wrong, what she could have done differently to keep Malone alive.

I diverted our attention. "Princess, I'll need some repairs. Where can I land?"

"Hangar bay two is still available. I'll meet you."

"If it's all the same, we can meet in your office."

She nodded. "I'll be waiting."

Wren terminated the transmission, and the screen reverted back to the image of Torian and Rulusian warships standing off, each waiting for the other side to start a battle so they could finish it.

I watched Rione again. Her eyes were glossed over, emotion ridges were back to being a lighter shade of her regular bronzed skin. If I was to guess, she was numbing herself to the pain. I was just glad she was still alive. Seeing her in this much pain, though, ate at my heart.

I turned my attention forward and watched as we drew closer to the station. Jeanie redirected our path toward the hangar bay.

I shivered, knowing we hadn't ended up safer on the planet, and we still weren't safe on the station. Rione and I would have to discuss our options.

I could hardly wait.

• • •

The landing skids touched down, thumping through my seat. The entire cockpit remained silent, just as it had after we terminated our conversation with the Princess.

Jeanie had no reservations about chiming in, though. "Aston, I've placed an order for a new pair of atomic displacement coils. I have made the assumption you would want to perform the repair yourself."

"That's right." She and I had been together long enough for her to know I never let anyone repair my ship, unless it was impossible to do it myself.

"The local parts supply center estimates they will not receive any in for at least the next three revolutions."

I cursed under my breath.

"Looks like we're stuck here for a little while," Rione mumbled.

There was something to be said for taking opportunities as they were offered. I went for this one. "At some point, we need to review our options."

"No time like the present."

Jeanie powered down, the lights inside the ship darkening. Rione's face took on a sinister appearance, and I was eager to find brighter surroundings. "Step outside."

"I'd rather not just yet." She turned away, blue emotion ridges evident even with minimal lighting. Her attempts at remaining numb hadn't lasted. With her long fingers, she wiped her cheeks, tear streams glistening. I wanted to help her, to comfort her. Unfortunately, I didn't know the first thing about trying to resolve someone else's grief. I didn't even know how to do it for myself.

"We're not safe here. You know that," I told her.

She nodded. "And apparently not on the planet either."

"That makes the choice fairly easy."

"Does it?"

It did for me. "Why wouldn't we just run for safety?"

"What then? Wherever we go, they'll hunt us."

I could think of several places where no one would ever find us. For the time being, I was willing to entertain her notions. "So, what do we do?"

"We take the fight directly to the source. We end this war and end the senseless killing on both sides."

I scrunched my forehead. "And how do we do that? Just the two of us, stopping a planet's civil war?"

"We kill the king and his sons. Lucian is next in line for the throne."

"You don't think she'll object to the idea. Even if she doesn't follow their beliefs, they're still family."

She turned to me. "I don't plan on telling her."

Shivering, I muttered, "This is insane." In fact, it was well beyond that point.

"It's the only way."

I shook my head. "Rione, you're not thinking clearly."

"My thoughts are perfectly clear."

"You're angry about Malone's death. You want vengeance. I know exactly how you feel."

Her ridges spiked bright red and I knew I'd gone too far. "You know nothing of how I feel."

Guilt over my own loss gurgled up. "I do."

Before she shot daggers through me, I held up my hand. "You wanted to know what happened before I showed up here."

She turned away. "It's not important anymore."

"I killed a man out of revenge. He nearly killed me in the process."

"Stop," she insisted.

"No. You have to know." I took a deep breath and exhaled. "I wanted him dead for taking the life of someone close to me."

She turned back, tears flowing again. "Then, you know exactly why I have to do what I did. I want my revenge."

Oddly, I did know. Given the opportunity to come face to face with Elijah again, I'd want the same thing.

She stood from her seat, then stopped and pointed. "Not a word to the Princess about this."

I sighed. "You're making a big mistake. Trust me."

Rione frowned. "I need you to keep your mouth shut."

"If I said no, you'd probably find a way to get me arrested, like our first meeting."

That elicited a weak smile from her, but no verbal response. As she moved past the divider, I followed her into my living area.

Jeanie, being the forward-thinker she was, had already lowered the exit stairs. As I climbed down to join Rione on the hangar floor, I considered her plan. One thing she hadn't mentioned was whether she planned to go it alone.

It was sometimes eerie how Rione seemed to read my mind. She and Jeanie tended to have that trait in common, even though one was a machine, the other flesh and blood.

Rione grabbed the duffel she'd packed before heading to the surface, turning to face me. "Are you joining me?"

Ordinarily, I'd have been on my ship and running for safety, aside from waiting three more revolutions for parts. But I'd come back time and again to the promise I'd made myself to protect Rione. She was making it more and more difficult to keep.

But for now, I was stuck. "Yes."

A wider smile passed over her lips. "Good. I'm going to need all the help I can get." She turned toward the double metal doors and started off at a brisk walk. "We shouldn't keep the Princess waiting."

• • •

The Princess turned from the window as we stepped into her office. Without a word, she stood from her chair and walked around the desk.

She embraced Rione, then stepped back, her hands still on the Lazarian's shoulders. "He was a great man."

She nodded in silence.

"If you need someone to talk to..."

"I'll be fine," Rione mumbled.

Lucian's pale face contorted. She knew enough to realize different results wouldn't come from pushing the issue. Instead, she stepped around her desk and took her seat. We followed a moment later as she motioned toward the two other chairs.

Rione got to business. "We need to find our leak."

Lucian held up a hand. "Let's back up. What happened down there?"

"We were preparing to strike a transportation hub. Like I mentioned, they ambushed us. It was a massacre."

Wren looked back and forth between the two of us. "We're lucky the two of you made it out alive."

I nodded in agreement, just before Rione mumbled. "It doesn't feel lucky."

The Princess folded her fingers in a weave. "No, but the one thing we can't do is let their deaths be in vain."

Finally, an evil smile passed across Rione's face. "They won't."

Lucian was taken back, and couldn't help but wonder, "So, what are your plans?"

Again, the Princess looked back and forth between us. I redirected my stare at Rione, allowing her to answer. She finally leaned back in the chair. "Aston and I are going back underground to track down the leak."

"But how?"

Rione shrugged. "I haven't figured that part out yet. Between the two of us, we should find a starting point."

Lucian continued. "The rest of the rebel leadership has been notified of the most recent developments?"

"I wouldn't know by whom," Rione started. "We were the only ones to make it out alive."

She nodded. "I'll break the news to them, and let them know to expect you."

I interjected my own opinion. "With the leak still out there, it may be good to keep our plans secret."

"Valid point. But how do you plan to get back down to the surface?"

Rione turned to me. "We need to hash out a plan."

"Would be a good idea," I said. Unfortunately, with my ship out of commission for the next three revolutions, I didn't have the first clue how we'd pull it off.

"Be careful," Lucian said, grimacing, "whatever you plan to do."

Even now, as we were secretly plotting to assassinate her flesh and blood, I couldn't believe it was our only way to end this civil war.

But in all reality, it was.

Chapter Twelve

We stepped inside Rione's quarters, where the silence was thick enough to cut with a knife. She walked over to her closet, tossed the duffel on the bed and rifled through her dresser for more clothes. She bumped against an open drawer and the electronic photo of her and Malone fell over. She picked up the frame and glanced over the picture. With a deep sigh, she flipped it face-down and resumed her packing.

A shiver of fear rushed through me as memories came flooding back. I'd been with Leah just like this, packing for a journey. Then, we'd been carrying out our plan of escape, and this time would be all about revenge. In the end, I couldn't shake the feeling brutal murders would be a common theme.

I confronted Rione. "You're sure you want to go through with this?"

She walked over to the closet area, responding without looking. "More than anything."

"Have you figured out how to carry through with these assassinations even if we find a way down to the planet?"

Rione turned to me, her lips a straight line. "If you don't want to join me, you can run away. It's what you're good at."

I sat there silent, unsure of how to proceed after her verbal slap in the face. She took my response as a signal to continue what she was doing.

This was one of those moments where everything could go right, or go terribly wrong. As she zipped the bag shut, I took a chance. “I promised myself I’d keep you safe.”

She turned to me with a look on her face that was either approaching nausea or pity, I couldn’t tell which.

For a moment, I figured we would have an argument over my admission, then she tossed the duffel bag strap over her shoulder before walking for the door. “I don’t need someone watching out for me. If that’s the only reason you’ve stuck around, you might as well leave right now.”

I went with my gut, since it was rarely wrong. “That’s not the only reason, Rione.”

She stopped and processed what I’d just said, bowing her head. But then she just kept walking, the opening doors allowing her out into the corridor. My soul crushed, I still couldn’t leave her to be massacred, so followed.

My admission apparently didn’t even faze her. “Have you come up with an idea to get us down to the planet’s surface yet?”

None were left to us. My ship was out of commission for three rotations, and if we stayed on the station that long, someone would make another attempt on our lives.

“We’ll come up with something,” I noted.

“Correction, you’ll come up with something. In the meantime, I’m going to figure out where to go once you do.” Rione stormed down the corridor with me on her heels.

The ROC would have been another choice for evading the multitude of ships out there, had it not been blown to bits by Commander Sevil. Of course, with so many ships out there between the station and the planet, and with everyone on high alert, there was no guarantee even a functional noise generator would allow us passage through the blockade.

In typical fashion, I was screwed.

• • •

Heads turned as we stepped inside the station's control room. Rione had a more frequent presence here, and I'd not had the reason to visit much, which explained the fierce looks I received from the Torian staff.

Princess Wren was nowhere to be found. This didn't stop Rione from walking to one side of the room, where a large tabletop display console rested.

She barked off orders to the nearby crew. "Bring up a map of the planet's surface."

Patterns of silver and white shimmered along the mock Torian surface. Rione moved her hands across the display, panning around, zooming in and out. All of it looked the same to me, cold, desolate and bleak. Somehow, the landscape made sense to her. She'd analyze each spot before moving on to another after a quick shake of her head.

"Looking for anything in particular?" I asked.

"Yes." She peered around the room, causing me to do the same. Everyone had returned to their duties, concentrating solely on consoles before them and keeping an eye out for any threats from the warships near the planet.

Rione focused on the map. I took the hint, and looked off toward the walls, where even more flat panel displays showed the standoff between Torian and Rulusian warships, magnified for clarity.

"I've got it," I exclaimed.

Rione stopped what she was doing and jerked her head to look. Her eyes went wide. "Not here. Outside."

I went with her instructions and set out through the double doors into the corridor. It didn't halt my curiosity. "What gives?"

"Prying eyes and ears shouldn't know our business."

"But you were scoping out the map in there."

"I could be doing anything with that map. You start announcing a plan to reach the planet's surface, and there won't be any mistake. We still have a leak, remember?"

I pursed my lips, but she had a point. I looked up and down the empty corridor. "We need to get down there in something small enough they won't detect it on scanners or see us visually, either."

"If you've actually got a plan, hurry up. I need to get back to those maps and scout out a landing zone."

"I think an escape pod would be just the thing."

At least she didn't roll her eyes and head back into the control room. Not yet, anyway. "Where would we get an escape pod, let alone pilot it where we need to?"

"With all of these Rulusian ships around, surely one of them has escape pods."

Her brow furrowed. "The warships they have all contain pods the size of your ship. The only ship that would have anything close to the size you're looking for would be a Rulusian freighter."

And unfortunately, the only one I knew of was Captain Dillager's, and he was probably halfway back to Rulusia by now. "Any others out there?"

"I can check, but I'm pretty certain they only sent along warships."

And just like that, my plan was shot to pieces.

There wouldn't be an opportunity to come up with anything else. The station wouldn't have anything small enough to get us down to the surface. "Maybe we can get hold of Dillager?"

"Doubtful, but you can give it a try." She looked back through the doors into the control room. "If it were me, though, I'd use your ship's communication devices."

I motioned toward the control room. “You really think one of them is the leak?”

“I don’t know if we can really discount anyone at this point. We know Ba’lor Bilhari was in direct league with the Torian king and his ministers, but obviously he wasn’t the only one. If a Rulusian could take his treason to that level, anyone could.”

“Well, I guess I’ll be doing it from my ship.”

“Give me a moment, and I’ll come with you. I think I’ve narrowed it down to three potential landing zones.”

She led me back inside to the map display. This time, not a single crew member turned to look.

I stared at the flat panel displays showing both battle groups. I called out to the room. “Are the Torian warships still positioned in interstellar space?”

One of the personnel sitting at the far side of the room responded, “Yes.”

“Are they still verbally threatening the Rulusians?”

“Negative. They’re maintaining total communication silence, despite the Rulusians instructing them to move back across the border.”

I muttered under my breath. “They’re not going to understand anything besides a violent response.”

Rione responded in kind, “Then we’d best hurry.”

I moved closer. “Are you finished yet?”

She nodded. “Just uploading the coordinates.” She pulled a crystal wafer out of the frame surrounding the wide oval display, and clasped it in her hand. “Let’s go.”

A flash of bright white light filled one of the side displays. A Torian called out, “New contact. Analyzing.”

Rione barked out her question. “We aren’t expecting any more Rulusian ships, are we?”

"No, ma'am."

I thought I recognized the configuration of the incoming ship. "That can't be."

Rione turned to me. "What?"

"It looks like a Rulusian freighter."

She focused on the screen, then spoke to the crew. "Magnify."

The ship's image grew large enough to fill the screen, and not a moment later, someone belted out information we definitely hadn't anticipated. "Rulusian freighter Green Four has returned to the system."

I realized they'd been on their way back to Rulusia for burial of the dead and punishment of a killer, and suddenly my heart sank.

This couldn't be good.

"Incoming transmission," the female communications officer told us.

Rione gave a quick response, looking up from the circular table display. "Put it through."

I leaned in close. "I thought we didn't trust anyone to have this conversation in front of them."

She turned, scowling. "I don't plan on going into details. I want to find out what they're doing back."

When we turned back to the display, Dillager's massive bald head was front and center. "Rione? Aston? I was expecting the Princess."

"She's currently away. Is there something wrong with your ship?"

His brow furrowed. "Nothing I'm aware of. Do you know something I don't?"

I interrupted. "We weren't expecting you to return."

He turned to me with those big black eyes. “We met a warship returning to Rulusia from training exercises. They agreed to transport the prisoner and our fallen crewmates.”

“I would have thought you’d want to be there to hand over the dirtbag yourself.”

He took a deep breath, his shoulders lifting high, before he exhaled. “I would have liked nothing better, but reports are flowing across the galaxy that a battle between the Torian and Rulusian fleets is imminent.”

A smirk flooded Rione’s face. “I’m afraid that seems to be the case. Mind joining us on the station, where we can discuss the situation in private?” She turned back to a nearby officer. “Arrange a docking location for their shuttle.”

A moment later, he called out. “Please proceed to holding area alpha. Shuttle docking is approved, ring two, port seven.”

Dillager attempted a smile. “We’ll see you soon.”

• • •

As we passed through the commons area, I looked over the Stardust storefront, now covered up in black plastic and waiting on repairs. The enormity of everything that had happened shook me to the core. But even worse, I realized we weren’t out of the woods yet.

Anxiety flooded over me while I glanced at our surroundings. Any of the few station visitors roaming about could be after us. I kept watch, waiting for someone to make even the slightest move, before we exited out toward the three docking rings.

Rione caught my random glances. “What in the world are you doing?”

“Paranoid,” I muttered.

She stiffened up. “You’re not alone.”

“So, how do you handle it?”

"Taking the fight directly to the source of the problem *is* how I'm handling it."

We stopped in the second docking ring, alongside the seventh airlock hatch. Down the docking tube, the shuttle had arrived, but its hatch was still closed, meaning the pressures still hadn't equalized.

I looked around to make sure we were actually alone. "So, do you think Dillager will go along with the plan?"

"Yes, without a doubt."

"He'll be involving Rulusia in a plan to assassinate most of the royal family of Toris."

She shrugged.

Another thought ran through my head. "You know, he could be the leak just as much as anyone else."

"Doubtful. But as far as he's aware, he's just helping us reach the rebel forces on another strike mission."

I pursed my lips. I didn't like this conversation's direction. "You're not going to tell him, then?

She laughed. "The truth? Not a chance. I'm sure even the Rulusian public wouldn't tolerate their forces being used for political assassinations."

The airlock hatch at the far end of the tunnel clunked open. My heart sank, but I wasn't sure why. Concealing my true intentions and fabricating cover stories were second nature to me. Unfortunately, this wasn't just a case of self-preservation, but utter malice. Rione wanted revenge at whatever cost, and I was helping her.

My stomach rolled as Rulusians climbed out.

"Let me do the talking," she instructed.

"Gladly."

A handful of green-bodied men and women exited and waited for the beefy Dillager to join them. As he climbed from the tube, Rione wasted no time. “Captain, we mentioned we’d like this to remain private.”

Wrinkles formed on his forehead as his stare passed from Rione to me and back again. Seeing the serious looks on our faces, he turned to his crewmembers.

“Consider yourselves on shore leave. I’ll make contact when it’s time to return to the ship.”

The group disbanded and disappeared around the corner. Dillager drew his massive arms against his bulky chest. “How private does this conversation need to be?”

Rione responded, “It’s probably best if we talk aboard your shuttle. We still have a leak.”

He lifted an eyebrow, but then thumbed toward the tube. “After you.”

Rione took the lead, climbing inside and crawling along the metal rungs. I followed her in, while Dillager brought up the rear.

My feet clanked on metal grate panels inside the shuttle. Once Dillager lumbered in, he closed the hatch behind him. The lighting levels steadily rose.

“So, what is all of this about?”

Rione went for the immediate issue. “We need your help getting back down to the planet.”

He snorted. “I’m sure you’ve noticed there are two fleets out there, not to mention the ROC was destroyed during your last mission off our ship.”

I interjected, despite Rione’s instructions earlier. “Your ship is the only one with escape pods small enough to evade detection as we make our way down to the surface.”

He finally allowed himself to break out into a smile. “It certainly seems you’ve thought this through.”

I forced myself to reciprocate. “You could say that.”

"Of course, had we not shown up when we did, there's no telling how long you would have waited around for another freighter to come along."

I was about to comment on our blind luck, but Rione jumped to answer. "Fate is smiling on our plan."

I glanced over at Rione, and saw her emotion ridges peeking out from underneath her long hair. They were simply a lighter shade of her bronze skin, giving away her smile as a fake, at least to me. Another look at Dillager confirmed he was none the wiser.

"It would appear so."

She lifted an eyebrow. "So, you'll help us?"

"I'm happy to." Dillager reached his humongous hands up and gripped our shoulders. He clamped down harder than I liked, and if I didn't know better, I would have thought he was trying to crush the truth out of us. I was just glad he grabbed my good shoulder. "That's what we're here for, after all, to give assistance."

I wondered how long it would take before he learned of the massacre which took place in his absence. Hopefully not before we were on the planet, neck-deep into Rione's plan.

He released his grip. "So, what are you thinking?"

Rione responded. "If you can get your ship close enough to the border, and eject an escape pod without anyone noticing, we'll take care of everything else."

"Consider it done." His face turned serious. "How soon do you want to do this?"

Rione looked over at me for a brief moment, then back at the green hulk. "As soon as possible."

"We could leave right now." He motioned toward the front, where the forward control station waited.

I stalled. "What about your crew?"

"I'm sure they wouldn't mind a little extra leave, after everything's that's happened."

Rione jumped in. "Would you have enough people left to operate your ship?"

"It would be a skeleton crew, but we'd be fine."

"I still need to pack for the trip," I commented.

Rione sighed. "And I left my gear in my quarters."

Dillager's forehead wrinkled. "I take it this mission will be a bit longer than the satellite strike mission?"

Rione nodded. "Actually, we'll be involved in several different missions."

The statement set him back a moment, but he recovered nicely. "Sounds like the rebellion is finally going on the offensive. The spy satellite's destruction must have given them the boost everyone hoped for."

His comment rendered Rione speechless. I glanced over and watched tears form in the corner of her hazel eyes.

Dillager hadn't noticed. "Well, I wish you both continued success."

"Thank you," I responded, sensing Rione's worsening emotional state.

"I'll wait here. We'll leave when you return."

Without a word, Rione turned for the exit, yanking the hatch open. Her emotion ridges were fully exposed to me, and the red tint left nothing to question. Then, she disappeared into the airlock tube.

Her immediacy was not lost on the Captain. "Hopefully I didn't say something offensive."

I grimaced. "She's just having a rough time since the bombing."

That seemed to appease the big man. He nodded knowingly. “I imagine it takes a long time to recover from that sort of thing.”

I didn’t say a word, for fear of drawing out this conversation longer than necessary.

“Well, I guess I’ll see you both in a little while,” he remarked.

“See you soon.” I took my cue and followed Rione out the airlock tube.

Chapter Thirteen

Stepping back inside my living quarters, Jeanie was quick to call out, "Aston, I have good news."

I could use some for a change. "Let's have it."

"I was able to track down a spare set of displacement coils available in only one rotation instead of three."

Though good news in theory, I'd already painted myself into a corner. There wasn't any way down to the planet other than an escape pod. Beyond that, Rione also wouldn't accept my offer to run away from this horrible place.

I still didn't want Jeanie to consider her efforts wasted. "Get them here."

"Acknowledged."

I moved to the opposite side of the room, reaching into a small storage cabinet for a few sets of clothing. An empty duffel bag fell onto my boots. It used to contain millions of galactic credits, all since moved off into several secret accounts, but the bag and its former contents all caused my mind to go into overdrive. The money had been ill-gotten gains, involved in my escape attempt from Elijah, and Leah's murder.

Now, though, it was the only thing I had which could carry clothing for the trip. Without bothering to look, I shoved everything I thought I'd need inside, then tossed the bag onto my cot. Crawling under the makeshift bed, I unlatched a secret floor compartment.

Out of that, I grabbed a black palm-sized plastic case. You never knew when a few thousand credits would come in handy. On this trip, I had no doubt we'd need to provide some hush money or the like. Most Torians who didn't live on the orbital station were xenophobic, so there was little chance we'd be able to move around unnoticed. I was banking on Rione having some sort of plan to combat that issue.

I climbed back to my feet, dropping the box into my duffel. Reaching up toward my blaster tucked out of sight beside the airlock hatch, I realized how useless it had been against the government troops and decided to leave it where it was. Then, I was caught off-guard by Jeanie's voice. "You appear to be packing. Are you planning to move to more permanent quarters on the station?"

I stopped cold. My natural inclination was to lie through my teeth. She didn't need to know our plan. "Rione and I are leaving for a while, until things settle down."

"I will not be transporting you?"

"We're just worried my ship would be easily spotted." That part was the truth, surprising even me.

"Do you know when you will return to the station?"

"Honestly, I have no idea." Another truth.

"Perhaps we could arrange a rendezvous point?"

It was possible she'd detected my deceit. "We shouldn't need one."

Unfortunately, that was a big lie. Not only could we use her help, but I then realized we had no escape plan. A pod was our way in, but there was no obvious way out. Perhaps that didn't bother Rione and her current unbridled rage, but I still felt a need for self-preservation.

"It would be prudent to set one up," she said.

Now I was certain she knew something was amiss. I could have arranged for her to come to our rescue, but I wouldn't put Jeanie in certain jeopardy like that. There was still a blockade standoff for her to pass through. And even though she was merely a machine, I'd feel terrible sending her to an almost certain death.

"Don't worry, Jeanie. I'll return soon."

She didn't respond, and if she'd actually been programmed with feelings, I would have figured she was upset. I hefted up the bag and started for the exit.

One last stop at the door, I turned and tried to smile. "I'll see you soon. I promise."

Still no response.

• • •

Rione was nowhere to be seen as I stepped up to Dillager's airlock hatch, and neither was he. With a peek down the open access tube, I saw nothing more to indicate anyone was on-board. That was odd, considering Rione had ended up with a head start, and her quarters were closer.

I called out down the airlock tube, just in case. "Captain?"

Only a moment passed before Dillager appeared in the opening. "Aston, good to see you again. Come aboard."

I shoved my duffel inside the tube, crawling toward the transport. I reached the other side, and my boots once again hit the floor.

"What took you so long?" Rione's voice startled me. I looked over at the forward control station. She sat, staring at the controls

"Sorry," I mumbled.

She didn't respond, making her seem more like Jeanie than I cared to admit. As long as she didn't start acting like she was reading my mind, I'd consider myself lucky.

Dillager slammed the ship's airlock hatch shut. "It shouldn't take long to get departure clearance"

I took one of the bench seats along the far wall and buckled in. Stowing my duffel across my lap, I watched Dillager take the second seat beside Rione. He began communicating with the station.

He finally broke free from the first conversation, and turned to the Lazarian. "Go ahead and take us out."

Rione called out to us. "Releasing docking clamps."

Hard thumps echoed inside the compartment only a moment before she ran her fingers over the touch screen and engaged maneuvering thrusters. This shuttle was far worse than the last one we'd used, as my seat vibrated hard.

The ship rotated away from the station, until the freighter showed up in both forward viewscreens, each mounted beside a forward center post.

The huge aft engines lit off and the vibrations intensified. I started to say something, but couldn't even begin to speak with my mouth chattering in rhythm with the ship. I also had to clamp my mouth shut to quell the nasty, queasy feeling billowing up through my insides. I normally didn't get sick during space travel, and I sure as anything wasn't going to start here and now.

Dillager turned in his seat, his brown, jagged teeth standing in stark contrast to his dark green skin. "Reminds me of fleet training exercises."

I laughed. "Agreed."

"You want to puke your guts out, too?"

"Only when I'm talking.

"Not to worry. This won't take long," Rione told us.

Dillager turned back to the front, where the modified freighter now took up the viewscreens. We continued toward the freighter's docking port. She expertly moved her hands over the control pads in front of her, while a second screen popped up in each viewscreen and gave Rione a more intricate view of the docking clamps and the freighter's mating receptacles.

Closer and closer they drew, at a speed that caused me concern. I gripped the seat's armrest as I braced for an inevitable impact.

Then, just before we struck the other ship's hull, Rione applied a hefty amount of side thrust, enough to where my seat shook just as it had with the main engines. We slowed to a coast moments before the clamps engaged.

I let out a sigh of relief while Rione climbed from her seat. "Hope you didn't soil yourself back there."

I smarted off right back at her. "I should have figured you were a reckless pilot."

"Trouble is, you've been getting soft having that computer of yours at the controls. You don't remember what it's like to pilot your own ship."

I pursed my lips, wanting to dispute her claim. If it hadn't been so true, I would have.

"Okay, children," Dillager interrupted, standing and casting his gargantuan frame over us. "If you don't mind, I believe you have missions to get down to the planet for.

Rione sighed. "You're right."

He winked before moving over and opening the hatch again. "Of course I am. Now get in there before I have to kick both of your butts."

The Captain followed us inside the freighter, where Rione and I both broke out into a heavy sweat. I looked over at her, long locks damp and sticking to her face.

Dillager turned to the baby-faced crewman meeting us just inside the airlock hatch. "Take the shuttle back to the station and wait for our return."

"Return, sir? Where..." He started to question his superior officer, then realized his place in the pecking order. He corrected himself before the Captain's attitude soured. "Yes, sir." With that, he climbed out and closed the hatch behind him.

"Sure you have enough experienced crew on-board? I wiped my forehead as we trekked down the empty corridor.

He didn't bother turning to face me. "If I was taking a gunship into battle, I'd say they're a bit raw. For the task we're going to perform, they're more than capable."

We walked down the corridor and I snuck a quick glance to the left, into the empty crew quarters. My memory was spurred and my sorrow increased as I remembered Jaclyn and my shoulder's therapy session. That only drove more memories of our final time together. My heart sank.

As we passed through another hatch onto the bridge, I realized Dillager wasn't kidding about having a skeleton crew, with only four other crewmembers standing at their stations. He stepped over to the center chair and turned to the helmsman at the far side of the raised platform. "Take us toward the border."

He pressed a few buttons on the console, and the huge vessel accelerated and adjusted course. The forward viewscreen zoomed in on the starfield and planet, with all of the battle craft parked in front of it.

I looked over at the Captain. "So, you don't think you'll attract attention?"

"Oh," he said, his grin jagged, "I guarantee we will."

I glanced over at Rione, concern plastered to my face. Certainly, being in one of this ship's escape pods would help conceal us. But if everyone was focused on the freighter, we might have been better off blazing all the way to the planet's surface on a Rulusian destroyer.

As we drew closer to the other ships, my gut feeling grew stronger, gnawing at me. There were too many logic holes, not to mention the total lack of an exit strategy.

With one look at Rione, her arms crossed and entire body a stone cold statue, I knew there was no turning back from this suicidal plan. My loyalty, along with my promise to keep her safe where I'd failed Leah, would now lead to my ultimate demise.

Dillager turned to a female standing at the scanner station, the spot I'd often seen Jaclyn take directly opposite helm control. "Have we drawn their attention?"

She looked up and nodded. "Torian heavy cruiser is on an intercept course. The remaining cruisers are holding position opposite our battleships."

"Ah, our old friend, Commander Sevil." The Captain's lips curled up into a smile. "This will be an extra special treat."

My skin crawled. We'd already escaped the Commander's wrath several times. My luck didn't run on the positive side, and continually tempting fate was a bad idea.

The female officer sitting at the communications console had been on-board during the spy satellite mission. "They're hailing us. Sir?"

"How close are we to the border?"

The helmsman responded. "Kissing it, Captain."

Dillager turned to me and Rione. "If you two don't mind preparing an escape pod, I'd like to face this bastard at least once before he dies."

The implication seemed clear to me. "Certainly." I turned to walk toward the forward hatch, following Rione.

His familiar words carried past us. "Happy hunting." As we stepped out, I heard him bark, "Put it through," just before the hatch closed behind us.

The forward end of this freighter hadn't been touched through the massive modifications for conversion to a covert operations vessel. A good thing for us, as the engineers likely would have eliminated safety features like escape pods in return for a high-power scanner array.

"Last chance to bail on me," Rione offered.

"You know I have to come along."

She shook her head in disgust, entering into the crew quarters we'd passed before. Then, she turned and jerked to a stop. Her forehead scrunched hard, eyes narrowing. "Don't be a fool, flyboy. This isn't your fight."

"It became my fight the first time I came here. It's become more so now that the king issued a death warrant."

She moved a hand up to my cheek. "We probably aren't coming back from this one."

At least the uncertainty had been removed, and I realized she wasn't going into this situation blindly. Rione knew exactly where this path might take us. She just didn't care whether she lived or died.

And then, maybe I didn't either. "I know."

Her face took on an air of pity. "Don't risk your life out of a perverted sense of nobility and honor."

Now my forehead tightened. "I'm willing to die for you. That's my choice."

Her hand dropped. She turned back toward the center of the room, mumbling, "You always were plenty stupid when it came to making decisions."

We moved toward an alcove tucked away in the forward wall. Two access doors rested on either side, while a third faced us. Rione yanked this one open and we crammed ourselves into the tiny compartment, each taking one of the four jumpseats forming a semi-circle. At the center, a tall center console protruded from the floor. We strapped our gear into the other two seats, then hooked up our own harnesses. Rione pulled out the crystal wafer she'd used in the orbital station's control room, shoving it into a slot.

Out of my line of sight, she ran her fingers over a small keypad. A few moments later, she stopped and looked up from the activity. "Destination is loaded. Just need some sort of indication from Dillager."

Almost as if on cue, a small holographic image appeared atop the console. The Captain was all smiles as he clasped his hands behind his back. "Thought you might like to know the Commander is back to his old habits, threatening our destruction if we violate the border."

"Like the Torian fleet already has?" I smirked.

Rione interrupted. "He and his cronies are all about doing as they say and not as they do."

Dillager pushed the conversation along. "He and his crew are all hard at work keeping an eye on their scanner screens, watching for us to slip up."

Which meant they wouldn't be watching for us in our escape pod. I smiled. "Thanks again, Captain."

He nodded. "Both of you come back to us in one piece."

I tried my best not to give away the true nature of the mission. "Will do."

The transmission died and the compartment darkened. Background light fell from a dim ring embedded in the ceiling.

I caught sight of Rione's smile. "Ready?"

"Definitely."

She smacked the top of the console, and red lights flashed inside the compartment about five times. Abrupt acceleration struck as the pod jettisoned out of the ship.

Restraints tugged against my chest and bile rose into my throat. I figured one normally used escape pods to flee a far worse fate on the ship. Being as how we were inside the pod by choice, I couldn't stop wishing it was equipped with windows, or at the very least some external cameras. That would have at least given me some sense of orientation as maneuvering thrusters jerked us in every direction.

One look over at Rione and I could tell she wasn't faring much better. With one big swallow to try and force down my nausea, I tried to distract her. "We're both in pretty sad shape for a pair of pilots."

The escape pod rocked again from another brief course correction. She grimaced. "There's something about travelling through space in a vessel meant for it. This definitely wasn't."

Another series of harsh maneuvers sent my stomach churning. I watched Rione close her eyes and push out her words. "Won't be long now. That was part of the re-entry sequence."

My mind raced as her words struck me. In all this time, I'd concentrated on getting us past the blockade. What I'd failed to consider was what would happen once we passed into the Torian atmosphere.

This was why I sucked at making plans.

"Is there a way to get this thing to drop faster?"

The pod rumbled as we hit the upper atmosphere. Rione's eyes flashed open, and it was as if she read my mind. "Scanner sites!"

I kept trying to figure out the new plan. "No way to use the thrusters to boost our speed?"

She shook her head. "The only ones with any power are the ones that jettisoned us, and they're single-use. We have to rely on a chute from here on out."

"Chute?"

"Only way for this thing to slow down."

"Is there any way to delay the chute?"

I figured she'd respond back to the negative, given my track record. To my surprise, though, her face lit up.

I prodded, "What?"

She put her fingers back on the keypad as the roar outside the hull changed pitch and volume. Typing while she spoke, thrill jumped off her tongue. "We should be able to adjust the altitude where the chute actually deploys."

I wasn't sure how I felt about the whole notion of this guessing game. "They don't have it locked out as a safety feature?"

She pursed her lips. "I'm sure there are restrictions on how low we can set it, but at least we can avoid being hung out too long for target practice."

It truly was the best option we had available, assuming we could make the change in the first place. Judging from Rione's furrowed brow, I was beginning to doubt whether even that was possible. Then she pulled her hands away.

"Got it."

I was still concerned. "You were able to get us down below the scanners?"

"It took a while to find out how low I could set it."

I lifted an eyebrow. "You didn't answer my question."

"You don't really want to know the answer."

She was right. I didn't.

"And I don't suppose this thing has any sort of defensive measures?"

Rione grimaced, telling me all I needed to know.

Air roared past our hull, while the pod plummeted. A mechanical voice called out. "Chute deployment in five...four..."

I braced myself.

"Two...one..."

An explosion sounded off above our heads, just a moment before the compartment jerked. My entire spine compressed hard. I almost thought it would snap into a thousand pieces. Then, sweet release as the pod stabilized.

I looked over at Rione. We weren't out of the woods yet. "How long do you figure we have until they lock on?"

My own question was answered before Rione even opened her mouth. A klaxon sounded off, while red lights once more filled the darkness.

She looked around the compartment, then back at me. "They've launched."

There had to be some way to get out of this. I couldn't believe we'd come through so much, so many close calls with death, just to be killed inside an escape pod with no way to defend ourselves.

Then it came to me. "Blow the chutes!"

"Are you nuts? We're too far up. We wouldn't survive the fall."

"We aren't going to survive this, either."

She saw my point, reached up and pulled a corded handle hanging from the ceiling. Another explosion rang out above our heads and the restraints tugged against my chest as we plummeted toward our deaths.

Chapter Fourteen

I braced myself for the inevitable impact, with no idea how soon or how hard we'd hit. The klaxon thankfully shut off, but we continued dropping toward the surface.

A sickening crunch erupted inside the compartment. I cringed in response, but there was no accompanying crushing of metal or breaking of bones. The deceleration was hard, but not any worse than the rest of the journey.

Once all motion had ceased, I looked over at Rione. "What just happened?"

She glanced around the compartment. "I have no idea."

I reached out for the hatch release beside me. Motors whined as they pushed out, but the door barely shifted out of position. A muted buzz interrupted the process as the motors shut off.

Suddenly, things didn't look as cheerful.

I turned back to Rione, who had the same concerned look on her face as I probably did. "What happened? Where did you send us?"

Her face tightened and I saw the faintest of a red tinge along her ridges. "Once we blew the chute, the pod had no control over where it landed."

I grimaced. "So, we're lost?"

She smirked and shook her head. "We're close enough."

"Then can you tell me why this hatch won't open?" Her lips formed a thin line and I looked away. "I figured not."

Her entire face contorted as she stared at the ceiling. "I think I might have an idea where we ended up."

I was eager to hear any idea, with nothing close to one myself. "Where?"

Rione unfastened her restraints and rose to her feet. Before I could ask what she was doing, she'd already reached up to the very apex, grabbing hold of a separate recessed handle. After a quick twist, Rione jerked her hand away as the ceiling split into four triangular sections, all blowing up and out.

Clumps of ice and snow fell into the compartment and I brought my hands up to deflect the frozen onslaught. Rione, knowing ahead of time what she'd planned to do, had pushed herself against the wall and thus avoided the assault.

"Thanks for the heads-up," I muttered, brushing my clothes clean.

"Didn't want to get your hopes up, in case I was wrong."

I looked out the opening, where a tunnel had been carved out by the impact, approximately a kilpar long. Even through the thermal jumpsuit, frigid air seeped into the compartment, making me shiver.

"So, where are we?"

"Northern ice fields," she stated matter-of-factly.

Being as I didn't have the first clue about Torian geography, I probed for more. "And how far away are we from our original destination?"

"No way to know for sure until we get topside, but it shouldn't be more than a couple kilpars or so."

"Will these jumpsuits be enough to protect us?"

“We’ll need a little something extra.” She pulled on a small access panel and pulled two folded packages out. Ripping the outer wrapping, a thin body suit unfurled in my hands.

“Put it on,” she instructed me. I did so, wondering how much more protection another thin layer would provide. It pulled over my hands with glove-like coverings, and even slid over my boots.

I lifted an eyebrow. “So, *this* will help?”

She reached over without warning, pulling an exposed tab near my stomach. Before I knew what was happening, the suit ballooned up slightly. The cold chill which seeped down from the surface no longer had an effect. Even my uncovered face was warm, a gentle airflow moving past it from the suit. She grabbed her pack, and I did the same.

“Give me a boost,” Rione instructed.

I cradled my hands and lifted her through the open ceiling panels before she pulled me up. My breath formed little clouds of vapor as I looked up. “So, any thoughts on getting out of this hole?” The surface seemed even farther away. My heart sank.

Rione exhaled a foggy stream of her own. “We climb.”

She started off first, reaching up for a handhold with one glove. Trying to keep track of where she’d found her spots, I followed along, trekking up the icy crevice.

I was in no shape to make this climb, but there was no other alternative other than waiting for death in a frozen grave. The ice sank its chilling bite through my gloves, and only increased the aches and pains caused by attempting to heft my sizable frame up the cylindrical cavern.

I tried to look past Rione to gauge how far we’d come, to no avail. “How much farther?”

“Almost there,” she muttered between labored breaths.

Looking down, I saw the open ceiling panels of the pod below, making me realize how far I'd fall if something went wrong. I had no fear of heights, not in the least. Death or serious injury, on the hand, was another story.

"You coming?" Rione's voice carried down.

I looked back as she peeked down over the chasm's lip. Keeping my mind off impending doom, I continued climbing until Rione grabbed the back of my suit and helped me out.

I lay there a moment, steam blowing out from the thermal suit across the ice. Looking out on the landscape, I couldn't see past a canvas of fog giving us about a megpar's visibility.

Wind nipped at my face, bringing me back to the mission. I rose to my feet. "Lead the way."

She'd already started out in a brisk walk as I spoke. I followed the small, almost indiscernible tracks she left in the ice.

The gusts picked up, pelting us with snow and sleet. A chill sank deep into my bones, infiltrating even the thermal suit. It was almost as if nature was trying hard to foil our plan.

"Sure you know where you're going?"

She kept moving. "Just have to trust me."

"As long as we get there before we freeze to death."

Adding an impressive insult to injury, the fog ahead parted, revealing a cavern entrance in the sheer rock face.

"Told you," she smarted off. Even with her face turned away, I could still visualize her cursed smile. We trudged through the snow and ice.

She continued, "The camp should have more than adequate supplies."

"Camp?"

"One of several sites we used when shuffling groups around to avoid detection."

"Are you sure it's still there?"

"There was no reason to get rid of it."

Unfortunately, she mistook my intention. "You're sure the king and his forces never discovered it?"

We stepped inside the cavern mouth, putting a stop to the endless wind, ice and snow. She finally turned to me. "Nothing's certain, but he never found it when his spy satellite was still operational. I'd say it's safe."

She rummaged through her duffel, and pulled out a small handheld light bar, which cast an eerie glow upon the reddish walls of the cavern.

The stench I'd grown accustomed to on my last trip under the Torian surface invaded my nostrils again. Walls of rock closed in on us from both sides, to the point where we barely squeezed through. The decaying stone odor only intensified within the tighter quarters, and I focused all my attention on staying conscious.

"No wonder they couldn't find this place. I assume it's just as difficult from the other direction?"

"That's the best way to hide," Rione responded.

I couldn't argue with her logic. Instead, I focused on the future. "Now that we're here, have you figured out the rest of our trip?"

I waited a few more moments, but she didn't seem to be any more forthcoming. "I'd be interested in any details you could share."

We finally broke out into a chamber. Rione walked over, ignoring my comments as she knelt down at the center of the clearing, and fiddled with a device barely visible in the reflected light.

The small globe in her hand glowed bright, bringing our surroundings into clear view. When she'd called it a small camp, she hadn't been exaggerating. The cavern walls stretched up into the darkness, barely having room for more than three or four people resting on the ground. I noticed the heat levels in the cavern rising.

"We'll rest here." Rione pulled a pair of rolled sleeping bags out of chiseled cubbyholes in the wall, handing one over to me. The temperature became unbearable.

I pointed at the glowing sphere. "Any way to turn the heat down?"

She moved over to me, and pulled again on the same tab as before. The suit started deflating and my comfort levels returned to normal. She did the same for herself, then slipped out of the thermal covering, her jumpsuit glistening in the light. I did the same.

I rolled out my sleeping bag. "So, plan details?"

She looked up, her greenish eyes colder than the conditions outside. "I plan to take out the youngest, then the oldest son, then the king himself."

I waited a few moments, but still didn't receive anything more. Why was she holding back? "And so, how are we going after the...?"

"Axyl Wren," she interrupted.

And then it hit me why she wasn't offering up more details. "You haven't come up with a plan, have you?"

Her shoulders heaved, before she crawled off inside the confines of her bag.

"Maybe we can come up with one," I offered while crawling inside my own pack. "Tell me about Axyl Wren."

She propped up on one elbow. "A spoiled brat, born into royalty and eager to follow his father's footsteps."

"Surely, there's more we can use."

"According to Lucian, he has a severe addiction to women and alcohol."

Despite the fact I suffered from similar issues, it didn't give me enough to go on. "Anything else?"

As she pondered her answer, the bag became nice and toasty. Drowsiness enveloped me.

"Lucian doesn't speak much of her brothers. The only thing I know is where his palace is located and his likeness from photographs I've seen."

"And we landed near his palace?"

"As close as we could get and still use a camp."

I yawned, which set Rione to do the same. Once both of us finished, I placed my head down on the warm, cushioned flap. "I guess we'll start there."

• • •

"Rise and shine, flyboy."

Every muscle in my body ached. Our sleeping bags had been cushioned, but the stone floor was still hard enough to cause me plenty of pain. I stared at Rione, still in the same semi-reclining position I'd last seen.

"Do you ever sleep?" I caught myself recalling my invasion of privacy, when I'd brought an intoxicated Rione back to her quarters. Even now, guilt slapped my face.

"Of course."

"You certainly could have fooled me. What are you already doing awake?"

"Can't sleep when I'm this wired."

"Nervous?" Strangely, considering I'd almost been killed on my last trip to this planet, I wasn't as stressed as I probably should have been. The troubling thing was I'd become far too accustomed to facing down death.

Her voice had a thrill in it. "Excited."

I lifted an eyebrow. "Excited?"

Rione climbed out of her bag and rolled it up quickly without another word or glance in my direction. It was as I feared. She couldn't wait to kill Axyl Wren, to make him pay for Malone's death. Honestly, I couldn't blame her.

Trouble was, this first assassination wouldn't satiate her bloodlust, I knew that much from experience. There was no guarantee she'd rid herself of those demons through the remaining murders, either.

I pushed myself from the friendly, warm confines I'd nested in. "So, come up with any other revelations?"

"Of how to pull this off?"

"What else?"

She grabbed my pack once I finished rolling it up, and shook her head. "We're probably better off if we don't do too much planning ahead of time."

I nodded. "It does seem to work out better, flying by the seat of our pants."

"Then it's probably best if we get moving."

We picked up our gear. "Probably so."

• • •

Things were slow as we trekked through more narrow passageways. My hope had been that I would have grown more accustomed to the stench. Unfortunately, it didn't happen.

"I hope we eventually get to walk like normal people," I grumbled, watching Rione slide sideways between the stones ahead of me.

"Shouldn't be long now," she retorted. "Trust me."

I half-expected us to burst into a cavern just as vast as the one we'd destroyed during our last escape. Instead, we kept moving through narrow, stone crevices. My frustration grew as the walls closed in on us.

"Are we lost?"

Rione stepped aside and bright lights overhead gave me a glimpse of a far larger tunnel.

The universe truly hated me.

She nearly laughed. “I told you to trust me.”

I pushed myself out of the claustrophobia-inducing cavern, into a tunnel resembling another transit route. “Is this where we were the last time?”

Rione shook her head. “They all look alike, since they’re constructed the same.”

“Well, I’m glad one of us can tell the difference between them all, then.”

“Only have to know the ones along our route.”

I looked up and down the tunnel in both directions. “Empty like the last one?”

She shook her head. “Don’t worry. Unless they’ve changed the transit schedules, we should be fine.”

“Should be?”

She turned and scowled, making it obvious I would again just have to trust her.

We journeyed along the tunnel, our boots crunching in the thin layer of rock dust. I was in no shape for a hike and had no idea how far we’d traveled, before a rumble started in my legs.

Rione turned and grabbed my hand. “Go!”

We raced along the narrow tunnel, the vibration growing stronger. I looked over my shoulder, and fear gripped my heart as the corridor filled with the roar of an approaching transport. Its dark menacing face bore down on us.

I was jerked aside mere moments before the transport screamed by. My heart raced, thumping against the inside of my chest. I glanced at our new surroundings.

“I wasn’t sure we’d make it,” Rione interrupted.

That made two of us.

Dim bulbs were nestled into the four corners of this room. Before us was a three-wheeled little brother to the transport we'd ridden with the rebels into the ambush.

My hand was still in Rione's grip, just before she yanked herself away. Taking the hint, I moved the subject on to another topic. "What is this place?"

She straddled the smaller vehicle's body. "Get on! We need to catch that transport."

I jumped on behind her and she kick-started the unit. Its combustion engine roared to life as we sped back out through the narrow opening.

I barely heard her over the engine noise as we entered the main transit tunnel. "Hold on!"

I gripped her waist and she opened up the throttle. We raced along after the same transport which had just tried to flatten us. The little vehicle's three wheels did little to cushion the rough ride. Hover-technology had definitely spoiled me.

This beast had plenty of power, something one didn't find all that often in hovercraft. We closed the distance in nothing flat, the transport's aft end coming into view. I wondered what Rione had meant by 'catching' this transport.

It became painfully apparent as we gained even more ground. The width became near nothing between us and the transport. She screamed out to overcome the machine's harsh refrain. "Grab those handles!"

I looked over her head at the bent pipes jutting out next to the transport's aft emergency exit. "How?"

"Climb over me."

That would be easier said than done, but I trusted her. Barely keeping my balance while Rione matched speeds with the hover-transport, I did as she asked and perched on our vehicle's front wheel cover.

Then, I did something stupid and looked down at the ground racing underneath us. The motion didn't force me to close my eyes, not completely anyway. Instead, the distance between the vehicles now seemed to span a full kilpar or two, in my head.

But I didn't have a choice but to jump, so that's what I did. Grabbing for the handles, I slipped once, but tightened my grip and finally got some footing on the platform edge. I looked back at Rione, who was trying to figure out how to join me. I held as tight as I could with my bad shoulder, and reached out. "Take my hand!"

She grabbed for it, but couldn't keep the throttle going while maintaining control, pulling back. Another couple of attempts, and her emotion ridges flushed. Then, her eyes flashed wide. She fell back even farther, and I suddenly realized she was going to attempt something really stupid. Then, she did exactly what I figured, and gunned the three-wheeler toward me. Just as I thought she might ram the transport, she flung herself over the handlebars. I barely grabbed her hand before the three-wheeler buckled and flipped, tumbling end for end. Rione reached up and grabbed the other railing, thankfully before my pain became too unbearable.

Then the three-wheeler exploded in a huge fireball.

Chapter Fifteen

We watched the fiery remains while standing on the platform. I interrupted, with the gentle whistle of the air rushing past the transport's sides. "We should get inside." Rione nodded her agreement.

Reaching over, she pulled an emergency rescue lever, forcing the outer door to slam open. We climbed inside the next tiny compartment and shut the door behind us.

On either side, an exit door allowed paying passengers to leave the transport once they reached their destination. A window in each offered a reddish blur as the corridor sped past outside. Another hatch ahead of us led into the actual passenger compartment itself. I snuck a glance through a small porthole window. Around a dozen riders slumbered comfortably in individual cloth seats.

I chuckled under my breath. "Surprised they're still asleep. Would have thought our daring heroics and the explosion would have gotten some attention."

Rione smiled. "The miracle of modern soundproofing, combined with an early departure time."

I reached out for the inner door's release handle, but Rione pulled my arm away. "No, we stay out here. You forget, we're not on the orbital station. Non-Torians definitely stand out, and not in a good way."

I nodded, remembering the xenophobia these underground dwellers felt. "And with that in mind, what's our plan?"

"Once we reach the next stop, we'll need to rush off the transport before anyone sees us."

"Hopefully we'll have someplace to hide. Trying to conceal ourselves from an entire planet will be tricky."

Her facial expression soured. "I know a place."

And that was that. Rione snuck her own peek into the passenger compartment. I decided not to press her further. She had a temper I'd seen on more than one occasion, and I didn't feel like incurring her wrath. Hopefully it wouldn't take long to get to Rione's destination.

• • •

The transport didn't even come to a complete stop at the next station before Rione bolted out the side door, and I followed right on her heels. Thankfully, the early arrival time meant no one was standing on the platform as we disembarked. The two of us ducked into a dark alleyway between the buildings.

We caught our breath, leaning against the clay walls. Hopefully there wouldn't be much of this, considering how out of shape I was.

I watched the other riders exit the transport, walking off in the opposite direction for the station. "Where to?"

She peered around the corner, then back at me. "Think you can keep up?"

"That depends on how far we have to go."

She pointed out. "Just past the transport track. The tallest building. There's a room inside we can use."

I saw our destination, though it wasn't that much taller than the other surrounding buildings. It wouldn't be too terrible, once I rested up a few more moments.

Unfortunately, I wouldn't get the chance as Rione bolted from our hiding spot. I had no choice but to follow, lungs burning and pulse racing. I glanced back toward the empty transport platform as my boots crunched through the dust. Thankfully, the pod itself stood as a barrier between us and the station, which lessened the chance of being seen. I was certain we'd catch their attention quickly, once they recognized us as people not of this world, let alone our new labels of fugitives and terrorists.

We climbed up the berm at the far side of the track, scrambling toward another alleyway. I had a bad feeling, but decided to ask, just in case. "So, let me guess, it's on the top floor?"

She smirked. "You're a smart one, flyboy." I cursed under my breath as she continued. "One would think you'd get in better shape, going on missions like this."

"Hoping this will be the last one," I muttered.

"Just a little bit farther."

I sucked in a rush of air. "If I make it that long."

Mustering up all the strength and stamina possible, I rushed after her as we scrambled down the alleyway. The passage was narrow and lay in shadows from both buildings. A lone doorway rested in the wall to our left, and Rione burst through with me only a step behind.

The large, square lobby we entered looked like it had been deserted for several revolutions. The clay floor had been bleached to a lighter shade of reddish-orange, and had as many spider cracks as the walls around us. There were no pieces of furniture, no decorations at all, not even the smallest sense that actual residents lived here.

A set of lifts rested in the far wall and I gave a quick sigh; relief had finally come. At least I'd thought so, until Rione sprinted through a different doorway.

But then, I should have expected that.

I followed into a stairwell where she'd already made it to the next landing. "Come on, slowpoke!"

I grimaced, jumping up the metal stairs as we scrambled to the top floor. She eased the wooden door open and peeked out into the hall only a moment before she raced through. I followed, finally getting into a stride.

Our boots padded along the thin beige carpet. Halfway down the hall, she grabbed a doorknob and we disappeared into the room beyond. Rione closed us inside, snapping a slide lock in place.

Tossing my gear to the floor, I collapsed face-first onto the single bed. I wanted to pass out completely, but Rione was having none of it. "Don't get too comfy."

I turned my head, still speaking into the sheets. "Surely we have time to relax for a while." Honestly, I wasn't making a suggestion as much as supplying her with information. My entire body was objecting to all this cruel and unusual punishment.

"No time like the present."

I tried laughing, but even that was too much effort. "It's not like we'll miss our chance if we rest a while, at least until I can feel enough of my body to move."

Rione said something in what I figured was her native Lazarian. If I was to make a guess, it sure sounded like she'd just cursed me out. Funny enough, as comfy as the bed was, I really didn't care.

She realized the futility of her current approach, and tried something more direct. "We need to strike before they get wise to the fact we're not on the station anymore. It won't take long for anyone to put the pieces together and realize we'd been in that crashed pod."

She unfortunately had a point, which made my body object even more. "And do you have a plan yet?"

"We'll have to come up with one, once we check out Axyl's compound."

"So, no." I grimaced.

"More reason to move quickly."

Sadly, I knew she was right, so took a quick tally of my body parts and their conditions. I decided one last question was in order. "Is there any running involved?"

That elicited a short laugh from Rione. "I'll try to keep it to a minimum."

Her words brought no comfort, but I also stood the chance of Rione rushing off to do the deed alone.

"Okay." I planted my feet on the floor. Standing, I glanced around the rest of the sparse apartment. Other than the bed with which I'd grown intimately attached, a small dresser sat along the inner wall. That was about it for personal amenities. No kitchen, nor anyplace to clean up.

"Anyone actually live here?"

She grimaced. "They did."

"Did?"

Her expression soured. "One of Malone's men. He was involved in the botched raid."

We fell into an awkward silence. Rione turned and rummaged through her duffel. A few moments later, she pulled out more traditional Torian garb for herself, donning the full-length brown robe over her black jumpsuit. It hovered just above the floor, and still accentuated her curves somehow. She pulled the attached head covering up over her hair. Besides hiding her dark locks, it also covered up her emotion ridges.

Torian clothing or not, she wasn't anywhere close to passing herself off as one. The skin color differences alone made that impossible.

When she pulled another garment out and handed it to me, I decided it was time to point out the obvious. "What are you hoping to accomplish? This won't hide who we are."

"We'll disguise ourselves," she muttered.

"You don't think a change of clothing alone is going to help, do you?"

She rolled her eyes. "Just put it on."

I followed her instructions, figuring she knew what she was doing. I was a bit larger, in many directions, than the average Torian. The hooded robe fit tight, only possible by the shape-forming jumpsuit underneath.

Fortunately, the head covering was loose when I pulled it forward past my ears.

I glanced over and did a double-take at the sight of Rione's face. While dressing myself, she'd transformed her golden bronze skin into the palest I'd ever seen.

What the...?"

She smiled. "You just got through pointing out the fact clothing wouldn't be enough. Why the surprise?"

"But how...?"

"This isn't the first time I've needed to blend in down here." She pulled a thin sheet out of her bag, and stretched it taut between her hands, now sporting long, black gloves which disappeared beyond her robe's sleeves.

As she tried to put it on my face, I backed up and stumbled onto the bed. "What do you think you're doing?"

"Relax," Rione insisted.

My mind knew it was Rione, but my paranoid tendencies took visual cues as gospel. "Easy for you to say. I'm not the one trying to shove a piece of plastic over your face."

She rolled her eyes again. “Why would I try to suffocate you?” I didn’t bother answering. “This sheet conforms to your face, and alters your pigmentation.”

That didn’t ease my apprehension at all. “How long?”

“Don’t worry, it eventually wears off. I’ve used them for plenty of trips down here.”

My acceptance finally grew to the point I stood again. “Okay, let’s do this.”

“It’ll sting a little,” Rione warned. She hadn’t given me enough advance notice, likely on purpose, so I didn’t get the opportunity to fight her off again before the sheet blurred out my vision and touched my face.

I closed my eyes out of reflex as the sheet attached itself to my skin, digging into every pore. So far, Rione’s warning was overkill. This wasn’t nearly as bad as most of the medical procedures I’d experienced. Perhaps I’d drunk so much for so long, I’d permanently damaged my pain receptors. I heard ripping sounds and took a breath through my mouth, glad to be beyond the idea of suffocation. I opened my eyes. Where my vision had been obscured, it was now clear. This was nothing to be worried about, not to the extent I’d been reacting.

In an instant, my entire face flushed with searing pain, as if I’d just stuck it in front of a thruster exhaust vent. Where the sheet had dug into each pore before, it felt like tiny explosions were taking place in them now. Drinking hadn’t dulled my senses near enough.

I reached up toward my face with a brief yelp, but felt a pair of hands grab hold of my wrists. “Don’t touch. It’s still working.”

I looked at the woman I once called friend. “It’s burning my face off!”

Her lips formed a thin line. “It won’t be long.”

I struggled against her hold, but she kept my hands away from this contraption. “Touching it during the transformation will foul up the procedure.”

I continued my struggle. “That’s the point!”

Rione grimaced. “It’s the only way to move about freely down here.”

The pain finally ceased and I let out a sigh of relief. The device must have finished, because Rione finally released her grip. Falling to my knees and groping my face, nothing felt any different, which didn’t fit with the pain and suffering I’d just experienced.

“Let’s go.”

I lowered my hands and looked at Rione. “I hope I won’t have to go through that again.”

“Not if we finish this fast.”

That was all the motivation I needed. “Then what are we waiting around for?”

“Well, first off, you may want to bring along some money if we’re going anywhere the prince is. I’m sure it won’t be cheap.”

Grudgingly, I grabbed the money box out of my bag and attached it to my upper thigh. Thankfully, it was below the point where the robe held my waist tight.

“Any weapons we could take?”

“Right now, we’re just scoping things out.”

I grimaced. “Hopefully we won’t have a need for them.”

“Hopefully not.”

This was going to go great.

Chapter Sixteen

Even though we had disguises on, I still felt uncomfortable putting myself out there for the planet to see. Rione led the way, moving through the growing crowd. It was hard for me to believe this many people lived beneath the Torian surface in one city, let alone the entire planet. I kept my eyes planted on Rione's body to prevent losing her in the crowd of brown-robed residents.

The street we walked down didn't resemble anything I knew. Instead, a patch of reddish dust and rock spanned the distance between parallel rows of buildings. Pedestrians didn't have designated areas to walk, instead flowing through the street wherever they felt like.

A puny horn bleated behind me and I found myself barely a hair's width away from a tiny hovercraft's front bumper. I scooted aside and allowed the vehicle to pass through the crowd. Looking forward, I'd lost Rione.

Stepping up to where I'd last seen her, I cursed and looked around everywhere I could. Upset pedestrians stepped around me, hurling insults in their native tongue. My immediate need was more pressing than their inconvenience.

It had been a long time since I had a reason to freak out, but this certainly topped the list. I looked through the crowd, then scanned the buildings along either side. The walls all looked the same, windowless and unadorned other than small markings along each building's corner. How did anyone have the ability to know where they were, or where they needed to be?

I moved forward in step with the other pedestrians. My nerves stretched farther across the jagged edge. What was I going to do? I had no idea where I was supposed to go, and wouldn't know how to get there even if I did. I couldn't even make my way back to the safe house, having no clue which building it was.

A sharp whisper penetrated the air. "Flyboy!"

I jerked my head around so I could focus on Rione's voice. The crowd parted and there she was, standing inside another alleyway. Ducking and dodging through the crowd, I made my way to Rione's side. Her sour look gave me a preview of her coming question. "What happened to you?"

"Sorry. Nearly had a hovercraft run me down."

Rione shook her head, turned and walked off. This time, though, without a mob of Torians around, it was easier to stay with her as she ducked inside a building.

Making certain not to disappoint me, she turned and started up a staircase. As we reached the top, I expected to enter another corridor, perhaps even from the first building we'd used, considering I had no way of knowing whether we'd been walking in circles this whole time. Instead, the door opened out to a rooftop covered in dirt and dust just like the street below.

"What gives?" I glanced around. Crowd noise rose up over this side of the building's perimeter. A wall came to my chest.

"Best spot to keep an eye out."

She moved toward the edge, peering into the distance.

"We won't draw attention up here?"

She turned with a sly grin. "Not nearly as much as you were drawing moments ago."

"Funny," I muttered.

The mass chaos seemed a little less disastrous as I joined her. I still stood amazed at the population density, but it didn't come close to eliminating my confusion about what she hoped to accomplish up here.

Rione leaned over, arms atop the slab. "There it is."

I looked up. Our target now obvious, a palace rested in the background. It was built from a familiar clay construction, but the golden walls were quite an upgrade from the bland, drab reddish-brown of the surrounding city. Elaborate, large windows adorned every wall, while sculptures and carvings took up the corners. Space was no object, with the building surrounded by empty land. The full compound stretched an equivalent of four city blocks square, bordered by a clay fence.

"Certainly has benefits, being the son of the king."

Rione scoffed. "Luxuries built on the backs of the Torian people, I assure you."

"So, now we just wait?"

She kept her steely stare forward. "That's the plan."

I chuckled. "Oh, we actually have a plan now?" Rione didn't dignify my comment with a response, so I joined her in leaning against the wall.

There was no way to know how much time passed, listening to the ebb and flow of the crowd far below. Rione stood there still as a statue the entire time. I, on the other hand, wasn't used to this much idle time, let alone standing. Even while travelling throughout the galaxy, I could drink myself to sleep. Here, not so much.

Vladirian liquor certainly would've helped.

"Finally," Rione's exasperated voice whispered.

I tried to follow her stare. "What's going on?"

"Axyl's on the move."

I still didn't see obvious signs of movement inside the compound. "Where?"

"Right there." She pointed slightly to the right. "Between those two buildings. You'll see his vehicle pass through the front gate."

I strained to look, and sure enough, a long, silver hovercraft moved into the crowd.

"How did you find him in the first place?"

She remained transfixed, her voice distracted. "He was wandering the grounds. I figured he'd head out, but wasn't for sure until his driver picked him up."

There was a slight flaw in the plan. "And how are we supposed to know where he stops with all of the buildings in the way?"

"We watch which alleyway he ends up not passing, and rush off to meet him."

"Hopefully, he doesn't leave before we get there."

"A chance we'll have to take."

I kept my stare on the hovercraft's progress. It turned a few more times along its path. Then, they passed along a lengthy stretch of roadway before the vehicle finally stopped showing itself through sneak glimpses down the alleyways.

"There!" I pointed.

"Got it." Rione took one last look, then bolted for the stairwell. "Let's go!"

In no time, we burst back out into the alleyway. This time, I kept pace with Rione as she scurried into the crowd. I rushed after her, fortunate she knew how to get where we were going. Neither of us dwelled on the unwanted attention we received.

Crossing intersections and rounding corners, we covered an impressive distance in minimal time. I turned the final corner, my lungs on the verge of bursting. Axyl Wren's hovercraft was perched directly in front of a nightclub. Rione thankfully slowed her pace, giving me the opportunity to catch my breath.

While I did, it was a prime opportunity to scope out our surroundings. One Torian sat on the hood of the hovercraft, his back to us. I'd considered our current clothing traditional based on most of the residents, but this fellow had a black jacket and pants which closely resembled the clothing I normally wore. One boot was propped up on the bumper, and he slid a hand over his scalp, running through blonde stubble. A shiver ran through my bones. If I hadn't killed him myself, I would have sworn this was the back side of Lars Cassus.

Shaking those thoughts aside, I kept my mind on the task at hand. Rione stepped off toward a shop beside the street, where a rare window offered glimpses at clothing beyond. I walked up close to her.

"Looks like he's the driver," she muttered.

"Axyl went inside the club?"

She nodded. "Based on stories I've heard, it's sounded like he's pretty active on the club circuit."

"I don't suppose you've heard anything about how many goons he might have with him."

She shook her head, pretending to gaze at a long formal gown. "He had a pair with him when he was walking out the front gate, so I'd start with that, but there's no way to know whether more were waiting in the hovercraft or already in the club itself."

I peered over my shoulder. The driver hadn't moved. "So, are we doing this inside the club? You wouldn't let me bring a weapon, remember?"

She grimaced. "Too public. We need to find a way to separate him from the crowd."

"Again, the question is, how?"

"We'll have to wing it based on what we find inside."

Sadly, another plan being made up as we went along. "Let's hope an opportunity presents itself to us fast."

Rione nodded. "Trust me, it will."

We turned from the window and started across the path. As we approached the club's front doors, the driver turned to stare us down. He took an especially deep interest in her, then whistled. "Fine piece, that body."

She spat her words. "Eat dirt, scum."

I didn't have a good feeling about this particular part of our plan. The hoodlum proved me right, jumping down off the hovercraft and standing in her path.

"What'd you say to me?" He rattled off another choice phrase, a Torian insult I didn't know.

She peered up into his face, and I figured her emotion ridges were burning red under her hood. "Get out of my way, you piece of trash!"

"How about you make me?" He grabbed her left arm.

Before I could strike him myself, Rione smashed a clenched fist up into his chin. He stumbled to his knees, dazed and confused, a moment before Rione slammed the side of his head with her thigh.

So much for not drawing attention.

"Let's go." As the crowd paused to watch, I ushered Rione toward the club's front door.

My usual haunts, spots I sought out in my galactic travels, were quiet hole-in-the-wall establishments. I couldn't take two steps inside this room before my brain pounded against my skull. Flashing lights blinded me while thumping speakers echoed off the shadowed walls.

There was no possibility of holding a normal conversation in here. I leaned over and spoke directly into Rione's ear. "I thought Torians were quiet and reserved?"

She turned and did the same to me, her warm breath in my ear. "What gave you that idea? The clothes they wear?"

I walked along next to her, all while attempting to get a glance at the room. The repetitive flashes of light weren't enough for me to see much besides the vacant stares of young people dancing in large groups. We all apparently had our own coping mechanisms in life.

Rione led me over to the far wall as the music faded. Either that, or I'd gone deaf. The lights dimmed along with the absence of reverberation.

She reached a stool. "So, see anything?"

"Not sure how anyone can see in here at all."

I took the stool next to hers, just before the music and lights started back up. Rione leaned over to speak again. "Over in the corner, behind me."

I glanced in the general direction she'd offered. Once I knew where to look and acclimated myself to the strobes, it wasn't hard to pick out Axyl. A pair of muscular hulks stood on either side of him while a handful of ladies sat with crossed legs in a semi-circle at his feet.

Even seated, his tall torso stood out. The lines of his face were sculpted as if he'd started life as a rough ivory block. The hair upon his head was just as golden as his sister's, but barely covered his ears. He wore a loose-fitting white shirt, unbuttoned down his chest, while his black pants were tight and revealed far more of him than I cared to see.

From this distance, I watched his eyes. He looked over the women at his feet with a jovial, playful demeanor. Behind that, a harsh chill sat. There was the true Axyl, the one we'd set out to kill.

The question was how.

The background music concealed the prince's voice as he regaled his groupies with some sort of tale. They laughed and giggled when he stopped, which either meant they were all far better at reading lips, or his part of the room was better equipped for conversation. They also could have been feeding his ego, which was always a possibility with celebrity worship.

Rione's voice caught me off-guard. "He's got quite a collection."

I wasn't quite sure of the context, and thought maybe there was something I was missing. Another look didn't turn up anything further, so I looked back at my friend.

She leaned in again. "We always heard rumors of his playboy ways. I guess he really does keep a private harem."

I looked back at the row of women before the prince. Rione was making a fairly big leap in my opinion. They fawned all over him, as many tended to do around the rich and powerful. Still, there didn't seem to be any evidence to support her claim.

And then I saw markings on one woman, and then another, and eventually all five. Circles, jagged lines, and random dots interspersed in a semi-circle around the back of their necks. I'd seen them before, but not in their current sequence. It all looked like random marks and strokes to me.

Rione leaned closer. "Torian symbols. In essence, it means they're off-limits, forbidden for anyone but him."

"So, how do they get trapped into this mess?" I turned to her as the music died down.

"He picks them, and that's it."

I lifted an eyebrow. "They have no say in the matter?"

"Not if you believe the rumors..."

Assassinating this creep was getting easier to fathom. "Any closer to having a plan?"

"Actually, yes."

That caught me by surprise. “Well, what is it?”

The music and lights chose that moment to start back up. Her eyes had a maniacal glaze to them, driving my apprehension soaring to new heights.

She moved even closer, to the point where I swore her lips touched my ear. “I plan to join his harem.”

I jerked my head around so fast, I almost took off her nose in the process. “What?”

“I plan to be added to his collection.”

All my confidence in Rione’s mental faculties evaporated. “Absolutely not!”

“It’s the best way to get close enough to him.”

“We need to find another way. I’m not leaving you alone with him.”

“Don’t worry. You’ll have your eyes on me.”

That didn’t exactly instill me with much confidence. She couldn’t rationalize away the need to have a backup plan in case something went wrong.

“You have something in mind?” I asked.

She nodded without comment.

I knew enough to realize there was no chance of overcoming Rione’s stubborn nature. Pretty much as usual, I was just along for the ride. She patted my leg, then rose from her seat.

Another voice called from behind me, loud enough to top the background noise. “Can I get you something?”

A young man stood behind the bar, clothed in a tight black shirt. I glanced past him at bottles of alcohol, figuring it would draw attention, sitting at the bar and not ordering anything. That, and I needed a drink badly.

A smile crossed my lips as I saw a familiar yellow liquid, the bottle resting all by itself, waiting for me. Since it wouldn’t have done any good for me to try talking, I successfully pointed the barkeep's attention to the Vladirian liquor, reached under my robe and pulled out a yellow-rimmed golden coin.

Once the glass was in my hand, I gave a silent nod of thanks, and plunked down my payment. Then, I turned and tracked down where Rione had run off to. It took about three-quarters of the glass before I finally made out her hooded form weaving through the crowd.

I shifted my stare onto Axyl, still sitting with a scantily-clad woman straddled across his lap. His eyes, however, weren't paying her any attention, despite all the girl's attempts to draw it.

His hungry stare took inventory of Rione's form as she flowed across the room in front of him, crossing slowly from one side to the other. It never strayed as he examined every part of her body. There was no mistaking his intentions, since I myself had looked at several women the same way more than a few times.

Things were going exactly according to Rione's plan.

I watched the lust rise within him as he ignored the woman in his lap. She attempted to gain his attention, running her tongue and lips along his neck and bare chest. Rione knew exactly what she was doing, strolling up to a random Torian on the dance floor. Grabbing him by the shoulders, she gyrated with the music, surprising even me with her sensuality. I didn't know what it was doing to Axyl, but even I felt the familiar pangs of jealousy.

That was before Rione decided to start rubbing her body tight against this stranger she'd never met. The young man was shocked, but his smile grew, making it clear he wasn't about to complain. Axyl, on the other hand, dumped his young mistress to the floor and stormed toward the pair.

He grabbed Rione's arm and pulled her away. That was my personal trigger action, and I reached under my robe again. Cursing under my breath, I'd forgotten about my blaster being back on the station. It was then I decided to use my bare hands and rose off my stool. Rione must have read my mind, for she flashed me a warning look. I watched the two face off, my hands clenched tight.

The music died down, while a mulling crowd gathered. Rione and Axyl spoke to one another, the prince's face serious while Rione maintained her apathy. The exchange went on for a while, and I wished I'd ventured off for a closer look, at least to the point where I could listen in. As the music started back up again, Rione gave a series of nods. The crowd went back to their business, but her smile was enough to tell me she'd succeeded in her goal.

The prince clapped his hands and went back to his original seat, while Rione winked at me and we headed for the door.

Chapter Seventeen

As we stepped back outside, the same guard who Rione had taken down on our arrival now stood facing the opposite direction, leaning against the prince's hovercraft. His roving stare stayed on the thinning crowd. I followed Rione's lead as we merged into the flow out of his sight.

"So, what's the plan?"

Rione responded. "He's arranging for me to meet him inside his palace. I'm to be there in half a rotation."

This was really happening. It was a realization which sucker-punched me in the gut.

She continued. "We need to pick up some things first."

"And what exactly am I going to be doing while this is going on?"

"I already said you'd have eyes on me. Don't worry."

I didn't know how that would work, since I was fairly certain Axyl wasn't going to let me watch. Still, Rione's confidence had proven useful up to this point. I decided to just follow her lead.

The return trip took far less time than our journey to intercept Axyl, an improvement courtesy of the thinning crowd. This time, when we reached our original building, we entered through the front doors and thankfully rode the normal lift transport up. My legs and lungs were both glad for the respite.

Once back in the room, all the Torian garb came off and Rione, with her face still bleached white in comparison to the rest of her body, searched through the small corner closet. Taking advantage of a brief lull in the action, I flopped down on the mattress, yanked off my boots and massaged my aching feet. As a space pilot, I wasn't used to so much walking and running. This mattress, even flat against the ground as it was, provided far more comfort than my ship's cot.

I really didn't want to get back up.

Rione continued rummaging through the closet.

"Looking for anything in particular?" I asked.

A smile shot onto her face as she pulled out a thin metal box. "Found it."

Intrigue finally won out over what little creature comforts I was deriving. I propped myself up as Rione flipped open the case.

Her eyes gleamed. "Jackpot."

"What's in there?"

She pulled out two thin white patches, each about the size of a fingertip. "I wasn't sure whether they'd still have this equipment or not."

This told me far more than I wanted to know. Rione was still generating her plan on the fly. I repeated, "What?"

"Microphones and earpieces." She peeled apart one of the strips and carefully attached it on the side of her face, along her jaw, before doing the same to me. I barely even felt the device. A moment later, she'd pulled out a small black ball and tucked it inside her ear, then again did the same to me. This one, though, I did feel.

There was something very disconcerting about something foreign being shoved in a spot it didn't belong. I cupped a hand over my ear. "You're going to be able to get that back out, right?"

"Stop being such a wuss." She walked toward the closet, slamming the case shut. Then, I heard her mumbling voice with amazing clarity in my ear. "It's unbecoming."

"Nice trick," I mumbled.

She shoved the case back into the recesses of the closet, then turned back toward me with a smirk. "No trick, jut technology."

"And it picks up all noise levels?" Not that there was a risk of having background noise. There was little doubt in my mind what Axyl had planned. The fact I'd be forced to watch somehow, let alone listen in on this new device, turned my stomach and nothing had even happened yet.

I had a pretty vivid imagination.

"Yes. The transceiver picks up the smallest vibrations and adjusts the output before sending to the receiver."

"So, how do you figure on doing it?" I frowned, as clarification was in order. "Killing Axyl, I mean."

Her expression dropped. "I'll improvise."

"Doesn't sound like a recipe for success."

"They're not going to let me in without a search."

"But they're going to leave you alone with him?"

"Unless he's into performing for an audience, which is always possible."

She must have caught my disturbed glance, as her playful look migrated off for different pastures. "Don't worry. I never heard any rumors about that, and I'm fairly certain no one could choke off that information."

Her efforts at assuaging my concern were wasted. I had no doubt Axyl was as cold and calculating as his father, and just as deadly if an opportunity presented itself.

I just hoped we wouldn't test my theory.

Rione walked toward the mattress, then slammed her boot against the floor. Needless to say, it startled me, the first time at least. Though my apprehension settled with the next few subsequent stomps, my confusion grew.

"Now's not the time to be learning new dance moves."

She glared at me, before smacking her foot down again. This time, the reverberation changed tone and pitch. This elicited a wider smirk from her lips. "Hope you're better with weaponry than you are with that crack wit of yours."

Her reaction brought me up to my knees, as I peered at the spot where she'd just stepped. Rione felt around before pulling up on the ratty, worn carpet. To my surprise, she lifted a square chunk, revealing another metal case under the floor.

She had my interest. "More supplies for the mission?"

"You could call it that."

She flipped open the lid and pulled out a black object resembling a brick. Then, she handed it over to me without another word of explanation.

Looking over the device, turning it back and forth, examining the various seams, I still wasn't any closer to a breakthrough. "So, what am I supposed to do with this?"

"That's how you're going to keep an eye on me while I'm inside."

I glanced at the brick again. "If you say so."

"Flip it open."

I held it closer to my face, finally figuring out the purpose of the seams. I pried on them all, folding out a barrel from the front, a targeting scope on top, and a pair of tandem hand grips on the bottom.

She pointed at the device in my hands. "We'll have to rely on that if things go wrong."

"And what is this?"

"Tactical version of a neutron disruptor. Hits targets pretty accurately from about a kilpar out with its concentrated fire algorithms."

I whistled. "And why couldn't we use this outside the compound?"

Her mood soured, proving to me there was no good reason. She was set on killing Axyl face-to-face, to be the last person he'd ever lay eyes on. I knew that feeling, more than she could imagine.

I brought the targeting scope up in front of my eye. The opposite wall showed up crystal clear in the digital display, black crosshairs centered.

Rione stepped closer. "But here's the real benefit of the neutron disruptor." Opening my other eye, I watched her rotate a small knob on the scope's side. I focused back on the display, where the view had changed. At first, I thought she'd knocked the focus out of whack, as everything seemed a bit blurry. Then, trading glances with the far wall, I realized it was something completely different.

Rione chuckled. "It's seeing past the wall, at the next building. Well, sort of."

"It sees through walls?"

"It runs a continuous scan at a set distance. As you adjust the range, you're getting the controller's approximation of what's there based on its readings."

I adjusted the knob some more, and moved through the next wall, finding myself in another apartment. Various furnishings were strewn around the room, all appearing as light shadows with fuzzy edges.

"You'll notice that the more surfaces you move through, the less clarity objects have as more approximation is used."

I pushed the device a bit farther until it moved through another wall. This time, a dark shadow appeared, taking the form of a slender female. The edges were clouded, but it didn't take much imagination to know she was showering. I brought the display back to the previous room.

"I think I've got the hang of it."

"Just realize that though you're able to see through walls, the power output is limited. It should knock a hole through one wall easy enough, assuming a regular thickness. I wouldn't count on it passing through a second."

I folded up the weapon's extremities and gripped the brick in my left hand. "Tell me what I'm supposed to do."

"Keep an eye on me. I'm certain you'll know if anything goes wrong, between the visual and audio cues."

I only hoped things wouldn't get to that point. "So, what do we do until you have to arrive at Axyl's palace?"

"I need to make sure our deception is complete, that he isn't suspicious. I'm going to need those credits you brought to buy a few things." She pulled on her Torian garb once more, then started for the door.

• • •

The crowd was almost non-existent when we exited out the apartment building's front doors. We only traveled a few blocks, then turned a corner into a fledgling commercial district. I was caught off-guard as Rione pulled a door open and walked inside a shop. Giving an awkward glance at the sheer black curtains covering its display windows, I regained my composure and followed.

And then, I lost it once more as my sight was flooded with images of lingerie and other unmentionables. I was sure my face flushed as overwhelming heat burned through my altered skin pores.

Honestly, I didn't know why this place embarrassed me so much. I'd seen women around the galaxy dressed in far less and sometimes even in public.

"Don't gawk."

I blinked hard, watching Rione rummage through outfits on a nearby rack. Cautious, I moved up to join her.

As I came within earshot, I finally mumbled, "What exactly are we doing here?"

She continued rifling through racks of clothes. "Hm?"

"Here. Why?"

"You're a big boy, Aston. I'm certain you know what kind of visit Axyl is expecting."

I did. That was the problem.

Rione continued, "So, it's going to be necessary to act out the part."

"That doesn't explain why you had to bring me along, least of all to this place."

"Had to?" A sly smile broke out. "What happened to your need to keep me safe? Wouldn't that mean maintaining a constant watch over me?"

My frown grew.

"Don't worry. We won't be here long."

Unfortunately, no matter how long we were stuck here, it would seem an eternity longer. I stood in silence, listening to metal hangars grind against the shiny tubes holding them up. I glanced around the rest of the small shop, and confirmed my worst fear; I was the only male in the entire place.

"How about this?"

Rione held up a thin sheet of black lace someone had convinced themselves would make a fine article of clothing.

"What about it?"

She grabbed another hangar off a rack behind her which held a slick, black two piece outfit, then held it in front of her, tacked behind the translucent fabric. I'd have been lying if I said it didn't have its intended effect on me.

"Will this keep Axyl distracted?" She modeled off the garments, which didn't improve the situation. I remained speechless, frowning. She chuckled. "I'll take that as a yes."

And with that, she scooted around the racks. I debated whether to follow along, while I felt more and more sets of eyes tracking me. Then she moved toward the sales counter, and I rushed to join her. Escape was finally near.

The cashier rang up her order, then gave the total to Rione, who promptly turned to face me with an expectant look. I pulled out my money box, handing over several golden coins.

As she started making change, the thin, young thing running the register cracked a smile. "Looks like someone is going to have an exciting time."

I couldn't bring myself to smile back.

Rione's hand patted my forearm, catching me off-guard. "Yes, quite exciting."

The salesgirl's deep curls bounced back and forth while she sacked the goods. "Well, have fun, you two."

Rione grabbed the bag in one hand, nestling her arm in the crook of my elbow. "Oh, we will."

Then, we rushed toward the exit. The stares coming our way were now filled with scorn. Rione broke away as we entered an area with narrower distances between the racks, and she moved a lot faster than I did. The stares followed her, and it became apparent the negativity wasn't directed at me at all. In my humble mind, I could only figure these ladies were only browsing in hopes they might find something they could eventually use. Rione, on the other hand, had a sure thing as far as they knew.

Again, they had no idea what our true plans were.

Rione's hearty laugh broke the silence as we exited the shop and she turned to face me. "Can you believe that?"

Her jovial attitude was catching. A smile finally crept onto my face. "What?"

"They actually thought you and I, that we..." She busted out laughing again. My smile disappeared.

I hadn't really given it much thought, but it made perfect sense why the shop had made me so uncomfortable.

Part of me desired my friendship with Rione to progress into something more. If I really wanted to dissect the matter, it had been that way for longer than I cared to admit. I'd successfully pushed all of those feelings aside, since she'd already been involved with someone else. Now, circumstances had changed.

My stomach knotted up with guilt. Malone had been her lover. I forced myself to laugh with her. "Imagine..."

Rione looked around the empty street and something akin to fear and paranoia filled her eyes.

Fearing the worst, I inquired, "What's wrong?"

"It's almost time. We need to hurry."

She pulled my hand and we rushed through the streets toward the safe house.

Chapter Eighteen

For better or worse, my stamina was increasing. The level of exhaustion wasn't nearly as bad as it had been before. I didn't have an overwhelming urge this time to plop down on the mattress when we burst into the apartment. Rione dropped her sack of unmentionables on the floor and scrambled for the corner closet.

I also needed to prepare for our task, snagging the neutron disruptor which Rione had shown me earlier. After I picked it up, I looked back at her hanging a long, black overcoat over the closet door. She shuffled the robe over her head, then started to unzip her black jumpsuit before she realized I was staring.

"Some privacy, if you please."

I turned and faced the empty gray wall. The mere sound of the suit hitting the floor made my cheeks flush red.

She chuckled under her breath. "Who would have thought a flyboy would embarrass so easy?"

"Only on special occasions," I muttered.

"It suits you." The lingerie bag rustled.

"I'll take that as a compliment."

"You've always been full of surprises."

I gave a slight chuckle. "I'd say the same of you."

I envisioned Rione in the same garments we'd purchased. No matter how I tried to clear my thoughts, I couldn't stop myself. It was all I could do to keep my focus on the wall. The torment between lust and civility rose within me. I closed my eyes to help, but it didn't.

"Okay. You can turn back now."

As I did, her dark black overcoat stretched to the ground and covered everything my mind had subjected me to. Rione leaned against the wall and pulled on her original boots, before zipping them up one at a time. A portion of the coat draped open, offering me a fleeting glimpse of her black undergarments. On top of that, she'd apparently used more of the bleaching pads, as she had pale skin in far more places now. I forced my normally involuntary breathing to function.

All I knew was that if this didn't keep Axyl sufficiently distracted, either he was already dead or his harem was one huge cover for his true feelings. Rione's boots clopped along the floor, as I walked over and joined her, weapon in hand.

She glanced down and her lips formed a thin line. "We should probably find a way to help you conceal that." She rushed back to the closet and rummaged through it a moment before yanking out another overcoat identical to her own.

As she handed it over, I couldn't help wondering aloud. "Won't these outfits stand out?"

"The city's going to be mostly empty for a while. Everyone should be asleep at this point in the rotation."

When I tossed the coat on, the feel of the leather made my skin crawl. It reminded me too much of the jacket I'd had to destroy. I looked down at my covered arms and half-expected to see Leah's blood caked there. I closed my eyes to shield the memories, but then heard Rione's boots continue toward the door. I tucked the brick underneath the flaps of my jacket.

• • •

The two of us walked side-by-side toward the palace we'd seen from the rooftops. I was finally starting to get a feel for the general city layout. The trick, of course, being that once we'd killed Axyl, I didn't figure on sticking around, or ever coming back to this place again.

That was, if we made it out alive.

Not a single word was spoken as we passed between dormant buildings. Rounding corners, I kept expecting to see more citizens walking or congregating. After a few more turns, though, it became apparent that wouldn't happen.

I finally broke our silence. "Does it seem odd we're the only ones around? Certainly, people should be asleep as you said, but the streets are completely empty."

"Axyl has the entire town placed on a curfew and lockdown." That didn't give me good feelings about being out and about.

We turned down a final street before I saw the compound, what I could see over the clay fence, anyway. Without warning, Rione cut in front of me and started down another alleyway. Uncertain of her plan, I followed. She jerked through a side door into another apartment building. I raced in, charging up the stairs behind her.

She led me up in a near sprint, finally barging out onto the rooftop. Another half-height wall waited for us, identical to the first we'd used, beyond which lay the ornate palace and its compound. Rione ducked down as we approached, urging me to follow suit. Then, we fell to a kneeling position beside the barricade.

"Ready your weapon," she instructed in a cold, calculated tone. "I have to leave now."

I pulled the device open and inquired, "Is there a signal you can give me? Just in case something goes wrong?"

"If it does, you'll know, even without a signal."

Unfortunately, she was right. The trouble was I didn't know whether I'd be able to help if and when it happened.

"Good luck," she muttered.

"You'll need it more than I do."

She patted my upper leg with a weak smile, then scrambled for the door.

I watched as it closed. Despite my best intentions otherwise, I couldn't stop envisioning Rione in ways that weren't appropriate, especially considering my attention needed to be on the task at hand.

Lifting myself up, I positioned the weapon atop the clay slab. I gazed through the targeting sight, moving along the roadway until I saw the gate Axyl had left through earlier. Rotating the range knob, I got a closer look at the first Torian guard Rione would meet.

His face was like stone, emotionless. I figured boredom had long since set in. At least it would have for me, had I been in his shoes. Cycle after cycle, going through the same motions, it wore a person down.

Rione's voice entered my ear as clear as if she sat beside me. "Approaching the gate. You ready?"

I pulled back the range a few clicks until I saw her moving toward the Torian. "I have you in sight."

"Here we go..."

The guard turned to watch her approach. Once she drew close enough, he held up his hand. His voice was as clear as Rione's. "Stop right there."

I centered the black crosshairs on him and they turned red in response. I didn't figure there would be a need to strike him down, but I wanted to be ready, just in case.

"State your business."

Rione was calm. "The prince requested my presence."

I watched the guard carefully, my finger itchy on the trigger. “Stay right there,” he instructed her.

The guard stepped over to a small guard shack. I maintained my red crosshairs with every step he made. Once he entered the clay and stone structure, I lost both sight and sound of him. First, I thought I should adjust my range. Then, reason finally stepped in. There wouldn’t be any way for me to pick up audio, regardless.

Mere moments later, he stepped back out into view, the gate finally rolling aside. He came into range of Rione’s transmitter before speaking. “They’re waiting for you at the front doors, main residence.”

“Thank you.” Rione strolled past him.

The guard turned his back to me. Males were mostly the same the universe over, and he kept focus on Rione’s body as she walked up the path. The steel plate gates closed once again, cutting off his view. He returned to his post.

“And here you were worried,” Rione mumbled.

“Still a long way from the finish,” I reminded her.

“Don’t worry. Axyl won’t know what hit him, and neither will his security staff.”

I lifted an eyebrow. “So you’ve figured out how you’re going to take him down?”

A lengthy silence followed.

“Hopefully they don’t take you too deep into the building,” I offered.

She moved up to the doors. “It should be fine. From the maps I’ve seen, Axyl’s bedroom is located along the outer wall, second floor.”

Just mentioning his bedroom made my forehead heat up.

“Now,” she continued, “before they think I’m talking to myself, how about we end this conversation?”

I didn't bother responding, instead tracking her movements through the display, adjusting the range as necessary. Finally, Rione reached the massive front door fashioned from golden Arcadian wood. She lifted her hand, but before she had the chance to knock, it pulled open. Another pale-skinned Torian appeared in my display, holding a phase pistol. My guess was he wasn't a butler.

His voice was gruff. "The prince has been expecting you. You're late."

"Had to find something appropriate for the occasion." I smiled, barely holding back a laugh. The guard wouldn't hear anything, but Rione would. I couldn't risk a reaction.

He ushered her inside and slammed the door. It was finally time to put this neutron disruptor to a real test that didn't involve peeping on complete strangers.

I reached up and adjusted the display until it passed through the front wall. Two dark images, the guard and Rione, walked up a set of stairs. It took some coordination on my part to keep the display centered and adjusted on the pair. Unfortunately, the images grew more blurry as the guard led Rione deeper into the building.

They reached the second floor and broke off to the left. No one spoke, but I did hear Rione's boots clopping against a hard wooden floor. At least I knew I still had audio coverage.

Other dark images passed across the display, guards walking in the opposite direction as Rione. Others stood still as statues. No one spoke a word. My original concerns about her safety, however, were quickly eclipsed by one far more problematic.

How was Rione going to get out of there after she'd killed Axyl?

"Right here," the guard barked, drawing my attention back to the present.

Two additional figures stood on either side of Rione and the first guard. With no way to see them in detail, it was impossible to know what their intentions were. Equally unfortunate, there was no way for me to take out all three guards at once, even if they posed a threat.

Rione came to an immediate stop and the first guard's image merged with her own, then one of the other two did the same. I now had no way to know who was standing in front of the others. I tried adjusting the knob, but both images disappeared, then reappeared, at the same time.

"Arms up. Spread your legs," the guard continued.

The image shifted as Rione complied, but she still spat out bitter words. "Is this really necessary?"

"Afraid so."

"You're just trying to get a cheap feel." From the sounds of his pat-down, I believed her.

"Guess working here does come with some fringe benefits after all." He started guffawing, and then I heard two other distinctive laughs. "Pull off your coat."

She maintained her silence to try and move things along. Heck, I wanted to blast a hole in her molester myself, and I would have if I could tell which figure he was.

Arms dropped and her coat's rustle was followed by catcalls and whistles. It was definitely the truest test of Rione's resolve. She wanted to murder Axyl Wren, and badly.

I heard her grunt multiple times, and my palms grew damp as I imagined the horrors she was being subjected to.

Sweat rolled down my forehead, before the guard finally declared. "Well, looks like she's safe."

The figure finally split into separate entities, and as a sign of passive-aggression, I tracked the guard with a set of red crosshairs.

Rione's mumbling voice rang out in my ear. "Not for a lack of searching." Fortunately, the guard didn't hear her. I dared not respond.

The other two figures reached out and opened a set of doors on squeaky hinges. Rione walked inside. Finally, she was being given access to Axyl's inner sanctum.

"The prince will be in shortly."

Chapter Nineteen

"Quite a place," Rione commented under her breath.

Her blurry, darkened figure moved across my display. "Was a bit worried about you a moment ago."

"Why's that?"

"Didn't figure you'd put up with much manhandling."

"It was all I could do to keep myself from beating down every single one of them."

A smile crept onto my lips. "I don't doubt it."

She moved around, pausing at uneven intervals, scoping out her surroundings, and hopefully figuring out the assassination plan. Hopefully she'd have time to work them out before the prince arrived.

Or not.

The doors squeaked open and another figure emerged onto the display. "Your highness," Rione announced, making no motion of honor such as a bow or curtsy.

His voice was far too sinister. "You're late."

I heard the rustle of clothing, then saw her overcoat drop to the floor. "I had trouble finding something I thought you would enjoy."

His voice didn't falter. "No one keeps me waiting."

I moved onto his image, the crosshairs turning red along with my anger. It wouldn't take much incentive to make me flinch and pull the trigger.

Rione, on the other hand, kept her cool far more easily. "My sincerest apologies, your highness."

His arm moved away from his body, and I figured he pointed down at the floor. "A mere apology isn't enough for your disrespect. On your knees!"

My finger twitched and I barely kept myself from breathing too heavily, knowing Rione would hear.

She surprised even me. "Yes, your highness."

I watched in disbelief as her image stepped forward and dropped to the floor. I didn't really want to think about what was going to come next.

"Now, you're prepared for an appropriate apology."

I honestly couldn't figure out how Rione was maintaining her composure. "Please forgive me, your highness. There was no reason for my tardiness."

I moved the crosshairs up to the top of his image. If I took this fool out, it was going to be with a head shot.

"I suppose that is acceptable."

"Thank you, your highness."

He moved away, and then crawled atop his bed. If Rione was going to do the deed, she'd better enact it quickly. Getting molested by the guards was one thing, and she'd proven herself capable of pushing through that. I didn't figure she'd be able to stomach the idea of going through with Axyl's planned activity.

Frankly, I couldn't either.

"I believe you know what to do," he insisted as he adjusted to a different position and the bed squeaked under his weight. A moment later, music filled my ears.

Without a word, her image moved closer, gyrating in sync with the music as she slowly closed the distance between them.

"I think you'll enjoy this game," Rione cooed.

Chills ran across my skin. She had a plan and neither I nor Axyl knew what she had in store.

"Such an ornate bed you have," she stated, moving toward the unsuspecting victim.

"It's good to be a prince."

I heard fabric rubbing against a surface, but couldn't make out the context. The prince's next words didn't help any. "What do you think you're doing?"

"Something your highness will thoroughly enjoy."

His skepticism faded with a laugh. "I just might."

Rione climbed on top of the bed, their images sporadically joining as one. Axyl's groans of pleasure nearly made me vomit, even if I figured both of them were still clothed.

At least I hoped so.

"Give me your hand," she demanded.

He laughed again. "I know where you're planning to go with this."

I smiled. His guess wasn't as good as he thought.

"Then, the question is whether you're going to go along with it, and do what I ask."

Rione's arm reached up toward a blurry dark image at the bed's headboard. Fabric ran across another hard surface, and it finally dawned on me what she was doing.

She was tying him down to the bed.

"Now your other hand," Rione demanded. I sensed Axyl's end was near, and only hoped he didn't do the same.

But his other arm came up, just as she'd told him to. Who knew a man used to so much power and control would yield all of it to someone he didn't even know, all for the idea of carnal passion?

But despite all that, it seemed to be working.

"I'm ready," he insisted. It was as if he realized how much power he'd given over, a few moments too late.

"I'm not."

Even I couldn't help but break out a sly smile. I heard the now familiar sound of Rione pulling more fabric into place, watching as her image was propped near the prince's feet. All the while, I expected Axyl to object, but none ever came. Of course, faced with the prospect of being pleasured by Rione, I'd have done the same thing.

Sadly, given my track record, I'd have expected her to try and kill me. Apparently, Axyl didn't stumble across the same type of women I normally did.

I needed to find a higher class of woman.

Rione tied the prince's feet down and stood at the foot of the bed. Another fabric rope was pulled free. Like me, it got Axyl's attention. "I have nothing else to tie. What do you plan with that one?"

"Oh," she murmured, "I have extra-special plans for this."

"I'm looking forward to it."

On the display, Rione climbed atop the prince. His voice changed pitch, a sure indication his confidence was slipping. "Wrapping it around the back of my neck...you definitely have odd tastes."

The poor bastard never saw the end coming, not until it was too late. Rione grunted and strained, cinching the makeshift noose across Axyl's airway. His chokes and gasps, barely audible in my ear, brought a sense of relief to my heart, as he was incapable of speech. His guards were unaware of what was happening.

All things considered, I was glad when he finally succumbed to his fate, falling silent forever.

Rione was still livid, riding the high of premeditated murder. She gave the fabric another tug. "That's for all the lives you've needlessly taken, you rotten son of a..."

I interrupted, urgency flowing through me. "Get out of there, before you're discovered!"

She grunted her displeasure with being unable to inflict more punishment on her victim. She rose, standing beside the bed. "Fine."

Heavy breathing echoed in my ears as she moved to the spot where she'd dropped her overcoat. Even with our target eliminated, I wasn't able to relax. That wouldn't happen until Rione and I had escaped.

I adjusted the display back to the hallway outside his room. Three figures, the guards Rione had left, still stood at the doors, barely moving, none too concerned with what happened behind the closed doors.

"Well, here goes," was Rione's only advance warning before the doors opened and she morphed onto the display.

The same guard who'd escorted her up announced himself. "That was fast."

Rione's voice had a playfulness one wouldn't expect from someone who'd just killed a man. "I picked out just the right outfit for him."

He laughed. "I don't doubt that."

"Now he's asleep. I guess that's my cue to head home." She turned and shut the doors.

"Smart girl."

Without another word, he led her back the way they'd come. I couldn't believe they were going along with this, that no one checked her story. A smile crept onto my face. We were actually going to get away with this.

I tracked the pair down the main staircase, without a word spoken. Finally, they reached the front door and Rione gave some parting blabber. “Well, it’s been fun.”

“And the prince knows how to contact you if he wishes to see you again?”

I held back the curse that tried to pass my lips. He opened the door for her. Finally, Rione responded. “I’m not sure. It didn’t really come up.”

“I’ll escort you back home, so I can relay your location.”

I froze at his statement. Fortunately, Rione kept her composure and kept walking. “That’s not necessary.”

“I insist.”

Now that they stood outside the building and walked down the path, I saw his facial expression. This had nothing to do with Axyl or what Rione had just done, nor with trying to keep tabs on her.

He was going to force the same treatment out of her she’d presumably given the prince.

My crosshairs turned red as I moved them over his head, while they moved toward the front gate. This would make things far more complicated than they should have been. The desire was strong inside me to take this beast out, but Rione needed to exit the compound first.

“Open up!” The guard barked out to his counterpart.

The steel plates began their slow grind out of the way. I began pondering potential problems with the weapon currently under my itchy trigger finger. I had no idea how this weapon operated, specifically how long it took to recharge between shots. I hadn’t considered that important information before. Now, two guards were in close proximity to Rione and it was crucial to her survival.

“Let’s go,” he ordered Rione.

The second guard wasn't sure what was going on either. "Where do you think you're going?" He asked his comrade.

"Just mind your own business."

He held a hand up against the other guard's chest. "You're not supposed to abandon your post."

I saw an opening in this petty squabble and whispered instructions to Rione. "Keep moving. Start running once you're past the guard station."

I wasn't sure she'd heard me, not until she moved through the open gate. As I figured, neither guard noticed, focusing on their argument.

A two-tone beep came out of nowhere, catching me off-guard while I watched Rione. I refocused on the two fighting guards. Her former escort pulled a transmitter off his belt, annoyed. "What?"

He listened to words I couldn't hear, but it soon became obvious. "Slow down. What do you mean, dead?"

My eyes went wide and I moved my crosshairs onto his head. I forced my words out for Rione's benefit. "Run!"

He looked up in disbelief. "You! Stop!"

I pulled the trigger without hesitation. A long continuous white beam fired from the weapon in my hands, crossing the distance and striking the target. All I saw was his body standing without his head, only a brief moment before it crumpled to the ground.

I cursed at the device's sheer power, but then heard another voice call out in my ear. "Stop or I'll shoot."

Moving the crosshairs onto the second guard's chest, he trained his own weapon on Rione as she ran.

I quickly discovered the answer to my concerns about this weapon. The crosshairs turned red, and I pulled the trigger. The beam fired off again, and his body lay in two separate pieces on the ground.

Klaxons sounded off throughout the compound, a fact I could hear without my ear receiver. I moved the display up and adjusted the range just in time to see guards pile out the front doors of the palace.

Rione's voice echoed in my ear. "Get down to the street level. I'll meet you there." I rushed toward the stairs, collapsing the neutron disruptor as I went.

She was anxious as I met her out front, jerking her head around from side to side, watching for our pursuers. No words were spoken as we bolted down the empty street. As we turned the last corner before our building, sirens rang out, echoing against the walls in an eerie chorus.

I glanced around again at the vacant street. If anyone saw the two of us, we'd be cooked.

Rione interrupted my thoughts. "The warning system being activated was inevitable. Focus!"

I did exactly as she told me and matched her step for step. We reached the safe house building in record time.

While we waited for the lobby lift pod, I tried conversing. "So, won't everyone be on the lookout now, especially for you?"

Her lips formed a tight line as the pod arrived. The doors closed behind us and we started up the shaft. "It's definitely going to complicate matters."

That was a major understatement. "But we have a way to get past them? Different disguise techniques?"

Again, no response until we reached our floor and the doors opened to an empty hallway. "We'll find a way out."

I personally didn't see how.

We rushed into the room without incident, and Rione yanked her outer garments off. At first, I stood there dumbfounded, as this was the same woman who'd gone out of her way to maintain her modesty earlier. Reason returned quickly, and I rushed over to the closet to grab a set of clothes for myself.

"If we hurry," she said, "we might be able to make the last transport to Icthus, and the second palace."

"And if we're too late?"

"Then I hope you're up for a hike." She turned to me, then grimaced. She finally realized she'd disrobed in front of me. The lace undergarments were form-fitting and exactly as I'd envisioned them. Her perfect curves had never been in question, given her wardrobes of the past, but seeing them now left nothing to the imagination.

Despite my difficulty doing so, I looked away for her benefit. "We'd better hurry, then."

I grabbed my duffel, shoving the neutron disruptor inside. Rione strolled over in a pair of dress slacks, digging it back out. "All of our weapons stay here." She shoved it back into its original hiding spot.

With a grimace, I at least took comfort knowing my Mark II was still safe and sound back on the station.

"They definitely have the means to detect whether we're carrying weapons onto the transport."

My shoulders slumped. "I have a feeling we'll need them."

"We'll improvise."

I pulled on the white dress shirt, black suit and pants. Rione soon filled out a pale blouse. I donned a matching fedora and she snorted. "We look so stupid."

"I didn't have much variety to choose from," I noted.

She held back a laugh. "Just a personal observation."

It was only then I wondered about the cheery attitude Rione was exhibiting. I'd have been lying, though, if I considered that in stark contrast to what I'd felt, killing Lars in my own rage-filled search for revenge. I'd taken joy in killing him, and would have done it all over again. I just didn't remember my joy leading to this much cheerfulness externally.

Granted, I was unconscious shortly after, which might have explained it.

"Well," she said with a sigh, "here goes nothing." With that, she grabbed her duffel and I followed suit, before we raced out the door.

The sirens were still going strong as we left the building, which gave us an actual benefit, drawing dormant citizens from their homes. They all looked up and down the street, trying to make sense out of the utter confusion.

I figured on being caught, hauling our bags past everyone, but they were all pre-occupied with the warning sirens, and we slipped past unnoticed. I maintained my focus straight ahead, Rione at my side. Murmurs from the growing crowd rose and fell like an ocean's tide. My paranoia rode those waves as we rushed along the makeshift streets, taking a normal route to the transport station.

"Things are going too smoothly."

"Don't knock it," she muttered.

"I'm thinking we should have just kept our weapons and gone in the back way like we'd left the station."

She shook her head ever so slightly. "Running across the tracks definitely would get noticed now."

We continued rushing along, crossing a footbridge over several transport troughs before we reached the station. Only the center ticket window of the three was open.

A chubby Torian sat atop a cushioned chair. His attention was with the distant sirens as well, echoing off the rock walls all around.

"Two tickets to Icthus."

He looked at her, stunned, as if she'd materialized out of thin air. A moment later, his puffy cheeks relaxed as he finally processed her words. Turning his attention to a nearby touch-screen, he brought up a schedule. He lifted an eyebrow.

"The last one out should arrive shortly."

I pulled out credits to cover the fare, as a smile crept upon Rione's face. So far, she was right on the money. This entire escapade was going far better than I expected, all things considered.

Which in my mind, was a terrible harbinger of things to come.

"Here you are." The attendant handed us each an electronic wafer. "Transport will be arriving and departing from platform C." He thumbed toward an open corridor beside the ticket counter, marked signs directing us.

Rione thanked him, then we rushed off.

"Surprised they didn't even bother to search our bags," I muttered as we pushed through the empty hall. Reddish-brown stone fashioned the walls, while far more comfortable-looking benches were sporadically laid out along each side. Dim lights hung from the ceiling, their light just enough to see the signage hanging on either side of the corridor.

"They usually do."

"Think they're laying a trap?"

"His mind was on those sirens. They haven't gone off since their underground power stations were destroyed."

The enclosed corridor began a steady decline, before we reached the platform exits. Third on the left, an illuminated sign directed us down a spiral walkway to the concrete slab below.

We were just in time, as a dual-tone alarm sounded off from overhead speakers, moments before a hover-transport sped out into the open and came to a stop in front of us.

"Great timing," I muttered.

"More good fortune," Rione insisted as the doors opened.

Waiting for a handful of passengers to disembark, we finally boarded. Rione led me inside the travel compartment, which was almost an exact replica from the one we'd hitched a ride on for our arrival. All in all, I preferred boarding this way.

A smoky haze rested near the ceiling, one slight difference I noticed right off the bat.

"Tickets, please."

I turned to the left, where an older Torian sat on an inboard-facing seat. His blue eyes were extra-pale, and his skin was creased and cracked. His black suit jacket and pants were a grand departure from the townsfolk we'd seen. The same could be said for the permanent frown etched onto the man's face.

"Tickets, please," he repeated, impatient.

I handed over my electronic wafer. His fingers shaking, the man fumbled around before finally inserting it into a handheld reader. Holding the screen out as far as his thin, frail arms allowed, he focused his eyes. With a grunt, he returned the wafer to me, before repeating the process with Rione.

"Seats twelve and thirteen." He motioned farther down the center aisle.

For better or worse, most of the compartment was empty, with only three other travelers scattered in random seats. I wrinkled my nose at the smoky stench, and motioned toward the ceiling. "Is this normal?"

The old man kept his blank stare forward. "Filtration system's busted."

I knew it was only a matter of time before the universe would return to beating me down. Finally, its first stage was exposed.

The old man let out a long breath of air as if someone had just jumped on his chest, then turned back toward the entry hatch in expectation of additional passengers.

It was just a hunch on my part, but I didn't figure there would be any.

And in the back of my mind, I couldn't stop hoping for that to be the case. The fewer people on-board, the less likely we'd be discovered. With all of that weighing heavy on my mind, I was caught off-guard when Rione pushed past me. Her voice dripped sarcasm. "Ladies first? What a gentleman."

A buzz sounded off, just before the old man's nasally voice bellowed. "Everyone in your seats. Buckle up."

Rione and I were the only ones standing, so I hurried my pace to catch up to her. Numbers were marked on the sides of each seat. She slumped into one of two facing each other, the forward-facing one. As I grabbed the headrest for the other, the transport lurched forward, causing me to fall flat on my face.

"Need to work on that timing." Rione chuckled.

"Take your seat," the old man's voice called out as I felt the acceleration forces subside. Now at the transport's constant velocity, I rose with my face flushed and took the seat across from Rione.

"Best relax while you have the chance," she commented, a trace of laughter still on her tongue.

I looked into her green eyes. "I'm not sure that's going to be possible just yet."

She looked around the compartment and I did the same. Two of our fellow riders were seated near the back end of the transport, one on either side of the main center aisle in staggered rows. The third passenger sat closer to the front of the transport, huddled up in his seat, facing aft with his eyes closed.

All things considered, maybe now was the best time to get some sleep, to bring myself down from the emotional high of both the assassination and escape. I leaned my head against the cushion and closed my eyes.

A klaxon blasted its obnoxious repetitive tone over the speakers. My eyes shot open and my nerves snapped right back into place. Rione appeared calm and collected at first glance, but one look into her eyes was all it took to figure out how frantic she was. That only cemented my own fear.

Someone had found us.

Chapter Twenty

The transport decelerated as the elderly ticket-taker lifted a sphere transmitter out of his pocket. "Is there someone who can tell me what's going on?"

The responding voice was tinny over the transmitter. "Have all passengers remain on-board. We're dispatching a squad to your location."

The old man became frantic, with no good reason for it. He wasn't the one in the crosshairs of a government death squad.

"Time to get out of here," I mumbled to Rione.

"There's no place to hide from them down this track."

The old man spoke into the sphere. "Is there anything I should do in the meantime?"

I didn't have any idea what sort of help the old man thought he could render, but the response came quick. "Just keep the passengers on the transport. The squad will take care of the situation."

"We need to leave now!" I demanded.

Another look at the other passengers showed all three of them now awake. They glanced around the compartment, attempting to figure out why their regular plans were being disrupted.

We finally came to a full and complete stop. Rione whispered behind me, “We’ll have to take over the transport.”

“Shouldn’t be too hard,” I offered.

“Follow my lead.”

I did exactly that as Rione stood. She called out to the ticket-taker. “What’s going on here?”

“Stay in your seats. Someone will be along to sort things out.”

Rather than abide by his instructions, she stepped into the aisle and marched to the front. “We have important business. Why can’t they take care of this at our destination?”

I had this sinking suspicion the death squad was going to ‘take care of’ every person on this transport, away from the public eye. The old man jumped into the aisle with a feeble attempt to confront us. “Stay in your seats.”

Rione again defied his orders, starting toward him. “We can’t afford to stick around here waiting who knows how long for the government to show up. It’ll take even longer for them to figure out what they’re supposed to do once they arrive.”

Someone in the back joined in, but sadly not on our side of the argument. “Just sit down and wait like the rest of us.”

Rione and I continued forward instead. The old man barked into the transmitter. “I have a male and female becoming combative.”

“Subdue them. Use of deadly force is authorized.”

There was no more doubt, in anyone’s mind, who the troops were after. Rione sprinted, catching everyone off-guard, including me. The old man grabbed at a phase pistol hanging from his belt, and pulled it free a moment too late. She yanked it from his grasp and shoved him back down. He let out a yelp as he hit the cushion.

She turned to me. “Get up to the control room. You’ll have to manually override the automatic controls.”

"On it." I raced forward.

Meanwhile, Rione addressed the rest of our fellow travelers. "There's a slight change of plans. Everyone off the transport."

"Here?" I heard someone object.

The phase pistol blast echoed. "Any other objections?"

Moving through the hatch into the vestibule, I took one look at the compartment's front and pulled on the door marked 'authorized personnel only.' It didn't budge.

I looked and saw my problem. A small scanner plate rested beside the door, with a red light warning me off. I called back to Rione. "Need something to open the door."

She leaned down to the would-be guard. I heard the old man mutter objections to his treatment before the phase pistol echoed again. She turned and tossed his badge through the air before turning her focus on the two remaining passengers.

I caught the badge and swiped it in front of the scanner. The light turned green and the hatch popped loose.

Rione's commands continued behind me. "Now, take these two and get off this transport. Do it yourself, or you can be dragged off unconscious. Your choice."

I stared around the cramped control room. A padded stool sat empty at the center. There may have been a need for it before the entire operation became automated. I sat and stared out the forward viewscreen at the hewn-out rock before us. It went on forever, beyond even the reach of the transport's light beams, another unnecessary artifact from times long since past. It would come in handy now.

"Passengers are off. Let's get this heap moving." Rione's bellow broke me out of my trance, and I glanced around the sparse control room. The single throttle slider sat on the right. A big red button with 'emergency stop' plastered on top rested at the dead center of the dashboard. I grabbed hold of the cold, metal handle and pushed the throttle forward with no effect.

I cursed under my breath and tried to find the solution. There was nothing in plain sight atop the console, so I dropped to the floor and looked underneath.

After a few moments of frantic searching, I finally found what I was looking for. Tucked into the side plates, I found a small tee handle. Through the power of deductive elimination, I twisted it counter-clockwise and the transport jolted forward. A mechanical voice called over the speakers. "Manual override engaged."

Jumping back into the seat, I grabbed the throttle and Rione called out to me from the other compartment. "Thanks for the heads-up!"

I didn't bother responding, instead taking in all of the additional gadgets which had now revealed themselves in the console before me.

A cover plate had rolled out of the way, exposing a display screen just below the emergency stop button. It plastered our position on a small map of the nearby tunnels. The viewscreen flashed before various numerical parameters appeared. Most of the accompanying words were in Torian, which did me absolutely no good.

Fortunately, Rione walked in behind me while the transport settled to a constant velocity. "You ever handle one of these before?"

I laughed.

She glanced down at the tunnel schematic. "Looks like it shouldn't be much longer to reach our destination."

A voice broke out of nowhere. "What is happening over there? We've detected the manual override being engaged, and the transport is moving."

I glanced over at the sphere transmitter in Rione's hand. She smirked. "Figured it might come in handy."

"Respond," the voice commanded.

"Guess you'd better do what the man says," I said while turning back to the map.

"I'm afraid we simply must arrive at our destination."

There was a slight pause. "Who is this?"

Rione toyed with them some more. "I'm afraid that information is classified."

"Well, whoever this is should know another squad of troops has been dispatched from the opposite direction. We'll catch you even before you reach the station."

Rione switched the device off and tossed it to the floor. I cursed under my breath. Things were finally getting back to normal, and the timing couldn't be worse.

I turned to face Rione. "What other options do we have?" Our odds were minimal at best. At worst, I didn't even want to fathom the possibilities.

She stared ahead, her forehead creased. "I have no idea."

Frantic, I looked at the digital tunnel map. I mentally traced the path we were on, looking for anything we may have missed. At this point, I was covering any piece of ground, even the obvious.

A small stub off the main tunnel caught my attention. The coloring was barely different from the background color that indicated the solid rock we tunneled through, which was likely why I'd not seen it earlier. Even now, I didn't truly know what I was looking at.

"What's this?" I pointed for Rione's benefit.

She stared, then drew closer and squinted. "Almost looks like a track they don't want anyone to know about."

That wasn't as definitive as I would have liked, but it would have to do. Our time was running out, and fast. The round green dot representing our transport was closing on the stub rapidly. A red dot appeared on the map's track farther ahead of us, and had to be the troops heading us off.

"Guess we'd better hope for the best, then." There didn't seem to be any controls beside the throttle lever and emergency stop. That left touching the screen as my only option.

I pressed the faded area where the other tunnel showed. A loud buzz filled the compartment and I jerked my hand away. A mechanical voice spoke over the compartment speakers. "This is not your current travel path."

Finally, a breakthrough. I pushed the track in front of us and a green arrow appeared ahead of the transport dot. I didn't know what to do from here, though. I lifted my hand and my mood soured as the arrow disappeared. I pressed it again.

"Now what?" Rione asked.

"I have no idea." But then a thought sprang into my head. I dragged my finger along the tunnel path, breaking off onto the faded tunnel. The screen blanked monetarily, causing me a moment's disappointment before two buttons. The mechanical voice returned. "Your proposed route change involves a tunnel currently under construction. Do you still wish to change your current route?"

Being as the buttons contained Torian symbols, I turned to Rione. "Which of these is 'yes'?"

She knew our time crunch as much as I did, and reached past to push the left button. "Acknowledged. Adjusting current route," the voice told us. The map returned to normal, and the green arrow moved to the construction tunnel, flashing a few times before disappearing.

I caught sight of the tunnel opening in the viewscreen, just a moment before we turned off the main passageway and shot into the hole.

And then, just as fast, I saw warning signs posted along the tunnel walls. Again, Rione had to provide a translation. Her face went pale. "Tunnel's not finished."

It wasn't unexpected, considering the aforementioned construction. Still, we couldn't continue down this path.

"Should we stop the transport and get off?" I mused.

"We'll be trapped down here."

Looking back down at the map, I knew we were running out of time. Fast approaching the end of the line, there wasn't an opportunity to come up with a better option.

Or was there?

I grabbed her hand and bolted down the long corridor for the back. She didn't resist, at least not physically. "Mind cluing me in?"

I kept up our rapid pace. "We're going to jump."

She broke herself free from my grip and snagged our duffel bags. "Are you crazy?"

"What better escape than make them think we're dead?"

I kept moving toward the far aft door of the transport. "You've lost it, flyboy," she stammered.

"We jump off the transport, and they'll think we died in the crash."

"Except we'll be standing there when they find it."

I exited out the door into the aft vestibule, then faced her. "If you've got a better plan, share it."

She didn't, I could tell by her concerned look. Turning back to the still-closed transport door, I swiped the guard's passcard in front of the nearby scanner. A wild vacuum sucked at the compartment, and had I not grabbed a safety rail beside the door, it would have pulled me out the opening. Rione's body pressed against my own, until we found stable footing.

"So, your brilliant plan is to jump out of a moving transport?"

"As brilliant as any of my others." Which unfortunately wasn't saying much.

"Hopefully a tad more."

I looked out on the fast-moving ground below, and even I didn't know how I expected this plan to work. We were on a path with destiny, though, and there was no turning back.

Rione had a moment of hesitation, then shoved the bags into my hands and jetted for the passenger compartment. I complained, "What are you doing? We don't..."

"Trust me. I'm improving on your plan."

I watched her bend over a seat. My attention was diverted by the viewscreen filling with an approaching wall of unexcavated stone. I screamed out. "We have to go. Now!"

Rione yanked up one of the extra-wide seat cushions and was running for me and the open door.

"Hang off the back," she exclaimed.

It took a moment for her words to register, but when they did, I climbed out onto the ledge and grabbed hold of the ladder rungs. Without warning, she crawled between me and the transport, holding a seat cushion.

"Grab hold."

It was getting easier to take her orders. With her body pressed against my own, there wasn't much objection to wrapping my arms around her.

"Jump!" She kicked her legs out and jumped off the transport, sandwiched between me and the cushion.

The pod sped down the tunnel as we bounced. I didn't imagine Rione had done this too many times, but she controlled our movements, keeping us from wiping out.

As our makeshift life raft settled and slid along the ground, the transport struck the wall and exploded in a wide expanse of flame and debris. Waves of heat washed over us as we skidded to a halt.

I climbed off Rione and she jumped to her feet. "Find someplace for us to hide." I scrambled for the tunnel's right side. Meanwhile, she raced over and tossed the cushion into the flames. Hiding the evidence wouldn't matter, though, if we didn't find a way to disappear.

I scoured the walls for any sign of an opening. Rione sprinted to the other side to conduct her own search. Heat grew with the flames and sweat rolled down my face. I blinked away the dampness and continued the search. Hands groping along the rock, the sound of boots in the rocky dirt echoed down the corridor. I turned and saw a faint light probing the darkness.

"They're on their way," Rione called out to solidify what I already knew. I doubled my efforts, drawing closer to the destructive flames and heat.

I hit pay dirt as my hand and then my arm disappeared into a deep crevice. "Here!"

I heard her feet crunch as she ran toward me. Upon more investigation, the opening was just wide enough for us to climb in sideways. Voices from our pursuers grew louder. I didn't know how much room there was, but we didn't have an opportunity to find something better. Our bags between our legs, we squeezed in the gap.

"That's all we've got," Rione commented, coming to a stop. I still had a little bit to go before I could make myself virtually invisible, so pushed closer. Residual heat built between our bodies, fanned by the flames.

The voices were louder now, light beams glancing off the walls. Right then and there, I wished we would have found a way to smuggle weapons on-board the transport at the station.

Troops wandered into view and kept coming, one after the other. Weapons wouldn't have mattered. There were too many out there for us to have taken on by ourselves.

They were cautious while stepping closer toward the heat and flames. Each was set up in a set of golden body armor, their joints covered with black flexible material. Faces were completely protected with a sealed helmet, their visors reflecting the flames. My nerves went on edge as I heard a synthesized humanoid voice. "Search the area."

I held back a curse. Dozens of troops spread out in all directions. Though the assassination attempt on-board the orbital station had made it clear enough, reality finally sank in. These people would do everything in their power to kill us.

One particular soldier ventured off in our direction, and I realized my time should be spent figuring out how to get the jump on them first. We'd need to wrestle weapons away from two of them, then find a way to escape back down the tunnels without getting killed in the process.

In other words, we were screwed.

As the soldier drew closer, it became obvious I was in no position to gain control of his weapon. We'd picked this particular crevice for its prowess as a hiding spot, not for its tactical advantage.

I held my breath as he reached the wall, scouring it the same way I had earlier. There was no chance he wouldn't find the same crevice. And even though we were tucked away out of sight, I had no doubt his arm would reach as far as mine had. Then he'd be groping my chest and we'd be caught.

I felt Rione's body against my own. There'd be nowhere to hide from those miniature blast rifles. My mind raced as his hand reached the opening. There was no doubt in my mind we were caught.

Chapter Twenty-One

As his fingers probed our hiding spot, an explosion rocked the tunnel. Screams echoed, as balls of fire billowed past. Dirt and rock fell everywhere, including onto my face. I stopped myself from blowing it off.

Outside, the situation was far worse with even larger rocks falling. Bodies rested all over the floor, immobile. The synthesized voice returned from beyond my field of vision. "Tunnel's collapsing. Fall back!"

The guard's gloved fingers were right in front of my face and he decided not to disobey a direct order, yanking back. As they all bolted away from the exploding transport, I let go of a held breath.

Rione and I weren't out of the woods yet, even as the voices raced away. Debris continued falling, and each stone dropping in the main tunnel was larger than the last.

"Do you think it's safe to run yet?" Rione asked.

"It has to be safer than staying here." With that, I slithered out of our hiding space, dodging falling rocks as they grew and multiplied. Rione and I scrambled away from the burning transport. Another explosion rocked the tunnel behind us, knocking us to the ground. The entire ceiling collapsed where we'd been standing just a short while earlier. Dirt and debris flew past, and once everything settled, I glanced back. Only a few paces separated us from a stone-covered tomb.

A pair of transports accelerated away nearby. We were out of danger, for the time being. Rione climbed to her feet, knocking the dust and dirt off her outfit. "Now that they think we're dead, maybe it'll be easier to get at our next target."

I followed her lead. "Can't hurt, I'd say."

"Let's hope we don't run into any more trouble."

I didn't respond, even though I had my doubts. Trouble found us whenever and wherever we went. Combined with my plan-making ability, it made for a deadly outlook on life.

Instead, I simply followed along behind her.

• • •

Ironically enough, we didn't come across another transport or band of troops the entire jog along the now-destroyed spur line to Icthus. My feet were killing me, and I couldn't wait to find a nice, quiet spot to rest.

"Hope you have a spot to clean up once we get where we're going," I commented as we entered another vast chamber that looked identical to the first. Maybe we'd gotten turned around in the tunnels and returned to where we'd been. That was entirely possible, for all I knew, and would have definitely been a problem.

"Unfortunately, we don't have a safe house here."

I stopped dead in my tracks. "Where do we plan on staying, then? I'm sure even Torians notice people living on the streets."

Rione started walking. "I assume you brought enough credits to foot a hotel bill."

I sighed, and resumed my pace. "I suppose so." With my basic need of shelter now covered, I really needed a drink. Idly, I wondered if Vladirian liquor was present here, too.

Rione stopped and glanced around. I was suspicious. "You do know where you're going, I hope."

She grimaced. "I have to get my bearings."

I glanced off to the left, where illuminated signs told me what she needed to know. "Aren't those hotels?" I pointed.

She started off in that direction, without a word of thanks. Before I could comment, she continued. "Just wanted to make sure we wouldn't be too far away from the palace."

And just like that, a reminder of what we'd come here for. More killing.

We climbed out of the short trough as soon as we could, and made our way along concrete sidewalks bordering paved roadways. Where the streets of the first city had been lined with pedestrians before, hovercrafts ran back and forth here. Citizens regarded us with disdain as we passed. I hadn't yet seen my face, but my clothes were disgusting. Given Rione was a filthy mess all over, it served to reason I wasn't any better off.

Still, this much attention wouldn't be good for either of us. I leaned close and muttered, "I hope we're getting off the streets soon."

"Around the next block."

Having a goal in such close proximity made me pick up the pace, and the two of us rushed along the path until we finally reached the front doors of a rather non-descript clay building. The rest of the city may have helped its image, because otherwise it didn't look too much different than the hovel we'd used during the first assassination.

At least on the outside.

When we stepped inside, all thoughts of similarity were dispelled. Ornate Arcadian wood and Traliquin carpet lined every visible spot. Just as aversion had filled the eyes of every passer-by outside, the crowd inside the hotel stared at us with an extra dose of contempt.

To speed things along, I rushed for the main counter. Rione followed my moves step-by-step.

Once we reached the counter, a prim and proper Torian looked down his nose at us, the overhead lights glinting off his pale skin. “I believe you may have made a wrong turn outside,” he insisted.

I didn’t plan on dragging this out any longer than necessary. Pulling out the money case and flipping it open, the sight made him stare and completely blank on his dismissal. Money always made people a bit more tolerant. “We need a room for two, so we can get cleaned up, that sort of thing.”

“Right away, sir.”

While he turned to a terminal console, I glanced back into the lobby where we were still the center of attention. This wasn’t going well at all.

Rione interrupted the clerk’s search. “If we could get a room facing the park...”

He flashed a huge smile. “Oh, definitely.”

For a price, I was sure.

A few more moments passed, and I felt a flurry of stares burning the back of my neck. “Ah, here we are...” He picked up a pair of electronic passcards and scanned them through a reader. “Room six-fifteen should be everything you’re looking for. If not, just call and let me know.”

Then he relayed the price. I nearly passed out before handing over several coins.

Rione interrupted. “Let’s go ahead and pay for a second night. This seems like a nice place.”

I handed over a second set of coins. This would be an expensive mission. Hopefully we’d be successful, and make it worth whatever cost we paid. If we weren’t, though, I likely wouldn’t be living to worry about it.

“Very well,” the pompous clerk said, and handed a passcard to each of us. Motioning to our right, he hurried us out of his lobby. “Lifts are just down the corridor.”

My voice was low as we finally left the lobby and reached the bank of lift pods. "I hope people in the lobby don't remember us once we take care of business."

"I don't imagine the general public is going to be something we have to worry about. Government troops will be on high alert."

"Even if they think we're dead?"

"Make no mistake, security will be ramped up. They can think we're dead, but if this is all a rebel plot..."

That sobered me up quick. I really needed a drink.

One of the lifts opened, and we stepped inside the pod. Rione called out, "Sixth floor."

The rapid acceleration didn't seem nearly as intense after our recent excursions hurtling down through the upper atmosphere, then our chilling antics in the underground tunnels. This was rather tame in comparison.

"So, any idea how we're going to do this?" I kept the references low-key in case our conversation was monitored.

"I have a few thoughts," she said. I watched her face in the mirrored metal walls bordering the lift pod.

As we exited out onto the sixth floor, a sign across the wide corridor directed us toward our room. We sullied the beige carpet with our filthy shoes, which I was fairly certain had just been steam cleaned based on the damp, musty aroma flooding my nostrils.

Rione popped the door lock with her electronic passcard. We glanced back at the filthy trail we'd left.

"Maybe we should call housekeeping?" I offered.

"We'll be fine. I don't plan on sticking around here long after we take care of business."

I followed her in and shut the door. Lights sensed our presence and burst on. If there was any reason to consider our last hide-out a dump, this was it. A huge bed lay in the corner, with clean floors and a walk-in closet. The restroom to our right was full of shiny fixtures.

And then there was what we really needed, a shower cube.

But just like that, Rione stormed past. “I’ll be out in a bit.” She slammed the door, and her clothes hit the floor.

Beyond the barrier, the shower cube creaked open and closed, followed soon after by spraying nozzles. I dropped my duffel on the floor and walked across to the only window.

Pulling the curtains back just a bit, I peered out onto the city. Beyond the mix of residential and business buildings surrounding this hotel and others nearby, a makeshift park had been built. Fake grass had been brought in for aesthetic reasons from off-planet, and families played and enjoyed the scenery. It seemed so odd this many people would be oblivious to a civil war being waged.

I peered a little farther past the park, beyond even more commercial and residential zones, to the palace. I wished for a neutron disruptor so I could get a closer look through a targeting display.

Before I knew what was happening, the shower cube nozzles shut off beyond the closer door. I continued staring at the palace.

From this distance, it looked similar to the one used by the king’s younger son. Pale columns lined the front, with several large windows along each wall. For this one, though, the entire facility was U-shaped, with a huge parking area situated at the center of it all. Rather than a huge park surrounding it, as with his brother’s, this one was nestled tight into the surrounding neighborhood. A fence made up of black metal spires surrounded it all.

On top of the building, and at various places around the metallic fencing, troops patrolled, dressed in the same combat armor as we’d seen at the site of the transport explosion. It made sense. Even with the city’s relative calm, the elder prince had to know of his brother's death. Especially true, considering the level of security.

The door opened, drawing my attention back into the room. Rione exited out, now sporting a towel and nothing else. It hugged every curve of her body. I wished there was a way to set the shower cube on a colder setting.

I thumbed toward the window. "Are the security arrangements over at the palace normal, or do they know what's happened to Axyl?"

She moved over and peered through the curtains. I started for the shower, but before I reached the open doorway, Rione responded. "Looks like they've stepped things up. They don't usually have that many troops stationed at the palace."

I held onto the door frame and watched her still standing at the window. "So, does that impact our plans?"

I heard her sigh. "Somewhat. I'll see what I come up with while you get cleaned up." Being summarily dismissed, I closed the door behind me.

It wasn't until I stepped inside the shower cube and boiling streams took off layers of filth, dirt and debris that the enormity of what we'd accomplished hit me. We'd assassinated a government official. Justified or not for the fact they tried to kill us first, it was no small feat.

I leaned forward, my hands pressed against the back wall. If all went according to plan, we would kill off two more. I steeled myself toward the end goal. We had to go through with this. Not only were we in too deep, they would stop at nothing to kill us.

This was just like any other job I'd agreed to. Well, aside from the small fact I wasn't getting paid. And of course, it was risking my life far more than usual.

I'd started down this path to keep Rione safe as I'd been totally unable to do for Leah. A sigh crept across my lips as I shut off the cube. Yet again I'd let my loyalties blind me with respect to protecting myself.

Even knowing that, I wouldn't have changed my plans.

Chapter Twenty-Two

I stepped back out into the main room where Rione still stared at the palace. While I'd been cleaning up, she'd changed into clean clothes, a gray dress suit and slacks. I felt a bit under-dressed in my customary white tee-shirt and black pants. She still didn't turn around, even when I announced myself. "So, we're still under the same premise?"

"What's that?"

"You'll want to kill him face-to-face?"

She shook her head. "Too risky after the last time. His death is more important."

There was an awkward silence. I didn't realize she could overcome her bitter rage from earlier. I sure hadn't, even after I'd killed Lars.

"You're sure?"

"I want them killed. It won't happen if I'm dead." Whatever the reason, Rione being a bit more rational with her bloodlust was a bonus. "We need to get our hands on something that can strike from this range."

"Don't look at me. You made me leave it behind." It was too bad, too, because the neutron disruptor would have been perfect in my opinion.

"I know some spots in town that'll have what we need."

Running around the city didn't sound like a great plan, now that we were in the safety of a hotel room. "You think it's wise when they'll be on alert?"

"We'll blend in, don't worry." She finally looked at me, and grimaced. "Well, maybe once we get you fitted with something more appropriate."

I frowned. "When are we planning on heading out?"

"No time like the present." She turned for the door, leaving her gear behind. "Bring all the money you have."

• • •

We stepped out into the damp air of the surrounding cavern. Icthus was an odd contrast to the first city we'd visited. Electronic billboards were plastered on the sides of buildings, while a variety of hovercraft sped through the streets. It didn't fit with what I knew to be true, that these people were xenophobes who hated dealing with outsiders. All of this equipment couldn't have been manufactured on Toris itself.

I mumbled to Rione. "Why so different here?"

"Unlike his younger brother, Jabaz Wren actually has plenty of business sense. Axyl took money from most of his citizens under his governance, then squandered it. Jabaz, on the other hand, reinvested into infrastructure."

"But there's more than just infrastructure here."

We stepped around a corner and came to a stop in front of a storefront window where clothes were prominently displayed. She continued, "Jabaz knows complete isolation isn't the way to go."

Suddenly, I felt queasy. The whole notion of our plan was to bring a change in leadership. "So, why didn't we just kill his father and put him in charge?"

She shook her head. "Isolation from other species has always been only one part of the problem. He divides the citizenry into classes. The ones you see around here have it good, yes, but all of this was built using slave labor, Torian people who don't meet his standards."

"But slavery is illegal, even here, right?" That was the case everywhere else in the known galaxy.

"He doesn't call them that, but he keeps them in servitude by restricting their finances and giving them barely enough in basic needs to keep interplanetary rights groups happy."

"Nice."

She walked over and yanked the door open. "Now, let's get you into some more appropriate clothes."

After she mentioned it, I glanced around and noticed several return stares, so rushed inside the building behind her. Without the chance to say a word, Rione grabbed clothes off circular racks. Drowning out the conversations between a handful of customers and sales associates, an annoying musical number screamed out on overhead speakers. Staccato bass thumped in an awkward rhythm while it fought with an obnoxious drum solo, reminding me of the club where we'd first met Axyl. I tried tuning the music out, but it weaseled into my head and established residence.

Rione turned to me, all business. Maybe she could teach me how to ignore the destructive symphony raining down upon us. "Here, change into these." She shoved the hangars in my hands, then pointed toward dressing rooms in the back corner.

Walking off into the cramped little cube, she gave me one last bit of instruction. "We don't have time to waste, so get out here as soon as you're dressed again." With that, she slammed the door shut.

I quickly disrobed, the contrast between my natural skin and the bleached evident in the mirror. The business attire wasn't my style, but unfortunately for me, she was right. It was just like every other outfit I'd seen outside the store. We didn't have time to argue, so I squeezed myself into a light blue dress shirt and off-gray suit with matching pants.

Glancing in the mirror, I wondered if this type of outfit would get me classier jobs than the usual leather outfit I wore.

Knowing the spots I usually found work, I'd probably get myself shot. Given the price tags hanging from each item, my attackers would probably try to rip them off my corpse and sell it off to someone else.

Her harsh whisper came over the door. "Done yet?"

"Keep your pants on," I muttered and opened the door to reveal my new look.

She nodded. "Much better." I shut my mouth, still feeling out-of-place even if it didn't look that way.

"Come on. Let's get this over with." I scurried toward the front of the store, where checkout registers waited. The quicker we were out of here, the sooner we'd be on our way, and the faster I could get out of this stupid outfit.

The young woman who waited on us gave a sly smile, which didn't sit well with me. Neither did the amount she rattled off for the price of this single set of clothes.

Grudgingly, I handed over a pile of coins. It ripped out part of my heart with every golden-rimmed piece that hit the metallic counter.

As I set the last one down, and she rang up a receipt, Rione caught me off-guard with a fierce whisper into my ear. "Oh, crap. There he is."

I whipped my head toward the front windows. Across the street, a tall, sculpted beast exited a luxury hovercraft through its gull wing door.

"Your receipt, sir."

I turned back to the cashier, muttering a quick word of thanks, before Rione and I rushed for the front door. "What's he doing here?"

"I don't know," she insisted.

Odd happenstances were one of those things that you could never count on. They certainly happened a lot more often than you'd think, especially to me.

We stepped out onto the sidewalk, amidst the hustle and bustle of the citizenry. The crowd recognized Jabaz immediately, and if not for a quartet of burly guards clearing the area, the elder prince would have been mobbed.

He was a man on a mission, and I barely noticed as Rione started down the sidewalk, matching his pace on our side of the street. I rushed to catch up.

"We don't have the tools we need," I reminded her.

"I don't plan to do it here in public. I'm just scoping things out."

He ducked into a building, a jewelry shop according to its nondescript signage. "Is he a playboy like Axyl?"

Her voice was distant as she focused on the prince. "Not according to my sources."

I watched through the front plate glass windows as the chiseled young man didn't bother browsing. Instead, he rushed up to an older Torian sitting at the counter. There was no fear or awe in the shopkeeper's actions as he retrieved a black box from below the counter.

"Well," I muttered, "I don't imagine he's buying that for himself."

Rione didn't have an answer. She jerked her head around at the crowd around us. "We should get moving."

I wouldn't argue with that. Jabaz pounded the pavement back to his vehicle while we continued down the street. The prince's hovercraft jerked around the corner, racing past us. "Maybe we should just sabotage his hovercraft, and he'll take himself out," I offered.

"We'll get him soon enough."

We wandered around a while, leading me to debate whether my companion knew where she was going. At least she'd made the right choice with the outfit, as no one paid me any attention now. Rione, on the other hand, received more than a fair share of glances from male Torians.

All of this wandering around aimless became too much for me. "Is there a point to all this walking?"

"Can't make it easy on you," she said. "Really, though, I'm just trying to get my bearings. It's been a while since I've visited Icthus."

"Well, hopefully you find a landmark before long."

"Not to worry, it's becoming familiar. As long as my contacts haven't pulled up roots since I last saw them."

"Let's hope not." I didn't know how long she'd been out of touch. With the king having momentum on his side with the spy satellite, and now the most recent massacre, it would have been hard for any rebel sympathizers not to go into seclusion.

As we walked down another sidewalk, Rione brought herself close. "There's a small bakery on the left. Follow me in, and I'll do all the talking."

I peered up at the small shop she mentioned. From the lights on inside, it looked open. That was a good sign.

We ducked inside, and my nostrils were assaulted by the warm aroma of breads and pastries. It reminded me of my childhood, where the local baker took pity on me and my two brothers; three orphan boys who constantly struggled to keep our family home.

An elderly Torian stood up behind the counter. His voice oozed apathy, and I wondered if he'd taken over the shop since Rione last visited. "May I help you?"

A smile crossed the vixen's face. "I'm searching for something special, a spicy Olera bread in particular."

His forehead and nose scrunched, then he lifted an eyebrow. "It's dangerous to eat such things."

Disappointment flooded her voice. "You no longer make it, then?"

A weak smile formed. "I didn't say that. We do have a few loaves remaining, if you'd like to look through our selection."

The old man climbed off his stool and exited through a swinging door in the back wall. He held it open for Rione, but held a hand up as I tried to follow.

Before either he or I could say a word, Rione interrupted. "He's with me. You might say he's a friend of the family."

He studied my face a few moments, then laughed under his breath. "I did not recognize him as easily."

I stepped through the open doorway, saying, "Glad the disguises are doing their job."

"They're very convincing," he responded. "I don't believe I've ever seen such expert work." He looked ready to touch my face. Fortunately, he thought better of it.

Rione spoke up as he led us into the back. "Technology has advanced a lot."

"It always tends to."

The smell of yeast billowed from along the wall counter. If I hadn't known better, I would have thought we were really back here to try out the bread Rione mentioned.

Instead, the older man walked to the center of the room, pacing his steps. Glancing down at the floor, he tapped his foot and I recognized what he was doing a moment before the floor's response grew hollow. Satisfied, he lifted his foot and slammed it down one last time. Gears ground and a set of stairs formed down into the darkness.

He reached into a drawer and pulled out a small stick. Shaking it back and forth, the device lit up bright blue, before he handed it over to Rione. “I believe you’ll find what you need. Just let me know when you’re done.”

She gave him a slight hug. “Thank you. We’ll make it quick.” One more look at me to make sure I understood the gravity of her promise, and she raced down the steps. I followed into the enveloping darkness.

Mold and mildew permeated every crack, crevice and hole in the small concrete chamber we walked into. The stench overpowered me and made my head ache as soon as I stepped off the last stair. If there had been any doubt about the older man before, the sight before us erased any of it from my mind.

Weapons of all kinds hung along the walls. Rione rushed through, giving each one a brief glance. My eyes, though, focused on the far wall where I saw another neutron disruptor. I snatched it off its pegs.

Rione caught sight of my movements, and chuckled to herself. “You’ve found true love over there?”

Nothing would take the place of my trusty Mark II, but there were plenty of times I could use a device like this. Our current situation was one. She grabbed a pair of phase pistols, two knives and a short-barrel scattergun. “Expecting trouble?” I asked.

I walked over and grabbed a scattergun of my own as she responded. “I expect to run into it during our escape.”

I hadn’t even thought that far ahead. Grimacing, I figured she was right. I slung the neutron disruptor over my shoulder and joined her.

“How are we carrying all of these around the city?”

Pulling open some drawers at her waist, she revealed duffel bags that would work for our purposes. I didn’t know if they’d help or hinder us for blending into the crowd, but we shoved our stash inside anyway.

Rione led me back up the steps into the shop’s back room. The older man stuck his head past the door frame. “I trust you found everything to your satisfaction." Without warning, the steps rose back to floor level.

Rione responded. "A wondrous selection. Thank you."

"I hope they bring you great satisfaction."

We stepped into the front room. "They should."

"Say hello to our fair prince when you see him."

That halted us both. We turned to face him and Rione stammered, "Why would you think we'd see him?"

A twinkle glinted in his eye. "I've heard reports our youngest prince was discovered dead in his bed."

"We've heard the same," she said, avoiding facts.

"Following the orbital station bombing, it makes an old man wonder if both sides are raising the stakes."

We couldn't get into a discussion about our plan here and now. I put a hand on Rione's arm. "We need to go."

She smiled at the old man. "Not to worry, our days of civil war will soon come to a close." He nodded his approval as we scrambled out the door.

Pulling the duffels close to our body, Rione and I started down the sidewalk. As I'd figured, the extra luggage garnered a few more glances from passersby than we'd received after updating my wardrobe. It didn't help we were rushing along faster than anyone else, either.

I let Rione take the lead, presuming she knew how to return to our hotel. Surroundings became more familiar as we continued along, rounding corners and crossing intersections. I glanced up and saw our hotel standing a few blocks away. A moment later, I nearly slammed into Rione from behind.

"What are you doing?" I stammered under my breath. "We're almost there."

"Trouble." She moved aside.

Up at the next corner, a handful of troops in familiar golden armor and automatic blast rifles glanced through the crowd. An armored hover-transport pulled up onto the sidewalk. Another guard stood on the back. Both of his hands held a huge plasma cannon's handles.

Trouble was an understatement.

We ducked into a small entrance to a business that had long since closed down. I gave one more glance at the squad, who focused on the intersection they were stationed beside. "Guess they found out we didn't die in the blast. What now?"

"I don't know."

I glanced back and forth along the street, contemplating our next move. Then another squad took up residence on the last corner we'd passed. Getting Rione's attention, I nodded in that direction. She cursed.

One thing was for certain. I commented, "We can't just stay here. We'll stand out."

She turned her eyes upon me. "Just as much as if we walk through one of those corners."

"Think they know what we look like?"

"Even if they don't, we're carrying these packs."

There had to be some way to get out of this mess without getting blasted by those massive plasma cannons.

Another clothing shop sat across the street and the wheels inside my head rolled. I didn't bother letting it get any momentum, instead grabbing Rione's hand and sprinting across the street. She started objecting, but realized my intentions and clamped her mouth tight.

Someone else opened theirs. "You there! Stop!"

I didn't bother looking, nor did I obey. My feet sprinted over the opposite sidewalk.

"Stop where you are, in the name of the law!"

We hurried our pace.

"Stop or we'll open fire!"

Chapter Twenty-Three

I broke into an all-out sprint with Rione. I wasn't sure if the troops would open fire in a crowd, but I wasn't about to find out. We burst through the door and thankfully didn't have glass shot out behind us.

"Can we help you?" A young woman sorting through empty hangars greeted us as we rushed in through the door.

"Just browsing," I commented, running past without a clue what to do.

I eyed the rest of the store as we sprinted through the main aisle. Clothes, clothes everywhere I looked. A set of dressing rooms was planted in the far corner, with swinging doors at the back wall. There was nowhere to hide in this main room, so I guided Rione toward the doors.

"Hope there's a way out," I muttered.

Other shoppers ducked out of our way as we passed them all. They stared at us wide-eyed as if we'd just escaped the insane asylum.

The front doors slammed open as we reached the back wall. Yells and screams from customers and troops alike filled the room, but I didn't bother looking. I really didn't need to see the odds we faced, because there was no way it would fill me with any hope.

They gave another useless order. "Stop where you are!"

We bolted through swinging doors. Boxes rested on sheet metal racks, and spare clothes hung off shiny rods. The one thing we needed, though, was an outside door. I didn't see one anywhere.

Rione pulled my arm and we scrambled toward a ladder nestled in the nearest corner. "Where's this go?" I asked, a moment before realizing it really didn't matter.

She ignored the question, grabbing hold of the rungs and scrambling inside a covered cylinder above. I had no choice but to do the same, while troops thundered along the shop's tile floor in the first room.

Voices rang out below, expressing their confusion about where we'd escaped to. Rione shoved a metal door out of the way. It creaked its objection while flooding the tube with light.

"In there," someone shouted below.

Rione scrambled out onto the roof. I had a few more rungs to go, moving as fast as my hands and feet allowed.

The same voice echoed up the shaft, louder. "Give me that repeater!"

My eyes went wide. I raced up the final rungs and flipped over the lip of the tunnel. Blue beams of energy raced past in constant succession, the tube vomiting its contents up into the moldy cavern above. It would have made for a dazzling light show, aside from the fact they'd meant it for my death.

Rione pushed the metal cover back over, followed shortly by muffled screams from below as energy beams ricocheted down the tube. The wily young vixen grabbed the neutron disruptor out of my bag and pointed it at the hinge. With a point-blank shot, it melted into a useless piece of scrap metal.

"Let's go." She shoved the weapon back into my own hands and pulled a scattergun out of her duffel.

"Go where?" I climbed to my feet.

She raced for the rooftop edge. "Back to the hotel."

I stared at her long locks bouncing with every step. She couldn't be serious. "You don't think they'll find us?"

She accelerated without response, before jumping off the side. My eyes were wide, knowing I had to do the same. While sprinting after her, I only hoped I wouldn't plummet to a quick and painful death.

I planted my foot and tossed myself into the air like a child playing schoolyard games. Wind rushed past my face, and just as quick as I'd left the first rooftop, my feet landed on the next. I barely kept from rolling over.

"Run!" Rione yelled, as if we had another option.

I ran after her as we made our way for the next rooftop edge. With confidence under my belt, this one went even smoother. As we landed, shots rang out behind us, echoing whines chasing while weapons recharged. This third rooftop became a pool of debris as the shots missed and reddish-brown stones jumped into the air.

Rione switched directions and raced for a small outbuilding atop the roof. I glanced back and saw about a dozen troops who'd finally bypassed our makeshift blockade.

Rione ran for the structure, flinging open the metal door with me right on her heels. We jumped down the stairs two a time, the steps blurring as we rushed several stories to the ground floor. All the while, I expected to hear troops above and below us, trapping us between them.

Rione didn't seem concerned, as she reached the ground floor and burst out into another room. Offices, cubicles and other such bastardizations of life itself waited for us, the grand entrance garnering several confused reactions. Torians jumped to their feet to look over the short cubicle walls at us as we raced past.

I voiced my worry between short breaths. "Think they're waiting on us?"

"Only one way to find out," Rione exclaimed as we burst out into the lobby. To my surprise, not a single soldier was nearby. In fact, even the corner we'd seen earlier was now void of any military presence. It was hard to believe the king's side of the conflict was winning this war, considering their lack of tactical planning. We hurried to hide our weapons back in the duffels, to avoid scaring the crowd outside.

As we rushed out onto the sidewalk, voices yelled above. I glanced up, seeing troops still stationed on the roof a few buildings down. They hadn't even built the courage to jump across the first chasm. They weren't looking in our direction, which was fine by me.

Rione slowed her pace as we merged into the growing crowd and continued toward our hotel.

• • •

I kept looking back over my shoulder, still seeing no sign of pursuing troops. We finally made it to the hotel, stepping inside and over to the bank of lift pods. Not a single person in the lobby looked at us, which boded well for our chances.

Only after we were inside a lift pod and on our way up to the floor did Rione finally speak. "That was too close."

I nodded my agreement.

She continued, "After this is done, we only have one more to take care of."

We exited out the doors into a plush hallway as the lift reached our floor. The beige carpet had been cleaned again. At least this time our shoes weren't befouling the hotel's pristine image. I couldn't say the same for what we planned to do later.

With a swipe of her electronic pass, Rione barged into the room and I followed. We dumped the bags on the bed, and Rione marched over toward the window facing the palace. "Get your weapon out. Let's get this over with."

I brought out the familiar neutron disruptor, unfolding its various appendages. By the time I walked beside her, she'd already pulled aside the curtains and I peered out through the targeting display.

The device was almost a part of me as I twisted the knob and zoomed in. "Any idea where he might be?"

"Try the open windows. It'll be the only way you'll see his face with that thing."

"There are a lot to pick from," I complained.

Rione's voice was closer, the heat from her body drawing close to my shoulder. "His living room's on the lower floor, just to the left of the main entrance."

That gave me a starting point. I pointed the targeting display as directed. Through the palace's glass windows reflecting glare from streetlights nearby, I saw several plush chairs and couches surrounding a holographic projector at the room's center. I zoomed closer and glanced around the large room. Empty.

I shifted the weapon left. A dining area, with a table set for a dozen, still didn't hold a single person. "You sure they didn't figure out our plan and escape while we weren't looking?"

Rione drew closer to the window. "No, if they'd figured it out, the prince would never have been allowed to travel the streets on his own."

"Maybe they figured it out after. We didn't see squads in the streets until a little bit ago." She didn't have a response, which made me worry. I responded under my breath. "I'll keep looking."

The next area with a set of windows was the kitchen, also empty of any life. There was an extended gap without windows between these last two rooms, though, and on a whim, I moved back to the adjoining section of wall between them. Rotating the knob, the display passed through.

Definitely an eye-opening experience.

Even through the distorted image, I could make out cabinets and countertops, what had to be a pantry area. Two darkened figures gyrated their hips in a rhythm that left no question what I was watching.

A smile crept onto my face. "I think I found him."

I eased back from the display, letting Rione take a peek at the pair in passion. "Well, at least we know who the jewelry was for."

"I certainly hope so. Either that, or it's to help someone else cope with this happening on the side."

The activity continued, and I had to hand it to Jabaz. He definitely had a lot of stamina. I was just glad I didn't have to listen in.

"One last fling before he dies. Fitting, I suppose."

I nodded at Rione's remark, but didn't plan on firing my weapon until he came out into the open. Certainly, I assumed it was him, but needed verification. The last thing I wanted was to kill some innocent guy doing not-so-innocent things.

Several more moments, and even I grew bored with the repetition. I almost mouthed off about Torian males and their apparent stamina, but clamped it shut when I remembered Malone. That was a can of worms I didn't want to open up here and now.

Finally, the two figures collapsed into a single blob against a counter. "About time," I muttered.

"So, thinking he's headed to the kitchen or dining room?" Rione was enjoying the show a bit much.

I went with it, trying to avoid thinking about the fact I'd be killing a government official in mere moments. "He has to be famished after all that. Kitchen."

As the two bodies separated, they decided to put me in my proper place, and started the other direction instead. "So much for that," I mumbled.

The man entered the dining room first, and I recognized him immediately from the brief encounter we'd had on the street. His confident strides were long as he stepped out of the concealed area. The fact his windows were uncovered did not prevent him from savoring the moment. Too bad it would be his undoing.

As I reached up to adjust the weapon for its upcoming duty, I glanced at the woman, who had a little more hesitation at public display of her nakedness. My eyes shot wide open.

A curse must have escaped my lips, as Rione butted in and peered at the video display. I worried her yell would alert our neighbors to something amiss. "That lying, scheming whore!"

She looked far different in the buff than she had when I'd last seen her, but there was no mistaking the facial similarities of Celine, Malone's former lieutenant.

In fact, in our last encounter, we'd assumed she'd been killed in the government death squads' ambush, same as Malone and the others had been. She was not only alive, but sharing intimate moments with one of the leaders of the government she'd sworn to overthrow. It didn't take much to piece together the facts.

We'd finally found our mole.

Rione was livid. "I'll kill her!"

I focused my attention back on the task at hand, centering the crosshairs on Jabaz. I hated to tell Rione, but after I shot the prince, I doubted I'd have the chance to get another shot off before Celine bolted.

She rummaged through bags behind me. I tried to maintain her focus. "Stick to the mission. The prince dies and we focus on the king."

"Change of plans..."

That drew my attention away from the window. Rione pulled out the short-barreled scattergun, along with two long blade knives, all of which she'd picked up at the bakery. She'd completely gone off the deep end. "What do you think you're doing?"

"I just told you, I'm going to kill her."

That wouldn't help our cause. "What happened to the idea that risking ourselves wasn't worth it anymore?"

"It became worth it again."

Glancing back at the video display screen, I cursed as the prince and his mistress left the dining room behind. I followed their movements as they traipsed into the living room and collapsed onto one of the couches. There hadn't been any sign of guards, most likely he'd instructed them to leave the pair alone. It almost made me believe we could infiltrate the palace and do the deed up close and personal.

But then I wised up. The best way to do it would be from a distance, just like I usually did on my ship. Nothing good would come from us testing fate.

We now knew exactly who the mole was. Trouble was, the plan needed to be back on course. "Once we take care of the prince, and then his father, we can come back for her."

"Malone's death is her fault. I'm going to kill her."

"It won't bring him back," I mumbled, even knowing it wouldn't stop her tirade.

Before she had a chance to respond, I blinked hard. Why was I trying so hard to dissuade her from carrying out this particular act of revenge? If I had Elijah in my sights, my rage would be as much, if not more. Especially since I'd sworn to kill him the last I'd seen him.

"I'm going to do this. Stay here or go with me, it's your choice," she told me.

I wasn't going to let Rione out of my sight, and had no intention of being an eye-in-the-sky this time around. I dropped my weapon on the bed, and grabbed a scattergun of my own. "Okay, let's do this thing."

Chapter Twenty-Four

Rione didn't bother waiting for the lift, opting once more for the stairs. She pounded down the steps, her billowing rage enough that I held myself back several steps to avoid the inevitable explosion.

I'd mistakenly believed her when she'd come to her senses during the first assassination. Instead, her bloodlust had curdled beneath the surface. Seeing Celine had boiled it over. Anger was a powerful motivator, but it made people do stupid things. None of us were immune.

We reached the ground floor, and I assumed the risk of speaking. "Have you come up with a plan for getting in? It's not like we can storm through the front door."

"Not if we look like we belong there," she commented without anything more. I still took it as a good sign she was actually thinking up a plan.

She pulled her jacket closed while exiting out into another alleyway, and I did the same. I wasn't sure it would completely hide the bulges where our scatterguns were tucked away, but no one on the crowded sidewalk was the least bit suspicious.

I mumbled, "Where to first, then?"

"A guard shack along the perimeter fence. It's where vehicles enter and exit the compound."

I lifted an eyebrow. "We're going to storm it?"

"Sort of."

Again, I left well enough alone, as we continued through the streets. We didn't run across any more death squad patrols, which was a pleasant surprise.

The clay station stood beside the compound's iron spire fencing. The lone guard standing outside took notice as we approached. Based on his apathetic facial expression and the fact he didn't lift his automatic blast rifle at us, he hadn't been informed who we were. Rione caught him completely off-guard when she pulled her scattergun out and slammed the butt first against his chest, and then across his temple.

The guard's knees crumpled and I helped her drag the body back inside the small outbuilding. She looked him over. "He's about the right size."

"For what?" I asked, right as I figured out the next step in her plan.

"You're going to capture me and take me inside."

"And if they're all under orders to shoot to kill?"

"Then hopefully we kill them first."

That didn't give me a good feeling.

She undid the uniform's buttons and zippers and handed his pants over. I ignored the fact she was watching me disrobe and quickly slipped into the pants, then a shirt. I wished we would have gotten the drop on one of the death squad troops, since they had better protection.

Soon, I was decked out in the new uniform. Rione looked over the outfit. "Well, it'll do for a while."

I realized a fatal flaw in our plan as I looked down at the outfit. "Where exactly am I supposed to carry your weapons? I'm certain they won't let you carry any."

She'd thought ahead that far, based on her quick response. "Just carry them on you. If anyone asks, tell them you collected them as evidence."

"And why am I bringing you to the palace instead of to the local jail?"

I slung both scatterguns over my shoulder and clipped the phase pistols and knives to my belt. Rione smiled. "The prince made himself the region's only judicial power. Judge and jury both. Guess that power grab will be his undoing."

Another kink in this fine plan's armor suddenly reared its ugly head as I picked up the guard's rifle. "Considering the reception we received earlier, won't they think it's odd I'm bringing you in instead of killing you on sight?"

She looked at me with scrunched eyebrows. "We'll have to cross that bridge when we come to it."

I always enjoyed plans where success relied on luck and seat-of-the-pants strategizing. Good thing, too, since most of mine followed that direction.

"Well, we're ready to go." I hoisted the dead guard's blast rifle up and playfully chided. "Move!"

She slammed her fist down on a big green button, which drove the gate open. After I pilfered a set of electronic restraints from the dead guard and placed them loose on Rione's wrists, we stepped through the sliding bars and headed up the blacktop toward the palace garage.

As we walked, several guards stood atop the palace walls, staring the two of us down. With a rifle trained on my 'prisoner,' none took any action.

Jabaz's garage was open, with several sporty hovercrafts sitting in wide stalls, all three sides held up by arched brickwork. My mind was already planning our escape using one of these beauties.

Two guards stood alongside the only doorway inside the garage. They were far more concerned about our movements than the guards outside had been. Both lifted their blast rifles.

"Halt!"

We froze, as the taller of the two pointed his weapon at me. "What do you think you're doing, bringing a prisoner in this way?"

Well, so much for our plan.

"I figured this way was faster."

"Well, it isn't. Since you've already brought her here, what's the charge?"

Thinking on my feet wasn't my most charming ability. "She was attempting to climb the fence."

"And you didn't shoot her?"

"I wanted to give her up to the prince."

Their eyes narrowed. The other guard jumped into the conversation. "You know the rules. Perimeter guards are to shoot trespassers on sight."

I kept my cool. It was time to adjust the plan, even if it meant revealing a bit more than we should have. "I believe this woman is one of the two responsible for the assassination of Axyl Wren."

They stared back at Rione in disbelief. The second guard retorted. "Did you see any sign of her accomplice?"

"No. She came alone." At least we knew they'd been informed about our past deeds.

"Well, then, we'll take her to the prince."

Only after one of the two moved forward and reached for Rione did I interrupt. "I can't let you do that."

His forehead scrunched. "And why not?"

Why not, indeed.

I only hoped I wasn't digging a deeper hole. "I'm fairly certain there's a reward for her capture. I wouldn't want there to be any mistake on who should receive it."

There was no telling whether a reward had been offered or not. The two guards gave each other confused glances.

Exuding confidence was the way to go. “So, I’m taking my prisoner to the prince now.” I motioned Rione forward with the rifle.

The guards formed a blockade. “Our orders are clear. No one but the prince enters through this doorway.”

Without a word, I turned the blast rifle to my left, firing a point-blank shot at that guard’s chest.

As his partner hit the ground, the second guard took a different tactic and sprinted a few paces for a big red button mounted to the wall. Rione dropped to the ground while I turned and fired, catching him just before he reached it. The shrill sound would get more notice.

“We need to hurry this along.” I removed the electronic restraints binding her hands.

“What in the world was that for?”

“They weren’t letting us in,” I stammered.

“Now we run the risk of someone setting off an alarm and rushing the prince away.”

Improvisation always led to problems. “Well, then, we’d better reach him quickly.”

Muttering curses under her breath, Rione grabbed both scatterguns off my shoulder, and we rushed inside. Fortunately, no one was waiting as we entered a narrow hallway. Closed doorways sat on either side, and I only hoped no one would check on the commotion as we sprinted for a set of stairs at the corridor’s far end.

Gauging from the quick glance I’d gotten through the video display, I assumed this led into the main entranceway.

Rione stopped short at the staircase and turned to me, dead serious. “Shoot anything that moves.”

I was glad to know we were both on the same page as far as planning. At least up to this point. "Let's go."

We scrambled up the staircase, reaching the completely empty front entry room. Expensive Arcadian wood floors and trim were neatly shined. A glass chandelier hung from the ceiling. Even with all of this, there wasn't a single guard stationed anywhere.

"Do you think he sent them all outside so he could be alone with Celine?" I pondered aloud.

The mere mention of the traitor's name sent her across the room, sprinting with anger. I had no choice but to follow, all the while keeping watch for anyone concealing themselves in the shadows.

As we entered the living room we'd seen from outside. Jabaz and Celine still lounged on the round leather sofa, completely bare-skinned and oblivious to our arrival. They made no move to cover their bodies, or protect themselves from their coming death.

Instead, Jabaz simply raised a glass of red wine to his lips and drank. He stared at us and merely stated, "I'm surprised it took you so long to show up. We've been expecting you."

Chapter Twenty-Five

Rione pulled the triggers on her scatterguns, but nothing happened. The same when I tried my blast rifle. I blabbered, "What the...?"

Jabaz smirked. "The latest in dampening technology. It won't allow weapons to fire until we shut it down."

It explained why they hadn't shown the least bit of fear. "You were expecting us?"

"Of course," Jabaz remarked. "After we heard of Axyl's murder, it was only a matter of time before you came here."

Rione spat her words. "He's lying."

He continued, "I have to say you've done a fine job of concealing your identities."

I blinked hard. "If you knew we were coming, why didn't anyone stop us?"

He laughed like a man gone mad, and maybe he had. "You two are fools. We had to appear mostly unguarded to draw you out. My guards are on their way this very moment."

"Well, then," Rione started, "I guess there's no point in drawing this out any longer." She pulled her knives out and launched them both in the blink of an eye.

Jabaz hadn't anticipated this. The blades buried in his chest, bluish-white blood flowing out. He screamed out in pain and agony, yanking them out. When he did, both wounds began gushing onto the couch. The knives fell beside him, as he gasped for his last breath.

Celine screamed, her naked body cowering away from the corpse she'd been fornicating with not long ago. I turned and watched the doorway, expecting guards to arrive. The only bright side was they'd have to shut down the dampening field to shoot at us, and at least we'd have a chance to return fire.

The sound of Rione's voice drew my attention back into the room again. "And you, how could you?"

I turned, watching her move around the holographic projector and stalk toward Celine. This wasn't the time. "We need to leave."

She grabbed both of her knives again. "Not until this witch dies."

"They're coming for us," I reminded her.

"I won't take long."

Celine scrambled away backward, keeping her eyes focused on Rione. "It was my only chance," she bellowed.

"Tell that to Malone and all those who died in that ambush," Rione seethed.

Commotion closed in outside. Once the guards saw the prince dead, capture wouldn't be on their minds.

Celine chided the woman set on killing her. "Are you an idiot? There's no way our puny rebellion would win."

"Then why join it?" She scraped the blades against each other.

"In the beginning, it felt right."

"And something changed?"

Her eyes narrowed. "I saw the truth. Our king and his sons are far too powerful and nothing would change that."

"You contributed to the deaths of over a hundred men, including Malone."

The traitor spat her words. "They all made a choice."

"And so did you," Rione retorted. "Now you die."

A pair of troops stormed in with automatic blast rifles in hand. I pulled my trigger, and thankfully someone had shut off the dampening field, as a series of shots dropped both where they stood. A moment later, two more eased around the doorframe, far more cautious.

"Let's go!" I bellowed out.

"One last thing," Rione grumbled. She rushed for Celine and sliced each knife across the traitor's throat. Bluish-white blood gushed from her neck and final shock was plastered on Celine's face. Rione wiped her blades clean on her pants before stowing them away.

Weapons fire rocked the room and I backed up fast. Dodging behind the holographic projector, we sought protection from the guards' weapons fire. Those in front yelled out to the others, "Prince Jabaz is dead!"

That intensified their resolve. I smiled. They'd tried to set a trap and it backfired. Of course, our efforts would be for nothing if we didn't get out alive.

I fired off continuous shots, and Rione did the same as we raced for the only other exit, through the dining room into the pantry. I tried not to think about what I'd seen Jabaz and Celine doing not all that long ago, as we ducked behind cabinets and fired off at targets beyond the doorway. Several fell where they stood, but they were replenishing their numbers with every passing moment.

"Hope you have a plan of escape." I fired additional blasts into the living room.

"Strange, I was thinking the same thing about you."

This was about as I figured. “Is there another way out that way?” I pointed toward the kitchen.

She fired, striking two guards who tried retrieving the corpses. “Wouldn’t count on it.”

“We need to reach the garage, which is blocked off.”

These later guards were far better shots, and the blasts came in greater frequency. I snuck a peek around the cabinet I used for cover, and more stormed into the room. Unfortunately, these weren’t palace guards, but death squads decked out in the golden body armor we’d already seen earlier. Too bad their brain power had been fully depleted by weapons training, or they may have caught us before. Of course, their inaction may have all been part of Jabaz’s ruse.

All in all, we didn’t have a choice. “Let’s go.” I ducked off into the kitchen behind us. She followed, dodging shots. Once inside, and ducking behind more cabinets, I studied the room.

We needed a plan.

There were wide windows I’d seen from our hotel earlier. Other than that, nothing stood out. Troops flooded into the dining room faster than we could drop them. We fired blasts through the pantry separating the two rooms, then I turned for another look. Besides the cabinets and countertops, there was a small, metallic door mounted waist-high in the back wall.

“There!” I pointed.

She looked, and without responding, bolted for the new destination. I followed, sending a flurry of return fire through the opening for good measure.

Rione pulled the door open. “Hurry,” she called.

I jumped inside the cramped compartment, and she scurried in after. A handful of troops bolted into the kitchen to locate us. Without warning, I fired off my blast rifle in their direction, dropping them all. She slammed the door shut and we slowly dropped down the pitch-black shaft on a motorized platform.

"Let's hope this is a way out."

I nodded, even though she couldn't see me. A motor mounted above us whined, straining to maintain our speed, apparently never meant to carry two grown adults. I only hoped we wouldn't plummet to our death.

"I suppose it's an empty celebration," I mumbled, "but at least we're one step closer to our goal."

"Trouble is, if Jabaz wasn't lying through his teeth, they know we're coming."

"We'll just have to come up with a better plan when we get to the king, then."

She took on a defeated tone. "If we make it out of here."

"We will," I said, though I wasn't convinced myself.

The platform finally came to a stop with a heavy clunk. The door popped open automatically, and Rione slammed it to its stop. "Guess we'd better keep these open. Don't need it heading back up."

She shoved one of her scatterguns vertically into the opening to keep the door from shutting while we climbed out into a dank, dimly lit cellar. The stench reminded me of the chambers we'd passed through on our arrival to the planet.

"So, any idea which way to go?" I pondered aloud.

"No clue," Rione responded and we each set off around the compact room to get a feel for what our next move was. Light levels slowly rose to give us visibility, as if the canned luminaries hanging from the ceiling were running on motion sensors. The room was about forty paces square, and filled with wine racks and other assorted shelves of cans and jars. Four walls fashioned from the decaying stone had no doors or other openings. A Traliquin rug rested on the floor, in the corner.

I moved along the wall, fumbling with my hands, but couldn't see any sign of another exit. "How does anyone get down here to retrieve this stuff for the kitchen?"

"Good question. I'm not seeing anything."

This wouldn't work if we had no other way out. "I'm certain they don't come down the same way we did."

"I don't know how else they'd do it," Rione muttered as she fumbled through the storage racks.

A sickening metallic clang echoed inside the chamber and both of us flinched. I sprinted over to the dumbwaiter and peered up the shaft. Another crunching sound hit and I saw light streaming across at the kitchen level.

I turned to Rione with fear in my eyes and voice. "They're busting the door open. We have to get out of here, now!"

"But where?"

There had to be some way people got into or out of this room. I just didn't see anyone, even servants, utilizing the dumbwaiter on a regular basis.

And that was when I laid eyes back on the Traliquin rug. I rushed over, knowing it had to be our way out.

"What'd you find?"

"Not sure yet," I told her, just before grabbing the edge and yanking to no avail. That made no sense. Who would put a rug down here in the first place, and then somehow permanently attach it?

The banging from the kitchen above continued, while I kept pulling. It was as if it wanted to come up, but something was preventing it. The edges were harder than the center, which had some give to it.

Rione rushed over, seeing my distress, and tried as well. "What in the world?" She commented.

I thought back. "Use a knife! Slice the center."

She pulled one out and cut down the center of the rug. As she moved along the rug, I pulled the flaps apart.

A voice carried down the shaft in a hollow echo. "We're through. Bring us some fragmentation grenades."

I cursed and dropped to the ground to search for our way out. We didn't want to be around for those grenades to drop in.

She stated the obvious. "We don't have much time!"

My hands gripped a large metallic ring. I pulled up and felt some resistance but exhilaration hit. "A door!"

I stood up, yanking with both hands. The door creaked and groaned as it lifted, revealing a small ladder. A grinding sound filled the chamber, as the rug fragments retracted toward the wall on an automatic track.

"Get in!" I demanded.

Rione bolted down the rungs and I oriented myself to follow, still holding the door upright.

Loud metallic pings rang out, like debris striking my hull out in deep space. Looking across the room toward the dumbwaiter shaft, several silver spheres bounced out into the room and fell with muted thuds on the dirt floor. Around the center circumference, green lights flashed in sequence, faster and faster.

My eyes went wide at the sheer number of grenades the death squads were using. They weren't planning on leaving anything to chance in sealing our demise.

"Go! Go! Go!" I yanked the door down. It smacked into me from above, striking my still wounded shoulder. The pain was intense, but I bore down and finally scrambled out of the way, just as the door fell into its spot. A moment passed, and a massive explosion reverberated in the chamber above. We weren't out of the woods yet, though, as the blast's magnitude rattled the rocks surrounding us.

I looked down but couldn't see Rione in the darkness below, so it was good when she called out. "I've got a floor down here, and a tunnel."

"Well, use it."

A few moments later, my feet touched down on the same floor that Rione had just found. It was a good thing too, because a moment after I had both feet on solid ground, the chamber above rocked again. This explosion was even larger than the one before. These death squad troops weren't leaving anything to chance.

"Run!"

"We'll be crawling. There's a tunnel," she said just before my face hit a rock wall and I fell on my butt.

This latest explosion had weakened the vertical tunnel above me enough to where a steady stream of rocks in increasing sizes fell. I scurried on hands and knees toward Rione's voice.

And then the area behind me collapsed, rocks and large stones smacking hard and fast against each other, followed by a deathly silence.

Chapter Twenty-Six

"There should be a light bar on your blast rifle," Rione told me.

I fumbled along the weapon's top with one hand. I flipped a rocker switch and bright bluish-white light filled the entire tunnel with an eerie glow.

I peered back the way from which we'd come, where a large pile of stones and rocks plugged the tunnel. In the pit of my stomach, I pondered what might have been. If we hadn't gotten out of the cellar when we did, or if the first blast had been strong enough to collapse our escape shaft, we would have both been sealed in a permanent tomb.

This assumed we hadn't.

I turned back toward Rione. Her face was covered in a blanket of dirt and dust, just as I assumed mine was. "You want to lead us out of here?"

"You've got the light," she mumbled. "Go ahead."

It was a tight fit, keeping the blast rifle against me as I squeezed past her and her scattergun. Our bodies passed in the narrow tunnel, and I looked into her eyes, catching an emptiness of despair that I hadn't expected.

I continued past her, then stopped. "Anything wrong?"

"I thought I'd feel different...better."

Reality hit me like the stream of rocks earlier. “Killing Celine, you mean?”

She nodded in the glow reflecting off the walls, which illuminated her like an ethereal being. “I figured it would absolve me of this guilt, killing her out of revenge.”

A lump developed in my throat. “I know how you feel.”

“It’s nothing close. I just feel empty.”

My lips formed a thin line. “Just remember we’re one step closer to our end goal.”

She let out a long drawn-out sigh. “I’m trying.”

I didn’t know how long we should stick around. “We should probably get out of here before they release another salvo of grenades. Don’t need to get buried alive.”

She looked down the tunnel “I just wish we knew where this went.”

“There has to be a reason for it. I don’t buy the fact that it was just used to keep servants from being seen.”

“Maybe it served two purposes, and Jabaz wanted an extra escape route.”

I peered down the corridor to the point where the light bar wouldn’t reach any farther. I found it ironic that a possible escape route for the prince was now being used as the same thing for those who assassinated him. “Only one way to find out,” I muttered.

“Lead the way,” she offered.

• • •

The tunnel went on forever, and without any idea of direction or orientation, it could have been a nasty trick sending us toward the planet’s center. What kept me going was the fact someone had planned this tunnel ahead of time. There had to be another end.

My back and leg muscles grew weary and sore. I turned and aimed the blue light toward my traveling companion. "Think we'll eventually get there?"

"I just hope there isn't a room full of death squad troops wherever we end up."

That was a sobering thought. Turning back down the stony rock tunnel, I redoubled my pace, even against my body's objections.

And then I thought I saw something up ahead. I turned back and handed the blast rifle and its light bar to Rione, who was understandably confused.

"Point this thing the other way. I think I see something."

She did as I instructed. With a little more darkness around me, I looked forward again. Despite the faint blue background cast upon the walls, I still made out a point of light up ahead.

I laughed with glee and turned back to Rione. "I think it's the end of the tunnel."

She looked past me and strained to see the same thing, before a smile finally came to her face. She returned the weapon to me and I strapped it over my shoulder. "Well, then, what are you waiting for?"

All grins, I raced down the corridor on my hands and knees. The point of light grew brighter and brighter as we approached, mirroring the hope inside of me.

"Almost there," I muttered.

I shut off the light bar, using the tunnel's end to guide us.

Once we'd reached the mouth of the tunnel, I rested there at the opening's lip, staring out into the small chamber. A cylindrical rocket-shaped vessel rested at the room's center, its clear canopy raised. Beneath it, a truss structure connected it to a set of rails leading to another tunnel along the side wall. Another doorway was hewn out of the opposite wall.

Rione released an abusive retort. "Move it, flyboy."

I crawled out of the tunnel and stood, stepping toward the doorway. Rione glanced around, taking in the rocket.

"The prince had quite an escape plan in place."

I gave a single laugh. "Which he never got to use." Peering into the next room, a metal ladder stretched up to a metal cover. Climbing up, there was no way to open it from the inside. This had to be the way servants made it to the underground cellar.

With no other option available to us, I walked back out where Rione studied the rocket.

The cockpit was empty of controls, aside from a big red button. A single seat rested inside. I glanced past her at the second tunnel. "I don't imagine we want to crawl anymore."

Rione shook her head. "We'll take this one in style. Well, at least as much style as this thing has."

I glanced at the single seat again. "I'd hate to point out the obvious, but there's only one seat and two of us."

She motioned me inside. "We'll improvise."

"I guess so."

I climbed into the cockpit, reclining in the seat before placing my weapon on the floor and buckling myself in. It reminded me of my time flying fighters in the Gryphon Defense Force, except I never remembered trying to shove two people into a single-seat cockpit. This was going to get interesting, and quick.

The situation didn't even faze Rione, who stepped into the cockpit, legs between my knees. Awkward didn't even begin to describe what I was feeling.

I was staring straight ahead and had a direct view of her chest, so was caught off-guard when I heard her grunt, "Oops!"

Rione grimaced. "Just bumped the button," she explained a moment before a klaxon sounded off in the chamber. The canopy began a slow descent, rotating down toward us. This wouldn't give us much of a chance to figure out the best position for the trip.

Rione was frantic, putting her hands up against the canopy in an attempt to stop the inevitable. Nothing would stop this rocket from taking us where it expected to. The engine at the back fired to life, catching us both unaware. I grabbed both armrests on my chair and then immediately watched in shock as Rione was thrown off-balance and landed on top of me. Without any more resistance, the canopy slammed shut and the rocket launched off into the tunnel.

Even with my past training, the walls were too close for comfort, making me ill as we raced along. I focused on Rione's face a breath away. A dim orange light was embedded into the canopy sill. Even disguised as a Torian, her features were all the ones I knew.

Her face contorted in confusion as we gazed into each other's eyes, the rest of the universe fading away. Completely oblivious to the fact we were one step away from assassinating the entire ruling family of a sovereign planet, our breathing increased and I felt the heat from our bodies building. It was just Rione and I in that cramped compartment, huddled against each another.

Her breath continued brushing my face, and despite my best intentions, arousal hit home. She was right on top of me so when her eyebrow lifted, there was no doubt she sensed it. There was no smart-aleck remark this time, as I would have expected. Instead, her face had a different look, one I hadn't seen from her before.

And then her face moved in, and our lips finally met in sweet bliss.

Chapter Twenty-Seven

It was surreal, an experience I'd thought of far longer than I cared to admit. Her body pressed against my own, heat building inside the compartment. The rocket's acceleration forces had ceased and we moved along at a constant clip. Even so, she didn't back away.

Her hands caressed my body, and I returned the favor, sliding underneath her clothing to touch the smooth silkiness of her natural skin. It was as if jolts of electricity passed back and forth between our bodies. I'd found Rione attractive from the point we'd first met, at least after she'd stopped shooting at me. A tension had always been there, and now it had seemingly been broken.

But there would be no time to take this farther. We finally separated, and Rione gazed into my eyes, a warmth there which had been absent for some time. She told me, "I've wanted to do that for a very long time."

"Me too." I gave a slight smile, though I wanted to ask about Malone and their engagement. Now wasn't the time.

"When this is over, we need to talk," she commented. I simply nodded my agreement.

The engine behind us sputtered briefly, causing the craft to jolt a bit from its constant speed. It returned to normal thrust levels, but I knew from experience what was happening. "This thing's almost out of fuel."

I suddenly had a nasty thought. I'd been anticipating that we'd be dropped off at the same spot the prince would have, but then realized his craft was built for one person and we'd loaded in two. The engine sputtered some more and then extinguished completely. I gave Rione a classic *we're screwed* look, and she returned it.

We still had forward momentum on our side, but I needed to see where we would end up. I tilted my head far enough to the side to peer past Rione. My eyes went wide at the sight of another tunnel opening, leading up to a sheer rock wall beyond. No longer was there concern over coming up short, we were going too fast. "We're going to crash," I said with fear crawling through my skin.

Before she had a chance to react, an explosion went off behind us. I glanced back, where a cluster of drag parachutes ejected. Rione clutched onto me as the vehicle jerked, trying to keep from flying through the canopy.

I couldn't look forward any more. "Is it enough?"

She turned her head. "It'll be close."

Based on my fighter pilot past, I'd say we'd lost about half our speed. I tried once more to look forward, but couldn't see past Rione. Instead, the mouth of the tunnel raced past the top of the canopy. I knew the wall was fast approaching and we'd be goners.

Suddenly, hiking through the tunnel hadn't been such a bad idea after all.

Then I heard metal crunching below us, and wondered what else could be wrong. I looked to the side. Sparks sputtered up past the canopy as if someone had installed fountains below us.

The truss structure beneath us had collapsed, as more wall height was visible than before. The added deceleration yanked us toward the compartment's front, and suddenly it became clear this was a purposeful attempt to slow the craft down.

"How much farther?" My only hope was this final method of braking would be enough. With twice as much momentum, it wasn't looking good.

"Brace yourself."

At first, I closed my eyes, not wanting to bear witness to my life's horrific end. Then, I came to my senses. If this would be my last moments among the living, I gazed upon Rione.

She turned, looking into my eyes with a mixture of fear and despair, before relief flooded us both. We'd both been saving each other's lives for as long as we'd known each other. At least we'd die together.

I wrapped my arms around her and held her tight, and she did the same to me. I felt the impact through every part of my body, most notably my still unhealed shoulder. The restraints pulled against my body, even as I heard the front of the rocket collapse and felt the entire compartment lift up in the air.

Rione screamed as the canopy struck the rock wall and shattered. I closed my eyes just in time, as millions of pellets stung our bodies.

Another jolt reverberated through my bones as the rocket fell back to the ground sideways. Then, an eerie silence fell, and I finally allowed myself to peer out at the world from a far different perspective.

"Is it safe?" Rione mumbled into my shoulder.

"Looks like it." Of course as I watched from my new vantage point, who could tell?

I released my grip so she could carefully climb out through the empty canopy frame. Then, I unbuckled the straps binding me and followed her out. Our weapons had made an unfortunate exit at some point in the process, and we walked a few paces over to retrieve them.

"So, where do you figure we are?" I asked.

"Some place that the prince figured would be safe."

She lifted the short-barreled scattergun. I followed her lead and did the same with my blast rifle.

I stared at the burnt, crumpled shell of a rocket, wondering how we'd made it out with our lives. Glancing around the rest of the room, I realized Rione would be the only one who knew where needed to go. Even then, she needed to know where we were to start with. A single opening was hewn into the rock far to our left, ornate in its design. It left nothing to choice.

"Well, I guess we're going that direction." I motioned with my blast rifle.

We stepped through the stone archway, the air moist with a moldy stench. It made sense, considering the prince had never used the escape route. It was possible he hadn't even remembered it existed.

Now, the two sons were dead, and only the king remained. Once we'd taken care of him, Princess Wren would be the only surviving member of the royal family, and she'd take her spot upon the throne.

"So," I started, "how do you think the people will react to Lucian's ascension?"

"I imagine it will be a tough transition period, but in the end, she'll still be the Queen."

When she'd first concocted this plan, she was certain this would end the Torian civil war. Now, it sounded like that wasn't the case. I left her change of heart alone.

We stepped through the archway into a small stairwell corridor. Each step up was hewn out of the rock. An eerie silence fell upon us as we walked, our weapons ready.

I tried to pass the time. "What are your plans after the war is over?"

"I haven't thought that far ahead lately."

The insinuation was clear to me at least. She'd had a plan with Malone, but now he was dead. I didn't exactly know where I fit into the picture, even with our confessions inside the rocket not long ago.

And though I was the one asking the questions of Rione, I really needed to ask myself: What was my plan after the war was over? I'd come here because I had no other place to turn to. I had Elijah Cassus after me, and now it seemed Leah's brother Uni was seeking his revenge as well. As paranoid as it sounded, everyone in the galaxy wanted me dead, as usual. How could I escape that?

The rocky staircase twisted around, leading up into another chamber beyond a second stone archway. This next room, however, put everything we'd seen so far to shame. Marble tiles, white and grey, lined the floor while thin, pale fabric rose toward a domed ceiling. I gazed up at the light tubes formed in a circle. "Certainly elaborate for an escape hideout," I mused.

Rione mumbled something I took as agreement, and we continued toward the center of the room. There were three other archways, made up of chiseled granite, along each of the remaining three walls.

"Which way?" I asked.

It wasn't necessary to choose, though, as primal screams bellowed from each doorway. Death squad troops raced into the room, and we instinctively lifted our weapons and fired off randomly. The energy burst from her scattergun spread on a conical path, striking multiple targets and sending them to the floor. Mine were single shots fired off on a repeating pattern, but yielding a similar effect.

"Ambush!" Rione called out too late, as we scurried backward, sending more shots across the mob that formed. The troops charged too fast for the scattergun's recharge time, and even my blast rifle began to bellow out its objection when its energy levels depleted.

A voice called out, deep and hollow. "Lay down your weapons, or you'll be executed on the spot."

As far as I was concerned, we didn't have a choice. Rione was more belligerent, but complied as well. We both tossed down our weapons, having come this far, only to fall short when it mattered.

Seemed to be the story of my life.

The mob of troops crowded in around us, weapons drawn. I'd been through this before, having had my ship boarded on more than one occasion. Unfortunately, this was a boarding party on steroids. They just kept coming, and suddenly I realized why the rebellion had been in such dire straits. The numbers disadvantage between them was too much to overcome, no matter how much firepower was supplied.

The death squad tidal wave finally came to a standstill, and the pool took shape around us. Yells and screams were too numerous to discern individual commands as weapons' barrels pointed at my face. I watched Rione, whose hands were plastered to the top of her head just as mine were. Emotion ridges burned red hot with the anger boiling within her.

We'd been so close, just to fall into an ambush. We should have known they wouldn't trust us to die in Jabaz's palace. All of these barbarians knew what we'd done to both of their beloved Princes. This made it even more confusing why we were still alive.

A hush flowed over the gathered. Slowly, a path emerged as they stepped aside in succession while another Torian stepped through. This one was in a white uniform, without any armor to speak of, far different than the other troops. I figured he was their commanding officer.

His echoes rattled around the room. "Rione Sc'lari and Aston West, you have been charged with terrorist activities, including the murder of government officials and destruction of government property."

Rione spat at the ground around the commander's feet. "Tell us something we don't know."

A snarl passed across the Torian's pale face. His bright blue eyes twinkled. "You've also been charged with the assassination of two members of the royal family."

I decided to take up the gauntlet. "And if the original charges bore death warrants, what do the new ones add?"

He stared at me, his tiny teeth sinister as they exposed in an ever-widening smile. "You'll first be subjected to torture." He started laughing maniacally, which set off a chain reaction through all of the troops. The resulting chorus drove fear deep within my heart.

"Bring them," the commander ordered. Several troops stepped up, shoving our backs to move us forward.

They marched us through the archway ahead, into another long corridor fashioned of marble floor tiles and granite walls. Up ahead inside recessed compartments sat chiseled stone busts all of the same man.

Rione cursed. "We're inside the king's palace."

This made perfect sense in retrospect. If Prince Jabaz was in trouble, and needed to escape his own palace, where else would he go but to daddy's side? Had we stuck around, we probably would have found another rocket for Axyl, too.

We reached the corridor's end, and passed into a main room that put both of the prince's palaces to shame. Golden chandeliers hung from spaced points around the room, polished and bright. Murals of the king at various stages in life were painted across the ceiling.

The officer bellowed, "Take them to the chamber!"

Even more archways led off to other parts of the palace, but we were shoved toward a small staircase tucked away in the far corner. Glancing back, most of our entourage had dispersed, leaving only a handful of troops directly escorting us, with two dozen behind them.

I turned my attention forward, where Rione struggled against their grip as they maneuvered down the narrow staircase. The struggle drew attention from both the squad behind us as well as the guards holding me captive.

I almost used the diversion to attempt a daring escape attempt, until I felt the cold, hard barrel of an automatic blast rifle press against my skull. “Don’t move,” came the rough, gravelly warning.

“Get down there, or we’ll drop you right now,” another told Rione as she ended up with a rifle against her head as well.

I tried my luck with a verbal attack. “So, why didn’t you kill us back in the chamber?”

Someone behind me guffawed. “Because the king would have had our heads. He wants you tortured and begging for your death.”

I certainly didn’t look forward to either part, but of the two, I’d rather not be dead. That meant biding our time until we had a chance to put an escape plan in motion. With all of these guards, it wouldn’t be easy. Nor did it bode well for our usual on-the-fly method of planning.

“Get down there,” the same voice said while the blast rifle barrel stabbed my back. “The king doesn’t particularly care if you’re wounded first.”

That spurred me along, following Rione and her escorts as the stairway morphed into a spiral job, emptying out into a dingy chamber tucked into the bowels of the planet.

Ahead of us was a rustic wooden door, propped open. I was pretty sure neither Rione nor I wanted anything to do with what lay beyond.

I’d inadvertently come to a stop, which I realized when the growling voice returned. “Move.” To add motivation, I received the butt of a blast rifle to my wounded shoulder, making me grimace. I plodded along the dusty floor. Tiny electric lights hung from thin wires, casting eerie shadows along the walls which danced along, taunting us.

"You rebel scum have no idea what you've done," the commanding officer pointed out. "Killing our princes was stupid on your part."

Rione seethed, "It would end this civil war."

The Torian turned, his eyes maniacal. "It still will. The king will crack down even harder and set examples of all dissidents, just as he does to you."

He stepped up to the wooden door. "Besides, neither of you are Torian. I don't know why you care."

I knew why Rione did, even though she kept silent. She'd told me long ago her own people had threatened to exterminate those like her who'd been born with emotion ridges. She'd felt obligated to help defend those facing a government doing the same to them.

My own motives were far more selfish. Despite my accidental involvement in the first place, I'd grown to care for Rione and the rebels, enough to serve as a natural hiding spot during my recuperation. Now it would be the location for my torture and death.

Funny how things worked out that way.

He shoved the door open wide and we were pushed inside. More small bulbs hung around the circumference of the room. Trails of water seeped down the walls, while the stench of mold and mildew floated about.

The death squads pulled us aside, where two metal posts stuck out from the floor. Attached to these were old-fashioned metal restraints on short chains, two each for our wrists and additional shackles for our legs. They made quick work of us, and we were soon locked in, unable to move more than a few paces in any direction, and unable to reach each other.

The satisfied squads left the room while the officer sneered at us both. "To think you could assassinate the royal family, you two must have lost your minds."

Rione spat a wad of saliva at him, falling short. "To oppress and murder your own people is lunacy."

He walked off for the doorway, grabbing the metal ring before stopping and responding. "Take it up with the king. He'll be with you shortly." And then, he slammed the wooden door behind him, a cloud of dust forming in its wake. As soon as we were alone, I faced Rione. As if I needed more evidence, her emotion ridges were still bright red. I started to speak, but realized I had no plan.

Various instruments were stacked against the opposite wall, sharp blades and barbed hooks on them all. I only hoped we wouldn't experience them firsthand. I shuddered at the mere thought.

A wooden table rested at the huge chamber's center. Additional restraints were latched into the planks, meaning we'd likely each be transferred there at some point. Even more tools of torture hung on the circular walls, along with whips and chains.

I was certain some might have gotten some sort of sick fantasy out of this treatment. Myself, this was frightening me more than the thought of a hull breach in the vacuum of space.

"We'll get out of this," Rione commented.

I was glad she thought so. "You have a plan?"

"We just have to bear through what's going to happen to us. An opening will present itself and we'll take it."

"Hopefully sooner than later," I mused.

"It won't be easy, considering what I've heard of their torture methods."

That didn't make me feel any better. "Well then, I certainly hope we survive."

"We will." She had enough confidence for both of us, which was good, since I had absolutely none.

"And once we get free?"

She turned and glared. "After we kill the king..."

"After that, then..."

That set her back a few steps. "I haven't thought that far ahead," she admitted.

The wooden door burst open. There was no way to know when our moment would present itself, but the sentence was about to be carried out right here and now.

Chapter Twenty-Eight

The stone busts had not done much to prepare me for the actual Torian king. He was far taller than most of his subjects I'd seen up to this point, standing a head taller than the death squad accompanying him. His face was weathered, cracks and lines exposed along his skin. I'd almost expected him to be a frail, old codger. Instead, age had given him a sinister look.

Around him stood four others in long maroon robes. I hadn't seen Torians dressed like this since their government had set me up to be killed on my first visit to the system, being a loose end to their genocidal plans. They were nearly as tall as the king, their faces concealed by their hood's dark shadows. The four broke away, and each took a spot alongside Rione and me. I didn't have a good feeling. During my last encounter, they'd stayed a healthy distance away from me, only serving as escorts for the former Minister of Defense.

The king's booming voice stole my attention away from his entourage. "There are two types of people who cannot be tolerated, traitors and killers. You are both."

I felt an urge to retaliate flare. "And since you're a killer, what does that say?"

A glimpse out of the corner of my eye was the only warning I received before a black metal-lined glove flashed across my jaw, sharp pain radiating through the bones. I pulled my restrained hand up to ensure nothing was broken, then turned and glared into the abyss where my attacker's identity hid. No words seemed appropriate, none that would keep me from being struck again.

The king continued. "Your kind has always been a thorn in my side..."

This time it was Rione who interrupted. "And we always will, as long as you rule with fear and tyranny."

And just like me, another giant pounded the side of her face with a black gloved hand. Rage built within me, but I kept myself in check to avoid suffering another blow.

"My people are all well taken care of. Simply because you miscreants spread your dangerous lies and falsehoods does not make it the truth."

Rione gathered up the contents of her mouth and spat a wad of blood mixed with saliva at her feet. Her tone was subdued, but still menacing. "And as long as everyone agrees with you, they're left alone."

One corner of his mouth lifted. "And when that happens, we have a lasting peace. I'm glad you understand."

I needled the king. "So, we can just agree to believe what you say, and you'll release us?"

His menacing dark blue eyes burned in anger and hatred. "You, Mister West, are finally going to die!"

"Hasn't been the first time I've been told that."

His eyes went wide, obviously having not experienced such snide remarks from others he'd tortured and killed. It didn't set him off his game as much as I'd hoped, though. He brought his face in close, his hatred seething while pungent breath rolled onto me. "Well, then, we'll ensure this experience leaves a lasting impression."

I felt the urge to fight. "Bring it on, old man."

He barked orders, nearly busting my eardrums. "Gentlemen, move to the next phase of your regimen."

Three of the four robed figures descended upon me in a flash. Clenched fists flew at me from every direction. There wasn't time to prepare for the blows alternating randomly between my face and body. I'd experienced beatings before, but never with gloves like these. I held back the screams of pain, but couldn't help myself from collapsing in agony. That was when I figured out the purpose of the remaining guard, who stood behind me. His mighty paws grabbed my shoulders and lifted me back to my feet.

The king belted out maniacal laughter. "Mister West, I'm surprised. Given your track record, I would have thought you stronger than this."

I coughed out my words, blood dribbling past my lips and dropping to the floor. My vision was blurry, and I had to shut one eye to clear things up. "That? I've had worse from jilted Balarusian females."

Comparing my abusers to the shortest, scrawniest women in the known galaxy likely wasn't my best move. It elicited another round of beatings, giving me an inside look into the life of a punching bag.

"Leave him alone," Rione called. I looked over with my one good eye still left.

"Not to worry, Miss Sc'lari, you'll have your chance."

They finally allowed me to collapse, but didn't let up on the physical abuse, kicking my already wounded ribs with huge black boots. One caught me in the back of the head, and the world around me faded in and out.

"Gentlemen, our other prisoner feels left out."

They stopped their beat-down just long enough to face the king. He pivoted, starting for the doorway. "I have other matters to attend to. Let me know when you're nearly finished. I want to witness their final moments."

One more kick struck my gut just as he left the room. Fairly certain several of my internal organs had popped open, I was glad to hear the crunch of the dirt underneath the massive guards' boots. At least until my brain, mush as it was, realized where they were heading.

Rione.

I fought against the intense pain and craned my neck, using my blurry vision to get a glimpse of her. I could do nothing but watch as they reached her, striking her with as much force as they had me.

She tried her best, but couldn't hold back the agony, crying out. That was the trigger I needed, dragging myself up to my hands and knees. The pain flowed like a river through every bone and muscle in my body, but I forced myself to continue. I spat a bloody wad onto the ground before me.

It was probably good our four attackers didn't notice my movements, or they might have returned to inflict some more pain and suffering on me. I moved to one knee without anyone in the room the wiser. Rione's cries grew louder and more pronounced as they inflicted more kicks and punches. She collapsed to the floor. Over and over again, despite her yelps and the fact she was already down, they continued attacking. My anger boiled as I watched. I couldn't bear to watch her experience such abuse.

Then one of the robed figures held up both of his gloved hands and stopped them. I finally breathed a sigh of relief, thinking this phase was finally over. Instead, his deep, growling voice went a different direction.

"Strip her down!"

My eyes went wide at the insinuation of what they planned to do to her next. Rage and fury saturated every nerve ending in my body, supplanting the pain and anguish.

As they grabbed at her garments, I sprinted to her aid, only to be jerked back when I reached the chain's end. Fabric was ripped off, revealing the bronzed skin which hadn't been altered. I tugged harder against the restraints, as she screamed bloody murder and crawled away in her undergarments. Screams echoed against the walls.

"Hold her down!" The one speaking had to be the leader of the group, and fast became the target for my bottled-up wrath. They grabbed her bare arms and legs.

Blood trickled down my wrists as the restraints cut into them. I no longer felt pain, just anger and hatred. I hadn't felt these levels since Leah had been murdered while I watched. It was hard to believe someone could do something even worse to another person I cared about. I wasn't going to let it happen.

The leader of the pack walked over between me and Rione so I couldn't tell what was going on until his gloved hands grabbed hold of her ankles and spread both legs wide. Rione's screams reached a fevered pitch.

I let loose a primal scream, catching the attention of the other three attackers. That was a mere moment before I ripped the chain holding my right hand from its mooring then whipped it toward them all.

The loose end of the chain bore in on the beast who'd dared to tread where he shouldn't, and wrapped itself twice more around his neck. I couldn't see his eyes, but he dropped Rione's legs and that only strengthened my resolve.

It caught the other three unaware, but when I yanked the chain with all my might, it must have blown their minds. My victim stumbled backwards to the ground in front of me, even as his three comrades released their grip on Rione. She scrambled as far as her own chains allowed.

With wide eyes, it was almost as if I stood outside myself, watching the mayhem. Being a man possessed, I grabbed the first guard's head and gave a quick, sickening twist. His body went limp in front of me. The other three yelled at me and at each other, their words utter nonsense to me. They pulled weapons from inside their robes, automatic blast rifles.

I ducked behind the beast's huge body just in time to shield myself from the incoming blasts. Figuring my victim would be outfitted the same way, I reached beneath the robe and snagged his weapon for myself. With it still strapped to him, I fired blind shots. The first, then the second guard dropped to the floor, collapsing into a cloud of dust, their corpses falling forever silent.

The third, however, took a page from my book, grabbing Rione and hoisting her up as a shield. I kept my weapon trained on them, but I couldn't take a shot from my current vantage point. With Rione in the crossfire, it would be impossible to get a clear shot.

He held the tip of the barrel up to Rione's cheek. She made no sound, but I saw the fear in her eyes. My rage grew, knowing I was helpless, just as I'd been with Leah.

The voice could have been a double for the first, even if it was a different guard altogether. "Drop your weapon and surrender, West."

Rione put on a show of bravery. "Don't do it, Aston. Our task is bigger than keeping me alive."

My heart wouldn't allow me to let her die. I kept my stance and aim locked on him, though. Her captor tightened his grip, pulling her body close and shoving his blast rifle deeper. "Do it, or she dies!"

Rione locked stares with me. Despite her bruised and beaten face, she gave me a wink, having just come up with a plan. It gave me enough resolve to firm up my aim. "I'll still kill you," I told him.

The beast bellowed, "You dare test me, heathen?"

Rione fell limp, forcing all her weight toward the floor. Her captor was caught off-guard, even more so when her head flopped forward, as if she was unconscious. He held her waist tight, so I could only wait for my chance.

"Cease this charade," he commanded her.

Without warning, she slammed her head back, catching him square in the face. Stunned, his grip loosened and she dropped to the ground, out of the line of fire. I shot continuous blasts of energy across the short distance, knocking him off his feet.

With our captors now all dead, it became clear what our next step was. "Let's find the king," I offered.

With a constant stream of shots, I melted the remaining chains from their posts. Rione grabbed one of the automatic blast rifles from another corpse, while I walked off toward the wall of implements in search of a key.

"This isn't going to be easy," she remarked. "Probably a suicide mission."

"It always has been." I found a lone metal key ring, just beside the door. Unlocking mine, I walked over and did the same for her.

"You don't have to stick around for this," she said.

As I released her, I looked at her face, trying to comfort her. She was strangely demure while she gathered her clothing, ripped and torn as it was. It wasn't anything familiar from her. "Don't talk like that. Of course, I'm sticking around."

"What about after we're finished?"

My lips formed a thin, grim line. "I haven't thought that far ahead," I mumbled, mimicking her own response.

Our awkward silence was interrupted by approaching boots outside the door. "Sounds like we're on the final road to redemption," I mused as we focused our barrels.

Chapter Twenty-Nine

The door burst open and a handful of death squad troops fell victim to our continuous energy bursts. We couldn't see anything beyond, and truth be told, we probably didn't want to.

We mowed down another grouping of troops storming up behind their fallen comrades before they finally realized the futility of a frontal assault.

Someone called out, "Sound the alarm!" That gave me comfort and fear, both. It meant not everyone had been sent down to investigate. It also meant we didn't have long before they did.

Another responded, "Yes, sir!"

I sprinted toward the doorway, firing in a wide swath in hopes of catching someone unaware. One of the decked-out death squad troops was running away toward the spiral staircase. Even though it wasn't my custom, times being what they were, I shot him in the back. He fell forward, a fresh corpse in this despicable civil war. I dodged for cover before getting shot myself.

The first voice continued barking orders. "You, go!" I couldn't gauge locations, as echoes bounced around the outer chamber.

"But sir," came the understandable objection.

"Do it!"

I peeked around the opening at another Torian running as he'd been commanded. I kept our safety in mind, making him another victim of my automatic blast rifle. His body fell beside his fallen comrade.

Rione joined me. This time, I heard no voices, only the sound of boots crunching gravel after Rione came to a stop. I peeked around and dropped yet a third Torian. I tried not to dwell on the fact I was getting good at shooting people in the back.

She whispered into my ear, warm breath against my skin. "How many more are there?"

"No clue."

"We can't just wait around in here. Someone will eventually find a way to call more troops in."

"You have another plan?"

"Rush through the doorway and catch them off-guard."

She was right. Picking them off one at a time would take too long, and we'd end up overwhelmed by numbers as we had at Jabaz's palace. "Lead the way."

Rione sprinted through the doorway; I was two steps behind her. She focused her spread left while I took the right. We mowed down another half-dozen guards congregated in the next chamber without any of them getting a shot off.

Now we had to figure out how to get to the king. All that, and we had to kill him in his own palace, overrun with guards.

As we ran back up the spiral staircase and closed in on the main floor, a stampede roared above our heads. It made us both stop in our tracks, with our eyes right at floor level. Peering across the main floor, I'd expected to see an entire firing squad waiting. Instead, death squad troops raced out the front doors into the city beyond.

"This doesn't make sense," I muttered as the last one exited. I moved onto the marble tile with caution, just in case they came back inside.

"No, it doesn't." We both stared at the mayhem outside the front doors.

Troops loaded up into hover-transports which mirrored the one we'd seen on the streets of Icthus. Without even a moment to take in their surroundings they sped off, leaving the palace in eerie silence.

This was going to be easier than I thought. "Any thoughts on where to find the king?"

"He could be anywhere," Rione noted.

"Does he have some sort of court area?"

"A throne room, but do you think he'd be there?"

"Unless you have any better ideas..."

She listed them off, counting one finger at a time. "Bedroom, kitchen, his treasury, walking the hallways, picking out the best weapon from the armory to kill us with. Should I go on?" She raised an eyebrow.

"Let's try the throne room. We have time to go on a larger hunt if I'm wrong."

"You're assuming all the troops are gone. I have a feeling he still has some waiting around for us."

I shook my head. "If he'd been aware of the trouble in the torture chamber, he wouldn't have just sent one squad of troops to take care of the matter."

She didn't have a good response for that, since she knew I was right. I didn't bother discussing how many squads had been instructed to leave the palace just now. With the king's life hanging in the balance, he shouldn't have ordered that to be done either.

I motioned forward with the barrel of my weapon. "I hope you know where we're going."

"I've seen some floor plans." And with that, she sprinted toward a side corridor lined with tiles covered with reddish-brown dirt from boots of the troops who'd just left. I followed at the same pace, since I definitely didn't want to get lost in this maze. Rounding several corners, I was actually surprised to see no opposition to our continued trek. Even I'd expected a few guards stationed around the palace to protect the king.

That raised another question, which I posed to Rione between heavy breaths. "What if the king already left?"

"Impossible," she commented in the opposite direction. "He wouldn't have left until making sure we were dead."

She had a point. He'd been near giddy with the idea of torturing and killing us. It was too bad he hadn't stuck around. We might have taken care of matters right then and there. That was wishful thinking, though, as there would have been far more guards in and around the room.

Rione looked back and forth at the bare walls, trying to get her bearings. I eyed her suspiciously. "You do know how to get there, right?"

She shot me an evil glare. "Yes, but these hallways all look the same. I'm doing this off memory."

Turning back to the front, she pointed to an elaborate set of doors. "There."

I walked up to the doors, taking one side while she moved to the other. Straining to listen, I didn't hear any sounds inside. There was no telling what I'd expected to find, perhaps a wild party or some ceremony celebrating our imminent demise.

I looked over at Rione. "Ready?" She nodded and we both eased our hands through the large golden rings.

As one, we yanked the doors open and scurried into the room. To our surprise, the king sat in his chair at the far end of a Traliquin rug. Even more surprising, there were no guards.

He jumped to his feet, his face full of shock and fear. Then, a gentle peace flowed through him, even as we raced down the path. He bellowed out a series of laughs. “I should have known better than to think you’d go down that easily, Mister West.”

He hadn’t been the first to make that mistake, nor would he be the last. We raised our weapons, targeting his chest. He held his arms out with open palms, as if to make himself a more apt martyr, making no move to protect himself. “Too bad your plan has backfired,” he muttered.

Rione sneered. “Doesn’t look like it. With you dead, Toris will finally be able to end its civil war.”

“You two are fools. Killing me won’t matter.”

I had a bad feeling about this. “Your daughter will ascend to the throne...”

His sinister smile grew. “If she lives long enough...”

Rione fired a single shot into her target. Fortunately, she’d targeted his leg, sending him to the floor. She jogged over and shoved the barrel in his face. “Spill it.”

Clutching his leg, he still had the audacity to keep laughing. “It’s too late for you to stop it.”

Rione fired another shot, and the king grimaced as it blackened the carpet beside his ear. She moved the barrel back into position. “Tell us.”

He licked his lips. We waited a moment, and Rione pressed the barrel harder against his forehead. Sweat rolled off the old man’s skin. Hopefully she wouldn’t kill him before we found out what we needed to know.

“The components used to build the spy satellite you two destroyed were launched on a series of heavy-lift rockets. We’d built extras for spares, just in case.”

Rione’s face soured. The king continued, “We’ve outfitted one as a final send-off for my daughter and her station.”

She shook her head. "Torians don't have the technology required to take out the station with one shot."

He chuckled, mostly under his breath. "We didn't until recently, you're right. Then I had the strangest visitor show up on my doorstep, someone with whom Aston here has a rather interesting past."

My eyes went wide. I mumbled the name. "Uni Zulch."

The king put on a weak smile. "Yes, he was most helpful for someone not of Torian descent. He knew of our troubles with Aston, and provided us a neutron detonator with all the specifications on how to outfit our rocket."

Uni, being a former Adelphi weapons designer, must have had several contacts willing to help him out. I lamented all the time about the entire universe being out to kill me. Some might have labeled it overactive paranoia, but everyone I came across certainly seemed to be.

He let out a wild laugh. "What surprised me was he didn't want any payment. He just wanted you dead."

I narrowed my eyes. "I'm not on the station."

"Minor details," he said with another series of laughs. "My plan was to kill you here, but why let a perfectly good weapon go to waste? My troops have already left to carry out my final plan." His laughter echoed against the walls.

Rione didn't know what to think. "But with both you and your daughter dead, who assumes the throne?"

"My various ministers and I put together an emergency decree after my first son's death. In the case of no living heir, they will run the planet in my stead, carrying out the same ideals I have ruled with for so long." His laughter rolled into the emptiness.

The man had truly gone stark raving mad.

So I did what anyone facing down a lunatic dictator would do, lifted my barrel and fired off a dozen rounds into his chest. His laughter finally ceased.

"Those troops have to be stopped," I told Rione. "We're the only ones who can do it." With that, I turned and raced for the door.

She was right on my heels. "Do you think we'll be able to get there in time?"

I didn't know how to answer, because I had serious doubts myself. This was the second time I'd been called upon to save the orbital station from complete destruction. This time, I wasn't sure I'd be able to.

• • •

We rushed through the corridors, my memory taking the corners in reverse. It gave me pause, even as I kept running for the exit. We'd actually done it, assassinating the royal family. Adrenaline pumped through my veins, until I realized none of it would matter if we didn't stop that rocket. Lucian would be dead, the king's ministers would assume control and our efforts would be wasted.

We popped out the front doors, and both of us stared along the lengthy driveway. On my right, a pair of empty hover-transports sat, similar to those taken by the death squads earlier. I could only figure they'd been for the troops we killed during our most recent escape.

"There!" I pointed.

"I'll drive," Rione informed me as we raced for one.

I jumped in the passenger side, which sent shocking pain racing up my spine with the lack of padding on the bucket seat.

It started like a champ when Rione smacked the button on the center console, though. She grabbed the dual control sticks behind the button and along the door armrest. Spinning the transport around, we sped down the drive.

I scanned the landscape for the first time. Much like the other two Torian cities we'd visited in our time here, the entire chamber was packed full of buildings. Everything appeared normal in the hustle and bustle of the citizens' lives. Little did they all know that they were now free from genocidal tyranny. At least for the time being.

Rione caught my attention. "Any sign of where we should be going?"

"Not yet."

I scoured the city for some sign of those troops. I didn't know how far they could have gone, but they'd have to visit a launch site. Considering this chamber had no exit hole above, let alone spare room to store a rocket of that size, they'd have to leave the city. I narrowed my focus on the outer wall.

And that's when I saw them.

"Over there, just leaving the city," I uttered and pointed off toward the right. The line of transports and personnel carriers sped along, leaving a small trail of dust in their wake as they left the pavement. Each one made a long turn before disappearing into a rock crevice.

"We're going to lose them," I told her.

"Not if I can help it." She gritted her teeth, and slammed both control sticks forward.

I held on for dear life as we accelerated, weaving in and out of traffic, pedestrians dodging our mammoth projectile. At least their screams and violent curses were silent inside the compartment. As we entered the heart of the city, our view was cut off by surrounding buildings.

I'd been out of the fighter pilot business for far too long, though, as the rapid turns and movements finally wore on me. Nausea reared its ugly head, and it was all I could do to keep from emptying my minimal stomach contents all over the rubber floor mats.

When we finally exited the city, and flew over the dirt road, she turned to me. "We're going to have the element of surprise, but just for a little bit. Get up in the turret."

I looked behind us, where a small crawlspace led back. My nausea had finally subsided, which was good. I pulled myself out of the seat and scrambled through the makeshift tunnel. Reaching the other end, I stood until my head pressed against a metallic cover. With all my might, I shoved it up just in time to see a tunnel opening, before we plunged into darkness.

I grabbed two rubber handgrips in front of me, and gears and motors clicked and whirred around me. Out of the transport's roof, two dark barrels rose, and then a helmet with a black visor popped up beside me. A narrow mechanical arm hoisted it atop my head. At first, the visor cut off my sight, but then without warning, everything became as bright as day. Crosshairs weaved back and forth around the screen, looking for a target.

I had a fairly good idea how this would work, but the specifics were beyond me. Nothing was as exhilarating as on-the-fly training. Unfortunately, this wasn't a game or some sort of pre-set scenario. Our friends' lives, and those of other innocents, hung on our ability to succeed.

Rione sped through the tunnel as my visor provided me everything I needed to see. My first target, the transport directly in front of us, trekked through the darkness, seemingly unaware of our presence. The crosshairs zeroed in on the other vehicle and hovered there. I pulled both triggers. The crosshair turned bright red a moment before the cannons fired off repetitive rapid-fire white blasts, striking the transport's hull.

The vehicle exploded, flipping onto its roof. Rione whipped the transport around the debris as I jerked down, yanking the cover closed behind me. Flames roared just beyond the armored hull, but I escaped the scorching heat. Satisfied we'd passed the danger zone, I forced the cover open once more.

The crosshairs didn't take nearly as long to zero in on the next target. Unfortunately, they'd noticed the huge inferno we'd caused. One of the guards stood, his own turret facing us.

Rione jerked us aside as the line of blasts strafed past. I waited for the crosshairs to hover over their hull, then pulled the trigger. Another explosion filled the tunnel. This time, the wreckage blocked our path, and Rione was forced to slam the controls aft and bring us to a skidding stop.

I heard her call from the driver's seat below. "Blow it out of our way!"

I focused the crosshairs on the burning inferno, and left it there, firing at will. A multitude of explosions rocked the vehicle, splitting it in two and finally offering a path forward. There was no chance to react, as we rocketed through the inferno, the heat from the flames flowing over me in unbearable waves.

And then just as quickly, we passed through the other side. I didn't see any sign of the next transport in line. Near-frigid air surrounded us in stark contrast to what we'd just driven through. A shiver passed through my bones, before I realized it wasn't just the cooler temperature, but another archway into the next cavern. Wherever we were headed, we'd arrived.

Rione punched our transport through the opening and I gazed up into the massive cavern, where a huge cylindrical rocket stretched up above us. She skidded to a stop, and I looked down over the precipice, seeing even more of the massive launch vehicle extending into the planet's depths. I fired the cannons at the rocket, but every blast ricocheted off the skin toward the cavern walls.

A flurry of yells filled the chamber. I glanced over at the rock face, seeing a small steel building embedded in the wall, along with the remaining vehicles.

"To our right," I bellowed to Rione when seeing the congregation of troops behind their transports and personnel carriers. The crosshairs had ignored my other movements, lazily moving back and forth. Now, they homed in on one of the transports, and I launched a salvo of bright white flashes.

The first transport exploded, then caused a chain reaction with the others sitting nearby, creating a far larger fireball than had been allowed inside the tight confines of the cavernous corridor. It enveloped most of the surrounding troops, throwing some of the others clear of the blast zone. None of them returned to their feet. Others had been lucky enough to escape the blast, but decided that this wasn't a battle worth fighting and ran toward a separate exit archway.

Rione caught me off-guard as she turned the transport and hurtled toward the steel structure.

The crosshairs hovered over individual escaping troops. Whatever it said about my own morality, I fired single shots and set each one ablaze where he stood. None of them escaped. We arrived at the building moments later.

I scrambled down the access tube and out of the vehicle, before we ran for the control room. Even through small rectangular blast windows, I saw three troops inside, distracted by their duties. My legs churned faster, knowing they had to be in the final throes of the liftoff sequence. We had to stop them.

"Shoot anything that moves," Rione instructed again, as if there was any doubt in my mind.

I yanked the door open and she led me inside. We lifted the automatic blast rifles we'd taken from the palace guards, spreading our destruction by taking down everyone inside.

I finally exhaled. "Did we stop it in time?"

Rione didn't have to answer. The excessive roar of engines filled the entire cavern, only to be silenced as the door finally closed behind us. We both watched out the blast windows in horror as the massive launch vehicle accelerated up and out of sight, leaving billows of white and grey smoke in its wake.

We were too late.

Chapter Thirty

I looked up at the escaping rocket in disbelief, while it rushed toward the cavern's ceiling, and the exit hole. With a glance over at Rione, her deep blue emotion ridges peeked out.

An overwhelming confidence fell over me. "We'll find a way to stop it."

She looked over, her eyes glazed. The color faded from her ridges. "Yes, we will."

Now we just had to figure out how.

Clouds lingered beyond the blast windows. I glanced down at the various consoles and display screens in front of me for brainstorming ideas. Many displayed camera angles of the rocket's original position, now blanketed with smoke. Others showed a different perspective, on-board the rocket as it sped up the launch tube. A small subset of displays to my far left held a completely separate look. Here, within another cavern, several interstellar transports and warships were parked.

"What's this?" I pointed for Rione's benefit. "Better question, where?"

She looked down at the screen, her shock and disbelief even greater than my own. "It has to be around here somewhere." She scurried off to other consoles, frantic.

We didn't have all that much time, but I now realized the answer. The death squad troops who'd tried to escape had given it away. "The other corridor."

We raced out into the thinning smoke, and jumped back into our transport. As the other tunnel came into view, I pointed it out from the passenger seat. She jerked the handles forward and the transport responded in kind, forcing me back into my seat.

She prodded, "You have a plan once we get there?"

I still didn't have a good answer. "Find a ship and stop that rocket, however we can."

"Seems to me we've been in this situation before."

It did bear a striking resemblance to my first visit to the Toris system. Then, we'd only had a pair of fighters with the barest of weapons stores. In the end, we'd helped the Torian government take out their attack cruiser with its own weapons. I was certain they wouldn't make that mistake a second time.

We shot through the sporadic cloud cover and into the tunnel. I didn't have the first clue how we'd stop the rocket, but there was always a chance we couldn't. We still had a chance at keeping the Princess in charge. "As soon as we get airborne, we need to get word to Lucian. Evacuate the station, just in case." Even doing that, I wasn't sure we'd get everyone out in time to avoid a neutron detonator blast.

Rione kept her eyes forward, her tone terse. "Agreed."

The trip was short before we sped out into the next chamber, as I'd expected. The video links had shown it, but I hadn't bothered to notice at the time, the entire chamber was empty of personnel.

I pointed to a ship that looked like a Rulusian freighter. Its long, sleek bullet-like hull shone in the dim light, almost as if it begged to be picked.

"That's what we'll take." I pointed and Rione turned us toward it.

The emptiness still bothered me. “Why would they have an entire chamber of ships with no one guarding them?”

“Does it matter?”

“As long as the ships are operational,” I mused.

Rione shot me a nasty look, then pulled to a stop just in front of the transport. We climbed out, racing for an airlock hatch open along the forward hull’s near side.

Sprinting into the ship, I marveled at the bare metal walls and floor. We scrambled toward the aft half of the ship, with no idea where we were going. Although the outside had looked close to a Rulusian freighter, the inside had no resemblance whatsoever. Literally, there was nothing here for the crew to utilize. Every room we peered into was empty as we searched for the bridge area. No furnishings, nothing.

And then it struck me, as I ran along behind Rione. I’d seen this type of place before, and it didn’t bode well for our chances. “A ship graveyard. They’ve sent them here to die.”

She came to a stop, causing me to collide with her. “What do you mean?”

“They’ve stripped the whole thing down. I’d venture to say every ship in this place is going to be the same way.”

“Well then, I certainly hope it has enough left over to lift off.” She sprinted down the metal corridor.

“Let alone stop that rocket.”

We continued down the corridor, and finally stumbled onto a bridge. The seats had all been ripped out of the semi-circular bridge layout, but at least the consoles were there, the physical shells anyway. It remained to be seen whether the guts had been left intact or not. And with time running out, we couldn’t find another way to stop that neutron detonator. This had to work.

Rione found the main power controls along the aft wall and tossed them on. The lights flashed on and the consoles flickered to life. The room was filled with a rough humming sound as everything started up. I figured it had been a while since this old bird had seen any type of action.

Unfortunately, as the screens finally displayed their intended functions, everything was in Torian script. Joy turned to frustration. “How exactly am I supposed to fly this thing when I don’t even know what I’m reading?”

She scrambled over, and started pointing. “Thruster controls, increase and decrease. Helm controls in all axes. Weapons control...” She tapped parts of the screen. Muttering a curse, she stepped away.

“What?”

“We don’t have any.”

It should have been a foregone conclusion, being in a ship’s graveyard, but the fact hadn’t hit home until Rione stated it outright. “How...” I started, but stopped, knowing the answer. Without weapons, there would be no way to stop that rocket from reaching the station.

She fiddled with another console and the forward viewscreen came to life. A moment later, the entire ship rumbled and shook. I watched the viewscreen as we lifted off from the chamber floor. Then it was my turn to try and get familiar with the controls before me. I’d once been told I could fly anything, which didn’t seem to be the case when we careened toward the floor. At least the controls were responsive, though, as I corrected my mistake and aimed toward an exit tunnel in the ceiling.

I only hoped our path would be clear. There was no telling whether this tunnel had been used recently, or if they’d blocked it off. At least then we’d no longer have to worry about the orbital station.

“Plan of attack?” I finally asked. Another opening appeared ahead and we were closing the distance fast.

“Still trying to come up with one,” she responded.

That made two of us.

We burst out of the launch tube and I finally allowed myself a chance to relax. Looking around for some sign of the rocket we were after, thin, wispy trails led up into the atmosphere. The sky darkened as we climbed in pursuit. As we finally reached a spot where the black starfield dominated the Torian atmosphere, I finally saw the rocket itself, still on its path of death and destruction.

Unfortunately, the Torian and Rulusian fleets were still out here as well. The two had finally started shooting at each other, flashes of every color spanning the darkness. I'd almost thought the Rulusians could help us destroy the rocket, but that chance was gone.

Now it was up to us alone.

Next to me, Rione gaped at the sight of all those warships battling. She muttered mostly to herself, "Time to get a message to Lucian."

She moved to another console around the semi-circle. I, on the other hand, kept my eyes on that rocket growing larger as we closed in. I increased our aft engines' power to help us along. At the very least, the Rulusian warships kept the Torians occupied, giving us cover. Hopefully, they wouldn't destroy us, thinking we were Torian, too.

The viewscreen shifted until the right side was taken up by Lucian Wren in her office. "Who is...?" Rather than relief at seeing us, fear filled her eyes. "Where did you two go?"

Rione responded, "No time to explain. Your father launched a neutron detonator at the station. Evacuate!"

Wren turned and mumbled her command off-screen, "Sound the alarm." She focused back on us again. "The Rulusians were caught off-guard by the Torian fleet's attack." Klaxons sounded in the background.

"It looks like they coordinated it with the launch."

"Can you stop it?"

I answered in her place. "If we knew how, we wouldn't insist on an evacuation."

"We need to keep you safe," Rione told the Princess. "I'll contact one of the Rulusian warships to pick your escape vessel up as soon as they can."

"Negative. I'll remain on the station. My father will not force me to flee, no matter what threat he sends."

Rione stiffened, and I understood the dilemma. Information on her father's death should be relayed directly face-to-face, not across the vacuum of space.

"Princess, I insist..."

"No, I'm staying. That's final." She terminated the broadcast, the viewscreen shifting back to the starfield.

We were now close enough to the rocket, the bright white flames nearly filled the viewscreen. I looked off toward the waiting orbital station. Flashes of light on the various docking rings told me the other occupants on-board were doing all they could to obey the evacuation order.

That spurred my memory. Even though we hadn't been separated for that long, I still had Jeanie in my corner. She'd bailed me out of tougher spots than this before, and I had to figure she'd be able to do the same this time.

"Take over," I told Rione. She must have caught my excited tone, figuring I'd finally come up with a plan. I didn't have the heart to tell her it was a tiny hope.

I fiddled with the communications controls, then sent out a communication. "Jeanie, are you out there?"

"Aston?" Her seductive voice was a welcome respite from the horrors I'd been through since we'd left the station. "Are you in trouble? Why are you transmitting from a ship with Torian registration?"

"No time to explain. There's a rocket on its way to destroy the orbital station."

"That does explain the evacuation order. I have already departed the station."

That was good news. "Can you access the inbound rocket, and redirect it?"

"Attempting..." She came back a moment later. "My attempt was unsuccessful."

"Can you detonate the device?"

"It does not appear this rocket has any sort of network interface on-board."

I cursed. There went the extent of my plan, right out the nearest airlock. "So, there's no way to stop it?"

"Remotely, it does not appear so."

Her comment spurred another plan, albeit more idiotic than anything I'd come up with to this point. "How would you go about stopping it other than remotely?"

"The neutron detonator is a fairly well-known design. It activates on impact."

I gulped. "So, once it hits something..."

"Affirmative."

Then there was only one way we were going to stop this rocket before it reached the orbital station. I looked over at Rione. "Does this thing have escape pods?"

Jeanie had the response instead. "It is designed with four located near the nose. From a quick scan, it appears there is only one remaining on your vessel."

I spoke to Rione. "Get to an escape pod."

Her left eyebrow lifted. "What are you planning?"

"I plan on giving it something to impact." The implication was clear. "Now, get to the escape pod."

"I'm not leaving you to kill yourself, flyboy."

"This isn't a discussion," I instructed her. "You need to get Lucian to the planet so she can assume the throne."

"I'm not leaving you," she repeated.

We stared at each other in a stalemate, until Jeanie broke the silence. "Both of you can take the escape pod. I am currently inside the Torian warship computer system. Positioning the ship for impact just beyond the weapon's damage range in relation to the station..."

The aft engines fired off, almost throwing us both to the floor. "I will eject the pod once you're both safely inside. Run, now!"

She didn't have to tell us twice.

"Thanks, Jeanie," I told her.

We bolted out the door and raced down the hall without words. The floor panels echoed loud as I sprinted alongside Rione. We finally reached the emptied crew quarters, and the small alcove where a lone escape pod remained. I jumped through the open hatch into the bucket seat, Rione climbed into my lap, and we made the best out of its restraint system. The straps tugged at us as the ship decelerated. We were reaching the impact point.

"Jeanie, we're in."

Her voice returned over a single, miniature speaker in the pod's apex. "I have been unable to access the pod. There appears to be a malfunction."

My eyes went wide. This had to be the reason they didn't salvage it off the ship like the others. Another curse escaped my lips. "Is there a manual release?"

Rione and I both scoured the compartment. Jeanie came back. "Moving the ship out of position..."

"No! Keep it here." I demanded. Her programming would force her to comply.

"You will not survive the impact."

"There!" Rione pointed down to a spot tucked into a recess beside my left calf.

"We're on our way, Jeanie." I yanked the handle.

With a quick slam, the hatch closed and explosions set off behind us, launching the pod. We had no windows or viewscreen, but the sheer force of the acceleration drove us into the seat. I only hoped we'd clear the blast zone.

Time passed and my breathing returned to normal. There would be no warning of the incoming blast wave. We would just be here one moment and if we were lucky, still here the next. If not, well, at least we had this time together.

I locked eyes with Rione and we lingered a few moments. Then, our lips met for what I hoped wouldn't be the final time.

The entire pod rattled, but we were both still alive. I didn't know what just happened, but the blast wave wouldn't have such a short duration.

"Something's clamped onto us," Rione surmised.

The pod jerked along, being pulled along. I had no idea where. We clunked against something. A few moments passed, and I waited for the hatch to open. If someone had captured our escape pod and brought it aboard their ship, what were they waiting for?

And then I felt what I'd expected to the first time. Our pod shook and shuddered as the shock wave hit. I held Rione, figuring it was our final moments. Then, the pod came to rest again. We'd survived the blast, and came out in one piece.

"I don't think anyone's out there," Rione commented.

"Let's see." I yanked the emergency release handle on the hatch. It jerked open as fast as it had clamped shut.

I didn't know how, but we were inside one of my cargo holds. Unbuckling the restraints, Rione led us out into the freezing cold, her breath forming clouds. "Isn't this...?"

I didn't let her finish. "Jeanie?"

There was no response. My fear shot through the roof. I opened the hold's hatch with the emergency release and raced for the front, Rione scrambling after me.

Entering my bridge, small energy bolts raced across every console, and the smell of burnt electronics filled my nostrils.

"Jeanie?" I repeated, this time with hope falling like an asteroid in the atmosphere. Still no response, the circuits finally cut out, and emergency backups kicked in. The lights dimmed, and I fell to my knees, catching a sob in my throat. "Jeanie, what did you do?"

Epilogue

"Okay, let's try this again."

I hovered over what I hoped was the last replacement part on-board. Flipping the master power switch underneath the cargo bay floorboards, the lights rose to their normal levels. At least that much was working.

I made my way back to the living quarters, wiping my hands on a work towel and looking around the emptiness. There was one more thing to bring back to normal. "Jeanie?"

Silence reigned for a long time, making me think the worst. There would be no fixing this.

"Aston?"

Excitement filled my heart and I gave a joyful laugh. "Glad to have you back."

"Do not..." Then without warning, the silence returned. Perhaps my elation had been premature. Without warning, she continued, "...feel back."

"Now that your systems are operational, I'm planning to head for a repair station and get you fixed up, just like new."

I didn't have to ask her how she'd reached us in time. From observers' reports, she'd pulled another in-system hyperspace jump to reach us before the neutron detonator impacted the freighter. "You saved our lives."

"Nothing...new."

I smiled and gave a short laugh. "That stunt nearly killed all of your systems. Not a wise decision." She didn't respond. "But thanks. I owe you big time."

I wanted to keep her talking, to ensure she stayed operational. Funny, Jeanie always seemed to have emotions she wasn't capable of, feigning worry over me. Now, I was the one with an emotional attachment to a machine.

"Now, it's time for me to get a drink. We'll head out for the repair station when I get back."

It was as if she knew hearing her voice would comfort me. "Acknowledged. Will...program course."

I smiled weakly and started out the exit hatch. My feet touched the landing bay floor and I ventured off toward Rione's quarters. Walking through the empty corridors, I found myself wondering if the end of the Torian civil war would signal a return to the station's popularity. Only time would tell.

I eventually reached Rione's door and knocked a few times. It slid open a short time later, and she looked out, a smile on her face.

"Just got the ship up and running. Thought you might like to join me in a celebration drink."

She smirked. "Not sure that's wise. The last time we sat together on this station, the place exploded."

"Exactly. We need better memories."

She stepped out and the door closed behind her, making her decision clear. As we walked, she jerked her head around, exposing her pink emotion ridges. "Jeanie?"

"She's functional, but damaged. Once we reach a repair station, they should get her back to normal."

"Thank her for saving my life."

"I will."

We walked toward the commons area. Once there, the sheer lack of visitors made it hard to believe the war had finally ended. One would have expected a celebratory atmosphere.

The owner of the Stardust had set up a temporary location in one of the other vacant shops, while the original underwent repairs. We walked inside the tight confines, where there was only room to walk behind a set of stools and take our places at the bar. The barkeep stepped up. “So, how are the heroes?”

“Thirsty,” I muttered.

He pointed. “Vladirian liquor, right?”

I nodded with a smile. While he walked off to make our drinks, I turned to Rione. “How are things with Lucian?”

“She still isn’t speaking to me.”

“Understandable.” Despite their differences, I assumed she still had some feelings for her father and brothers.

“She knows we did what had to be done,” Rione said. “The war’s over, and Toris needs her leadership.”

The barkeep brought back two glasses of the pale yellow liquid I loved in all its glory.

Rione looked up. “I didn’t order this.”

“Oh, my apologies. What would you like?”

She looked down at her glass of Vladirian liquor, then back over at me. “This will be fine.”

I warned her, “It takes some getting used to.”

We sat in silence. I didn’t feel like drinking just yet, since there was still one unanswered question in my mind. “So, what do you plan to do now? Stay on Toris, help them rebuild?”

She shook her head. “Now that the war is over, there’s nothing for me here.”

I absently ran my fingers across the lip of my glass. “You could always come with me. My ship’s not really equipped for more than one, but...”

"I'm sure we wouldn't need room for more." She placed a hand on my other arm. The implication was clear.

I hoisted my glass up. "To new beginnings." We both tossed the contents down our throats.

Sitting our empty glasses down, I looked into her eyes. She angled up the corner of her mouth as we stared into each other's eyes. "Drinking Vladirian liquor is fine, but I can think of a better way to celebrate."

"Oh?" I asked.

She grabbed my hand, and we stood from our seats. Tucking her arm into the crook of my own, she laughed under her breath. "I think you might even enjoy it more."

I smiled without comment as we started back toward her quarters. There was no doubt in my mind what she had in mind, and I couldn't wait.

To new beginnings, indeed.

Thank you for reading *Death Brings Victory*. Please enjoy this bonus excerpt, the prologue from Aston West's next novel in the series,

All Good Things

The lounge's rancid stench was what you'd expect out of a hole that criminals scrambled into. With his medical background, John could make out the smells of urine, blood, vomit and various other bodily fluids and excretions, combined with cleaning agents that had tried and failed to win the battle. He pursed his pale pink lips tight, trying to hold his breath as long as he could between quick draws of air that made him gag. Fiddling with a small crystal wafer hanging from his neck, he looked across the booth's table into the hazel eyes of his wife, Isabel.

She ran a tanned hand through her long black strands of hair, pushing them behind her petite ear. "I don't like this place," she whispered.

"Not much longer," he attempted to assure her.

"Another moment longer is still too long." She sighed deep, and broke their mutual stare to look off toward the doors they'd be using to leave later.

John had been second-guessing his decision to bring her along, ever since they left the transport to trek through this forsaken spaceport. He could almost pass off for someone intending to be there, as his Torian heritage gave him a near-albino appearance, aside from his bright blue eyes. He'd actually seen a few others of his kind while walking through the corridors, which he thought quite odd, considering his species had always been known for staying close to home. He, on the other hand, was nothing like the rest of his people. He'd ventured out into the universe to make his own way. And now, he was delving into a life of crime and profiteering that would have made his own mother retch.

Isabel's glamorous body, however, made her stand out in ways he had never expected. Certainly, she'd turned heads everywhere he'd taken her, even when they lived on Vetras, their former home. But here it was worse. Her looks made her the target for all of the drunken animals and other criminals to ogle. It was obvious that she wasn't supposed to be here, and that made her a target.

He shouldn't have brought her.

John waved off the scantily-clad waitress as she tried to drop off another round of drinks, despite her having already been foiled on three earlier occasions. The barkeep behind the opposite counter gave them dirty looks, not expecting anyone to nurse their liquor for as long as he and Isabel had.

John continued stealing glances at a digital timepiece on his wrist, a present from Isabel for their recent wedding. She fiddled with the diamond ring on her left hand, shielding it from everyone else's view in the establishment as she twisted it around her finger.

Finally, he breathed a sigh of relief with one last look at his timepiece. The moment had come. "Time to go," he mumbled.

He slid out from the booth, holding a hand out for his wife. A smile finally graced his face, even though Isabel didn't match his expression herself as they walked as a pair toward the exit. Watchful eyes made no effort to hide the fact that other patrons were keeping tabs on the two as they left.

Everything he'd done had been leading up to this point. Putting up with his former employer and her lunacy, stealing the wafer which now hung on a chain around his neck, and traveling to this disgusting armpit of the galaxy. His moment had finally arrived.

Their moment, he thought to himself, as he snuck another glance at his loving bride. She was afraid, and with good reason. But in a short while, they'd have millions on them, and could travel anywhere they wanted.

Someone was paying a hefty price for the wafer and its contents, exactly as John had hoped when he'd stolen it right out from under his employer's nose.

They moved quickly out of the room, into a sterile, white tile hallway. The stench didn't improve any, even though there wasn't a single soul in sight. Isabel latched her arms around his waist and squeezed him tight. "I can't wait to get out of this place." John could feel her shaking, but he wasn't sure if it was fear or excitement.

"It won't be long," he told her.

She looked up into his pale blue eyes, a smile finally coming to her face as she gripped his hand instead. "What are we going to do first with our money?"

"Buy a home, maybe a ship." John kissed her cheek. "Once we have it, we escape this hellhole and never look back."

"I can't wait," she told him, giving back a much deeper and more passionate kiss on his lips.

Having scouted out the location in advance, John knew where he was supposed to meet the buyer. That was about the extent of his knowledge, though. The transmissions had all been heavily-encrypted, and no identifying details had been given to him, even when asked. The only things John needed to know, he'd been told, was when and where the exchange would take place, and how much he'd be making in the deal.

His smile grew as he walked with his wife, until they finally reached landing bay four. Passing through an opening set of sliding doors, Isabel gripped his hand tighter. A ship faced away from them, its stub nose tucked into the darkened far corner as if it were being punished.

John's heart thumped hard against the inside of his rib cage. He didn't see anyone standing here, but he'd double-checked and triple-checked the messages before setting out for the meeting, and they were right on time. Isabel's fingernails dug into his skin. He was just about ready to bolt when a loud clank resonated through the enclosed hangar, followed by even louder whirring. He looked over at the ship again, and saw the aft cargo ramp lowering.

Goosebumps covered John's skin as he set eyes on the man who had to be the buyer. He was a beast, standing tall and decked out in a full body suit, jet black and glistening. Bristly blonde stubble adorned the top of his head, his face chiseled like stone. The suit flexed along with the man's muscular chest, as he marched down the ramp and strode toward them with a frown.

The beast lifted an eyebrow as he drew closer. "John?"

He simply nodded, and came to a stop with Isabel clutching his hand almost to the point of cutting off circulation. The plan had been solid, but reality was setting in. John and Isabel were no criminals, and this man no doubt was.

"Elijah Cassus." The bulky beast extended a hand with a sly smile. "I assume you brought what we agreed upon."

John finally got his nerves under control, and pulled the wafer out from under his shirt. He blurted out in response, "And you?"

Elijah thumbed toward the open shuttle ramp, and a large duffel bag that rested just inside the ship. "Right there. Ten million, as agreed."

John's earlier feelings of mistrust finally began to dissipate. "Then it sounds like we have a deal."

Elijah's thin smile grew, before he turned and walked off toward the shuttle.

John muttered to his bride before following, "Stay here. I won't be long."

As they drew closer, John glanced at the duffel bag. Even from his vantage point at the bottom of the ramp, he saw several small holes in the outside of the bag, as if a projectile weapon had been used against it. He was no criminal, but knew enough not to ask questions. The only thing that mattered was those credits would soon be in his hot, little hands. Ten million credits would go a long way toward setting them up for the rest of their lives.

John unfastened a clasp behind his neck as Elijah climbed the ramp and hoisted the duffel bag off the floor plates. He pulled the wafer and its lanyard off, clasping the chain in his hand. He determined then and there not to let loose of it until he had the money. Elijah turned, and the two of them stood in a standoff.

Isabel caught John off-guard by calling out from the other side of the landing bay, "What do you plan to do with this information?"

Elijah's tone soured as he growled, "It's of no concern to you, as long as you're paid."

John gulped, thinking she had fouled up the deal. He'd thought she'd been on the same page as he was, that they didn't care why anyone wanted the information, or what they'd use it for. The money was enough.

"But I have nothing to hide..."

John kept a close eye on the duffel bag and rivulets of sweat flowed down his temples. His heart thumped hard against his chest again. Elijah softened his tone as he continued, "I want to bring back my dead brother. We have an old score to settle."

John took in a long breath, forcing himself to relax. His employer, the woman he'd stolen the information from, had successfully brought her husband and daughter back from beyond the grave using nano-bot technology and programming, all of which was well-documented on the wafer. He had no doubt that this man would have just as much success using the 'death cure' on his brother. He ignored the whole idea of settling a score that Elijah had mentioned. None of that concerned him.

Elijah tossed the duffel down the ramp, and it landed on the hangar floor beside John. "Ten million, as promised."

John knelt down and unzipped the bag, before running his free hand through the solid credits inside. Each of the golden coins had a silver rim, which put the value of each coin at a thousand credits. All of his worries and concerns melted away at the feel of those coins against his skin.

Elijah's voice grew cold. "And now, I want the information you promised."

John looked up, distracted from his love-fest with the duffel bag. He flung the crystal wafer and its necklace toward the top of the ramp, where Elijah caught it mid-air with one hand.

"It's been great doing business with you." Elijah turned and stormed off. Isabel rushed over and knelt beside John, staring at the money. She squealed in delight and planted a passionate kiss on her husband.

"Oh, one last thing," Elijah interrupted. John glanced back up, seeing a disintegrator cannon in the other man's hands. Isabel screamed, before jumping up and sprinting toward the exit. John attempted to catch her, but she evaded his grip. A shot echoed in the emptiness. John watched as the energy blast struck her in the back, knocking her down with an awkward stumble. Her body quickly burned from the inside out, decomposing into organic ash while she screamed in pain and agony, writhing around on the hangar floor. Her voice carried even over the klaxon that had sounded off after Elijah's shot.

John's heart shattered into a million pieces as he scrambled toward her, screaming, "No!"

He was too late to do anything but watch her final moments, as her body completely decomposed. He ran his hands through the pile of ash, sobbing over his wife's death. He felt something solid and pulled out the ring that he'd given to her, which only made him an even more emotional wreck.

"Why?" He moaned, turning back to his wife's killer, who now pointed his weapon at John.

"The trouble with making deals with evil men, John, is you shouldn't trust them."

"But we gave you what you wanted."

"You were both loose ends, John, pure and simple."

John sobbed, trying to figure a way out of this mess with his own life intact. "But we wouldn't have said anything. I'm the one who stole the information to begin with. If I told, we'd all be imprisoned."

John kept trying to stall, hoping that someone, anyone, would come in and stop this madman. He held his hands out in front of him. "And ten million credits is obviously enough to keep my mouth shut."

"I always did despise blabbering idiots," Elijah snorted, before firing another blast.

John screamed even louder as it blasted through his hands and struck his stomach. The next few moments were more painful than anything he had ever felt in his life, as if his body were a garment that was being pulled apart at the seams. The seams were then seared with a blowtorch, only to be ripped apart again, and the process repeated.

His fingers were the first to disappear, and he watched Isabel's ring fall into his wife's ash pile at his feet. His watch soon joined it, falling off along with the river of ash that was falling from his arms as the weapon's effects propagated up both limbs.

John could feel his organs within his gut slowly being ripped apart, their functions shutting down, causing even more intense pain. His lower extremities turned to ash faster than the upper, and though he just wanted to die, he collapsed into Isabel's remains when his legs could no longer support the rest of his rapidly decomposing body.

While the pain and agony raced up his chest, he looked past the mound of ash up at Elijah who rushed down to retrieve the duffel. John knew his end was certain, but he had hoped that someone would stop this madman from getting away. As Elijah raced back up the ramp, all of John's hope was lost.

Gears pulled the aft ramp up off the floor, the grinding sound barely distinguishable with the klaxon echoing to no avail throughout the hangar. A maniacal laugh escaped his lips as the ramp slammed shut behind him.

John could feel his heart stop, and knew that the end was fast approaching. It was only then that he truly felt remorse for what he had done. His actions had killed both his wife and himself, and who knew what else this madman would do with the information he now had in his possession.

With no blood circulating, his brain shut down, bringing with it a reduction in the pain levels, albeit for a mere moment. And with that moment, he saw his watch lying next to Isabel's ring.

And then, darkness fell.

About the Author

Always a glutton for punishment, T. M. Hunter works a pair of jobs all day and evening. With whatever free moment he finds, he spins tales of drama and intrigue, penning stories from a vast number of different universes. His short stories have appeared in such publications as *Ray Gun Revival*, *Residential Aliens,* and *Golden Visions Magazine*. This novel continues the now-completed five-novel Aston West saga: *Heroes Die Young, Friends in Deed, Death Brings Victory, All Good Things,* and *Before the Dawn*. His short story collections *Dead or Alive* and *Dirty Dozen*, his novellas *Seeker, Fallen*, and *Stormrunner* and his novel *The Cure* are also fan favorites.

He currently lives in Wichita, Kansas along with his wife, an over-hyper monster of a dog who identifies as both a lap-sized puppy and a home security system, and a well-fed cat who rules the house with a set of deadly murder-blades and an on-again/off-again benevolent mercy in keeping her subjects alive.

www.ingramcontent.com/pod-product-compliance
Lightning Source LLC
Chambersburg PA
CBHW062018170626
46813CB00001B/210
* 9 7 8 0 6 1 5 6 4 1 1 5 7 *